THE ODYSSEY OF
EFFIE FROST

THE ODYSSEY OF EFFIE FROST

K. S. HOLLENBECK

THORNDIKE PRESS
A part of Gale, a Cengage Company

LIBRARY OF CONGRESS CIP DATA ON FILE.
CATALOGUING IN PUBLICATION FOR THIS BOOK
IS AVAILABLE FROM THE LIBRARY OF CONGRESS.

ISBN-13: 978-1-4328-9586-0 (softcover alk. paper)

Published in 2024 by arrangement with Kandie Hollenbeck.

Printed in the USA
1 2 3 4 5   28 27 26 25 24

For RD
the only man I know who
was named after a horse

ONE

Our cramped cabin stank of salt and mold. Weary enough to sleep through the smell and the lashing of the Atlantic against the hull, I would have been resting in the arms of Morpheus were it not for Phoebe's noisy prayers on the berth above me. Claiming her night and day devotions brought her closer to the bleeding side of the Savior, my little sister's prayers were more a parlor-room racket and proved an irritant in the dank quarters we shared. Just to irk me further, she drew out her devotions tonight, loudly thanking the Lord for another day in this "splendid world" and requesting for the hundredth time our passage be swift and free from toil.

She was wasting her words.

I believed God was paying us no mind. My knees had been roughened from kneeling by the edge of our bed and begging Jesus, God, and any angel who might be careening overhead to let us stay in Boston. All my prayers had been swallowed by the trees and sky. Jesus couldn't help me then and didn't want to listen to my grievances now. My uncle hadn't wanted to hear them, either. Due to our unwelcome status as orphans, we were at his mercy and now on this mail steamer headed toward California, where life was certain to be peculiar and unbearable.

"Think we'll find husbands?" Phoebe asked after a strident *amen.*

I had no interest in the wedded state. The doldrums of running a household and minding children seemed an undesirable life. Besides, I'd just celebrated my eighteenth birthday in November and didn't feel old enough for the permanence of matrimony. And Phoebe, just sixteen, was much too young and brash to become someone's wife.

"Aaron's letters talk of whole towns empty of the fairer sex," she carried on. "Whole towns without one female! Can you imagine, Effie? He wrote about one woman who rode into one town on a white horse and left a week later with thousands of dollars. Thousands! The men must have given her all their money, thinking she was an exotic royal."

"They didn't give her their money for nothing."

"Her company was enjoyed I suppose."

I wouldn't explain further. "Yes, dear sister, they paid for her company."

"I plan on choosing the cleanest one. I do not care to live with a man who makes the air melt around him. What type of gentleman will you choose?"

"I won't be making such a choice. I don't care if he smells like wet carnations. Now, go to sleep."

"Wet carnations do smell wonderful. But gardenias smell better."

"Just shush up and sleep."

"He has to smell nice and be important. I want to prance through town in shiny new boots, holding my nose high."

My sister's chatter ticked at my nerves. I wanted to sleep. If I had my way, I'd be dozing from here until California. It felt like we hadn't moved at all since pushing off the docks a week before, into the Atlantic's gaping sunrise. I was one of three hundred fifty souls aboard. In addition to me, Phoebe, and my cousin Beatrice, one other woman traveled with us, an Irish with her husband. She'd only spoken to us once, and this was to admonish us for traveling alone. I'd taken offense. After all, I had no choice in the matter. But the Irish was right. Traveling alone was daft. My pragmatic father, had he been alive, would have forbidden such a journey, and my uncle should have forbidden it, too. I would always believe that if it weren't for his favor and adoration of his only child, Beatrice, he would have never allowed us to leave.

When we were young girls, Beatrice would soil her dress, and within a week a fresh frock, prettier than the one she'd ruined, would be laid out on her bed. If Phoebe and I had ever dared ruin our garments, our parents would have tanned our hides. But Beatrice got away with all sorts of mischief. Once, she'd thieved some freshly baked bread from a neighbor. After the neighbor had accused her, my uncle had blamed a stray mutt and had my Auntie — God rest her soul — bake the neighbor a new loaf.

So, when my cousin's new husband, Aaron Criswick, chose to make his fortune as an Argonaut, and Beatrice couldn't bear the separation, crying herself to sleep every night with the lovesickness, my uncle agreed to fund her passage. I erred in voicing my concern about a girl like Beatrice traveling alone, reasoning my uncle would consider me rational and require a servant to travel with her as a chaperone.

I should have never breathed a word because when I came downstairs for a breakfast of soft-boiled eggs and soda bread on a cold January day of this year, he announced that Phoebe and I would be accompanying her.

"No. We won't." I recalled the tea being very hot and scalding my tongue. I also recalled my words sounding as if they'd come from the cuckoo clock that hung on the wall. I had never defied my uncle. Neither had I ever defied my parents. In that moment, both, if still alive, would have scolded me for my petulance.

My uncle had only responded with something about arrangements already being made and an order to "organize my belongings so as to fit into one small trunk."

Earlier today, we'd reached Havana. The steamer carried passengers, but its main purpose was to pick up and deliver mail. We hadn't left the boat, but Beatrice had received a letter from Aaron. Blushing with each omission, she'd read parts to me and Phoebe. Phoebe found Aaron's descriptions thrilling. I found them off-putting. These men who believed the ballyhoo about the bonanzas in California were witless and irrational. I wanted nothing to do with them.

11

The steamer rocked slightly, my thick, wool blanket scratchy but warm. Phoebe had shushed up, and I'd shut my eyes. Sleep was finally about to descend when Beatrice, still wearing her day frock, burst into the room.

"You awake?" she whispered.

Why was she whispering? If we'd been sleeping, she clearly wanted to rouse us.

In the dark, I could only make out the shadowy outline of Beatrice's shapeliness that men had always noticed and pursued. Glad not to be burdened by her beauty, I didn't mind my unremarkable face and slight figure. Nor did I mind the plain brown of my hair and eyes. It helped me go unnoticed. When alive, my father had called me a hearty creature. "Euphemia, you were born to live a century," he'd always say. I'd liked it when he'd talked like that. Maybe it was true. Maybe that was how I'd survived the scourge that had taken my mother, father, and both little brothers to heaven.

I did want to live a hundred years. I wanted to live that long to keep the memory of my family alive.

Beatrice was now shaking me, as she'd mistaken my silence for sleep. "You need to wake up," she said. "Someone's overboard. Come quickly!"

I wavered. We should stay in our cabins. But Phoebe had already crashed down from her berth and was shoving her feet into her boots. Travel on the steamer was tedious. Even I had to admit a certain thrill at someone falling overboard.

Once wrapped in our cloaks, we rushed up the stairwell to the chilly deck. Many passengers had joined us. As was typical, they either stared at us as if we were rare butterflies or evaded eye contact altogether. I peered over the deck rails into the water below. The night, dark and moonless, had blackened the sea into a gemstone. The water seemed far away from the dry planks of the steamer's deck. I believed I could have survived the fall but didn't know for sure. We couldn't see who was in the water, flailing and gasping. We only heard the music water makes when it's blooming, withering, and spinning.

"Who is it?" I asked no one. Others asked the same question. It seemed the most important.

We three girls watched along with the rest as the crew lowered a skiff into the water, attempting to find and save the poor soul. I wished the moon shone brighter or the sea suddenly land. I wished I was home more than anything.

My teeth chattered, and I tightened my cloak around me. It was too cold to be out here in the night air. Then I chastised myself for complaining, though I hadn't spoken the thought aloud. If I were cold out here on the deck, I could only imagine how bitter the water was. The man must have been feeling pinched and beaten blue by such a strenuous chill.

"Let's go back to our cabins," I said. "If we stay out here, we'll fall ill. And we cannot afford sickness."

Phoebe and Beatrice didn't argue, which was unusual. They must have been as cold as I.

Before we left the deck, an old man in a thick fur hat handed us each a stick of peppermint candy he'd pulled from his pocket. Phoebe thanked him and despite the grim circumstances laughed like a much younger girl at the delight and prospect of sweets.

"Do they know who it is?" I asked the man.

"Far as I can tell, we'll learn his name in the morning after a head count."

I grabbed Beatrice and Phoebe's hands and led them away. Later, when I was once again drifting off, and Phoebe had finally ceased praying for the gentleman's safety, I had to weep some for the man in the sea.

14

He had surely drowned by now. Dying was bad enough. But you shouldn't die so alone that no one knows you're dead until they count the living.

Once we'd reached New Orleans, Phoebe blamed me for having to stay on board. But it was the captain who'd forbidden us from going ashore while lecturing about the city's cholera riding like a pestilence on the steamy air and our vulnerability as the fairer sex. When Phoebe had protested, he'd chided her and said he couldn't spare even one crew member to act as our chaperone.

With the captain out of earshot, Phoebe called him a toad. Then she poured out a monologue about how she believed we should see as many strange "somewheres" as possible in our lives. "The captain is trying to pluck the adventure from us and stop me from living the way I see fit to live."

"He's concerned for our safety." I was pleased with the captain's edict. I'd deemed New Orleans wild and wicked. The man who'd given us the candy told me all about its medley of Latin tongues, voodoo temples, and quadroon balls. Though he'd gone ashore despite his description, I was satisfied to remain on the steamer until we reached Chagres.

Not Phoebe. She'd pouted the rest of the day and was still pouting while we ate our supper of hot rolls and beef steaks inside Beatrice's cabin.

"Here we are stuck on this steamer while the others are witnessing grand sights," Phoebe said, picking at her food. "You'd think we were being held captive!"

"Your savior," I said, "would not abide us mingling with such devilish activity."

"We wouldn't have to mingle," she said. "We could just watch it. Nothing sinful about seeing sin if you're not sinning yourself."

She was bending words up and rattling my nerves. Even if allowed, I wouldn't have gone ashore. The looks from the men on the ship were bad enough. I could only imagine what type of ogling three Bostonian girls would receive while prancing around the French Quarter.

Still, being this close to land brought out a longing to feel the earth beneath my feet again. Well tired of the sea and cramped spaces aboard the steamer, I felt I might run for miles once able to disembark.

"I hope to get a letter today," Beatrice remarked. "If not from Aaron, from Father. I miss him so."

I glanced over to her pining, heart-shaped

face. "We should have stayed in Boston, then."

She glared at me. "Yes, Effie, you've remarked on that more than once."

The journey was a lark. I couldn't help but say so. Before we'd left, I'd urged her to speak with her father. To convince him to have a servant chaperone her in our stead. She'd refused. Then she'd pulled charm from her quiver and aimed it my way, coating her voice in sugar. She needed family. She'd be too lonesome without us. She would miss me most of all.

"It's simple, then. Don't go. We'll all stay here," I'd replied.

"But I'll die without my Aaron," she'd cried.

I had not been able to resist comforting her. In truth, we were more sisters than cousins. If she'd gone on her own, I would have been achy missing her and written her letters every single day. I would have fretted every minute about her welfare. Beatrice, born just four months after me, often behaved younger than Phoebe. Sent on an errand once, she'd been swayed to give her money to a tall man in a hat in exchange for the best calico woven in the lost city of Atlantis. Carried off by the fiction, Beatrice had handed over all the coins from her purse and waited the entire next day for the fabric to be delivered. Though my uncle had never voiced his concerns about her gullibility, he must have been aware of how much Beatrice needed me.

With the steamer anchored, the rocking of the boat intensified.

"Why couldn't the captain let us wait on the docks?" Phoebe complained. "This rollicking and roiling could give us the seasickness, and we could end up dead."

My sister was alluding to the man who'd jumped overboard and drowned. We'd discovered he'd been wretched with the seasickness for days and could no longer endure the suffering. "Even if I did grow ill," I told her, "I wouldn't end my own life. The illness from the sea is temporary. Death is permanent."

Phoebe chewed on her thumbnail. "You don't know what you'd do."

"Effie's right. It's best we stayed aboard." Due to the steamer's agitation, Beatrice was clutching a blue teacup with both hands. "Aaron insisted we be safe, and frolicking in a strange city with rascals and pickpockets would not do."

I was pleased she'd sided with me. Typically, she and Phoebe banded together to put us all at risk of scolds and punishments by convincing me to participate in a silly frivolity. I had to confess that most of the fun I'd had in my life was due to the pair's prodding. I'd choose a good book and sit by a fire, or I'd sew, or study, or simply watch rain from a window over almost any amusement. But Beatrice and Phoebe had dragged me to the circus, numerous parties, and a few memorable balls. With their persuasion, I had swum in the ocean, picnicked in the woods, ice skated, sledded down dangerous hills, and even jumped in mud puddles with the leaves of the trees around me changing to gold, purple, and yellow.

But I doubted I would ever be pleased with Beatrice's decision to board this steamer. I was convinced it was hauling us toward catastrophe.

With the anchored steamer heaving up and down, we needed fresh air to ward off the sickness. So, after finishing our meal, we walked up to the deck. Studying the seaweed floating and curling in on itself, I breathed in the briny smells and could detect a slight odor of manure and sewage.

Leaning too far over the rails, her braids hanging like yellow ladders, Phoebe said, "I still wish we could have seen the city. Even the edges of it."

"Be careful," I said, "or you'll end up in the water."

"I wonder what that would feel like," Phoebe said.

"It would feel like drowning," I snapped.

"I wonder if I would see fish and whales under the surface."

"You'd see nothing but the dark."

Phoebe looked away from me. "I wonder what the ladies wear here. Or what they eat. I heard the food has a hot spice that burns your lips."

I didn't understand why she'd crave such a thing or why anyone ate food that burned their lips. "We are only stopped long enough to deliver and pick up mail. Even if we had been allowed off, we wouldn't have had time to experience such things."

Beatrice again expressed her hope for a letter. In every waking moment, she was far away in California with Aaron Criswick.

"You ever wish you were a boy?" Phoebe now asked.

"You ever wish your sister would stop talking?" My crankiness had been induced by a bout of queasiness I intended to disregard.

When the mail skiff finally returned to the steamer, we headed again to Beatrice's cabin. There, I unbraided and brushed Phoebe's curly lemon-colored tresses, and we played a game of whist that Beatrice won. Tired, and still somewhat queasy, I eased back to my own cabin, leaving the pair to their joshing and girlish stories. Upon entering, I saw that someone had slid an envelope under my door. I assumed the letter was meant for my cousin, but it was addressed to me. From my uncle.

I smiled, thankful that he'd taken a moment to write to me, rather than his daughter. Despite his decision to ship Phoebe and me off to California, he was a kind and decent man. He'd taken Phoebe and me in after our parents had passed. He'd fed, clothed, and sheltered us in our time of need, providing us with comforts for the past two years and ensuring we continued our education.

Holding the letter, my thumb against the wax seal, I treasured that the envelope carried a bit of home in its folds. I could almost smell my uncle's writing desk, the dark wood, the sour tobacco from the remains of a cigar.

I sat on the edge of my berth and slid my index finger under the wax seal.

Then I read the first sentence.

I read it twice more.

Dearest Niece, I am gravely ill. The doctor says I will die soon.

My uncle knew I appreciated forthrightness and grumbled significantly with those who hemmed and hawed. And this, I understood, was why he'd plunged straight into the dire issue at hand. In any other circumstance, I would appreciate the approach. I did not appreciate it now.

I have been aware of my poor health and nearing end for several months. So, you see, dear niece, this informed my decision to send you and Phoebe west with the light of my life, my dear daughter.

Gripping the paper, I read on with a gnawing in my stomach. The letter became even grimmer when he detailed how he'd spent his last dollars on our voyage and subsequent travels.

No more funds will be forthcoming, for none exist.

No more funds would be forthcoming? The room swayed and swooned. Perhaps it was the sea. Perhaps it wasn't. At the end of the letter, my uncle attempted to reassure me by detailing how he'd already written to Mr. Criswick, informing him of his illness and urging him to provide financial support, not only to Beatrice, but also to me and Phoebe. His handwriting then became difficult to read, as if written with a trembling hand.

I regret dying and regret more the uncertainty of your futures. I am confident, however, about your prospects in California, where fortune will be at Mr. Criswick's fingertips.

He then apologized for the abruptness of his death and his *un-granted wish to live longer.* Certain her delicate nature would not survive such news, his last sentence was an instruction not to inform my cousin until we reached California, *where she would have the strong shoulder of Mr. Criswick to weep on.*

From what I knew of Aaron Criswick, his shoulder wasn't of the strong variety. My uncle knew this, too. Of course he did. His optimism was hogwash. His decision to burden me and me alone with this secret was hogwash, as well. Why had my nature, delicate or not, been deemed strong enough to withstand such tragic and terrifying news? Lack of money was the biggest fear.

All we had in the world was the five hundred dollars my uncle had entrusted me with for the journey's incidentals and a few gold coins and silver dollars Phoebe and I had received upon Father's death. Those coins we'd sewn into the seams of our dresses prior to leaving Boston. But that would not be enough to live on for long.

With the steamer moving again, the next stop would be Chagres, but it might as well be a faraway star. I could hear the common sounds of gambling, oaths, and streams of consciousness born from too much rum coming from the other passengers. More than ever, I missed home, which seemed the only civilized place on earth. I'd always thought my uncle, known as a Boston Brahmin, was a wealthy man. How money was earned and gained had always been a mystery to me, and I'd counted on my father and uncle for everything. And everything had been provided. I knew my uncle had owned and bought property and land but was ignorant of how such transactions worked. Almost anything Phoebe and I might have wanted or needed, however, had been available. I'd presumed my uncle had taken charge of my father's estate and was managing it with care. But perhaps my father, who'd spent most his time giving talks about abolition, had been penniless as well.

I felt a solemn guilt along with my grief for never thinking or caring about the practical details of providing for a house and children. As the steamer gained speed, moving from the harbor, I wept not only for the loss of my dear uncle but for us all. My throat tightened. After my parents' deaths, I'd had difficulty swallowing. My uncle had the servants feed me warm chicken broth for days until my health returned. Here, grief and illness seemed a luxury I wouldn't be allowed. I doubted I would ever be allowed either again.

With the letter in my lap, I could imagine my uncle at his desk writing it, pausing to think of the best words. Dipping his quill in the inkpot. Considering how to phrase the darkest news I could possibly receive. He could not have believed what he wrote about Aaron Criswick's abilities to provide for us. A house cat had more ability to assume this role. My uncle, in his last days, had only this delusional optimism to rely upon. The reality, his daughter and nieces destitute and alone in a strange land, must have been too much to bear.

He understood as well as I the pale potential of my cousin's husband. Aaron was a tailor's son with a wide grin, dimpled chin, and complete ineptitude when it came to his father's business. My cousin had adored him from the age of seven. She claimed it was his laugh, which was constant and battled the silence I craved. He couldn't even keep from smiling in the daguerreotype from their wedding day, which then caused Beatrice to laugh, so now posterity would remember them as lark-loving fools.

I didn't know how Aaron spent his days. But I'd heard the gossip. Many whispered that his primary occupation seemed to be assisting escaped slaves in finding temporary shelter and then helping them continue their journey toward Canada. I'd also seen with my own eyes how he gave his father's money away to any impoverished soul he came across.

So my uncle was mistaken. In fact, I'd concluded the entire reason Aaron left to find his fortune in California was due to his inability to provide for my fickle cousin in Boston. I doubted he would ever find gold. I didn't think he could find gold if it were resting on the toe of his boot. Even if by some miracle he did, he'd give it away to the nearest ne'er do well.

The entire world had gone mad with California's discovery. The broadsides seemed exaggerated, almost theatrical. To me, those who'd left the only homes they'd ever known were all rash fools who'd surely choke on their chancy dreams.

The nausea tugged even more than before to consider that our futures were in the hands of one such dreamer, Aaron Criswick. But my uncle was right. Neither my cousin nor Phoebe could know. I'd have to tuck the news away until we reached California.

By the time I eased back into Beatrice's cabin, we were on open waters, moving toward our unkind future. My sister and cousin were giggling and playing cat's cradle with a string they'd found. It seemed both lived in another world.

"What's wrong, Effie?" Beatrice's cheeks were pink from the sun.

I tried to change my expression. "Did you receive a letter from your Aaron?"

She stopped the game and frowned.

"Well, we shall see him soon." I tried to sound as cheery as I could. "He's likely found the largest gold nugget that ever existed, and we'll live like queens." Saying the opposite of what I believed helped some.

Phoebe stood and bowed. "The Queens of California."

I curtseyed back, wondering if my boots were sturdy enough for what lay ahead.

Two

An excited energy infected the crew and passengers as we neared Chagres. Anxious to leave the steamer, we'd packed the night prior and were waiting on the deck this morning before most of the others had awoken.

To our consternation, when the steamer anchored, we were ordered to wait.

From the deck, we could see in the distance the snow-capped Andes. We'd been told that Chagres, itself, was a shabby little town made up of about thirty thatched huts. Skiffs had already transported most of the rowdy passengers ashore. A few just dove into the blue-green water and swam for it. But we were made to wait on deck in the warm rain. Apparently, we would not be allowed to leave until one of the crew members could accompany us.

Phoebe balked at this. "We should be able to get off the steamer with the others. Just because we're women, it doesn't mean we need to be looked after."

I disagreed. "You should be thankful for the captain's concern."

"I didn't ask to be minded," she kept on. "I'm just as free as these men and should be able to come and go as I please. I have the urge to jump in and swim to shore like the others."

I glanced out at the land and craved the stable sensation of my feet on the ground. "Patience is a virtue."

She rolled her eyes. Fortunately, Phoebe was easily distracted. "What are those?" She was pointing to a grove of tall skinny trees with wide jagged bark and giant plumage crowns.

"Palms, I think." I'd read about palm trees. I didn't know if they grew coconuts or dates or anything at all. The bark was odd, as if someone had nailed dark animal hides up and down the lanky trunks. As exotic as they were, I preferred the big leafy maples of Boston. Such tall, slim trees seemed useless. How could they provide any type of shade? We were starkly at the sun's mercy on the steamer's deck, and I craved to roll up my sleeves. At least their length shielded me from the mosquitoes that buzzed about us in clots.

Phoebe, ogling the ruins of San Lorenzo with its company of buzzards and pelicans, didn't seem to notice the insects. "Did you know pirates attacked that castle? Morgan and his buccaneers? One of the men on the steamer told me all about it."

Beatrice, swatting at the mosquitoes, glanced about quickly and nervously. I assured her the pirate incident had occurred a long time ago.

"They even killed the women," Phoebe said. Either she hadn't noticed Beatrice's nerves or was intent on provoking them.

A crew member approached us and removed his hat, revealing ears the size of clocks. "The captain cannot guarantee your safety here. He recommends you return to Boston on the steamer."

I considered the suggestion wise, but Beatrice waved her gloved hand at the idea. "We will of course be going on to San Francisco as planned. We didn't travel all this way to turn around."

"The captain figured as much." The man scratched at his beard. "Arranged for a flat-bottomed boat to take you down the river forthwith. Captain don't want blame for what might become of you after a stay in Chagres. Less a village. More a stew of yellow fever and collywobbles."

I wanted off this steamer and to walk on land. If I had my druthers and a better pair of boots, we'd walk all the way to San Francisco rather than board another boat. Disembarking this vessel only to board another to travel fifty miles down an unfamiliar river troubled me. Even Phoebe, as eager as she was, was now looking to me for reassurance. I chose not to show my anxieties. Rather, I thanked the crew member and offered my gratitude to the captain. And after at least another half hour, we were helped off the steamer and boarded the last skiff.

Finally on shore, the ground had stopped shifting about as if made from puzzle pieces. I stood in place and relished the moment. Soon Phoebe, Beatrice, and two crew members lugging our trunks joined me. We were instructed to follow a dirt path for several miles to reach the river docks. I was happy for the walk, however long and hot it might turn out to be.

After a mile, I changed my mind. This was the warmest I'd ever felt. Phoebe and Beatrice's faces were red and glistening. We could no longer tell the actual color of our frocks, as they were darkened by perspiration. When the rain stopped, the heat thickened into a wax. Sweat pooled on my upper lip and neck. Every slight breeze brought a moment of relief, but soon we were suffering anew until another puff of wind, as if blown from a stingy God's mouth, came our way.

Following several groups of men, all appearing amphibious from the sweat, I was grateful they paid us no mind. Some of the more ambitious and excited of the Argonauts had started down the path at a slow trot. But the heat had quickly overcome them, and they were now trudging along slower than any of us.

Beatrice stopped for a moment to drink water from a canteen a man had handed her. "Goodness, Aaron didn't write about this sort of summertime."

"It's only April," I snapped.

I watched a yellow mutt trot past us in the opposite direction. After the mutt came one fat hog. Then we passed several children as naked as the day they were born, skipping about as if they'd just left a schoolhouse.

Despite the heat, Phoebe seemed energized by the strangeness of it all. And not for the first time did I question our familial ties.

After a few hours, we reached this land's docks, though they bore no resemblance to the grand ports and docks of Boston. Many large empty canoes were tied to poles and tree stumps, sloshing about and knocking into each other. Wading in the water, natives shouted *"Canoa! Canoa!"* and waved the men over.

Even with all the boisterous activity and flurry around us, everyone surely heard Beatrice scream. I poked her in the side with my elbow to shut her up. Why was she shocked? She'd seen a naked man before. I had not. Neither had Phoebe. And we weren't screaming. That the natives who manned the canoes and labored on the shore wore nothing but hats didn't surprise me. We weren't in Boston anymore and shouldn't ever expect civility again. Phoebe covered her eyes, but I saw her peeking through her fingers. Beatrice tugged her bonnet over her face.

"Did Aaron write to you about this?" I couldn't help but laugh at how silly she looked.

We hurried forward and were helped down into a large flat-bottomed boat. With us were four men ranging in age, the youngest being no older than I and the oldest my uncle's age. They all seemed to have means, as their suits were of quality textiles and their nails clean. Clean nails seemed a sign of wealth, especially in a filthy place such as this.

The men introduced themselves as being from Virginia. The three older men were brothers with identical gray beards, and the youngest had a clean-shaven face as pink as a baby bird's. His name was Eugene Pierce, and he was the son of one of the bearded men. They, like the men at the docks, were headed to California for the gold.

"My husband's already there," Beatrice bragged. "He's probably already found more nuggets than anyone. He's clever like that. We're going there to join him. My cousins will likely find husbands, too. What is *that*?" She'd stopped talking about Aaron and was pointing at the water.

"A crocodile," Eugene's father told her, peering at the monster through thick spectacles.

The beast's giant head looked at first to be a floating tree root. Knobby. Dark. And slick. But for its wicked grate of teeth, I might have been able to convince my cousin of this, had the elder Mr. Pierce not stated the fact.

My cousin bit on the edge of her knuckle. "Are they dangerous?"

Phoebe turned and frowned at Beatrice. "You think it has teeth that long just to

34

chew on grass like a milk cow?"

"I suppose," Eugene said. "Crocs aren't as dangerous as some of the snakes living here."

Beatrice hugged herself and scooted to the middle of the bench. If the young man was attempting to ease Beatrice's mind, he'd failed. At least he hadn't said the reptile could bite her in half, which I knew to be true from a book I'd read. But I didn't want to think on that. If the boat capsized, I decided I would breathe in the river water as if it were air. That way, I could die swiftly and avoid being conscious while serving as supper for these river monsters.

Our flat-bottomed boat seemed much safer than the canoes, which were all over-crowded and at risk of capsizing. Under my breath, I thanked the captain for arranging it. Even with the better vessel, none of us was immune to the sweltering air. After a while, I began to envy the canoe pilots. Nudity seemed a rational choice. If not for modesty, I would have torn my skirt in half and ripped open the bodice that clung wet to my skin. My bonnet shaded my face from the sun, but it felt as if my head were being cooked inside a calico kettle. Phoebe kept reaching her hand into the river and splashing her face. At first I'd admonished her. Now I was doing the same. Beatrice's hands were on her lap. She probably feared a crocodile might bite off one of her fingers.

A Frenchman with a pile of black curly hair piloted our boat. Shirtless, an unlit cigarillo protruded from his mouth. He didn't speak English, so we couldn't ask him where we'd end up. I couldn't get back home, but I didn't know where I was going. It was as if I'd fallen into an unfamiliar dip, not being able to see over the horizon or back to where I'd been before. I was not only a stranger in this place, I felt estranged from myself. Loneliness, unlike any I'd ever suffered, began to overcome me.

But I couldn't permit it. I had to quell all emotion. I concentrated on this river, deciding to categorize and observe everything I saw as a scientist would. We were surrounded by red clay banks, and a canopy of foreign trees tangled above us. Beatrice pointed out a colorful bird called a parrot, and it was a grand and bright sight. How could such a bird exist? I listened to the jungle's jumble of chirps and howls.

Staring at the vibrant patchwork of orchids, I tried not to worry about our futures or dwell on my uncle's letter, tried not to close my eyes in order to pretend we were at home in our bedroom with its striped wallpaper and cherry-wood rocking chair.

We drifted past a tree bowing into the waters, creating a wrinkle in the flow. Near it, a worn canoe's nose poked lopsided out of the surface next to a platoon of rocks. What had happened to its occupants? Again, I was thankful for the flat-bottomed boat. The canoes were dangerous. With the rain again falling, one or more of them looked on the verge of sinking.

"Look up there!" Phoebe pointed at three monkeys above us. Making comical faces, they scampered back and forth on a branch, their long tails nimble and useful, almost as if they had an extra limb. Beatrice began to laugh at the sight. And we couldn't resist joining her.

As we meandered down the river, I studied everything I saw. The fanned-out ferns, herons, woodpeckers, water fowl, and a black bird with a giant disproportionate orange beak, which the oldest of our traveling companions called a *too-can.*

"How long will this take?" Phoebe asked the men.

"Three or four days," one of them said.

"Good," she said. "We should see about a thousand new things in three or four days."

We'd also be miserable, mosquito-stabbed,

pruned from the constant rains, and sun-burned. But I kept this prediction to myself.

The men helped the pilot row, digging oars into the dark-green water, while Phoebe and I — to pass the time — took turns making up names for everything we saw. I called the purple flower that climbed trees ripe plum blossoms. Phoebe named them little brothers because my brothers had loved climbing trees. Phoebe was far better at the game, so I let her name everything else. She called the trees with the wide frothy cano-pies church parasols. She named the birds that swam underwater swim-flitters. I liked that one best.

This helped distract some from my ap-prehension about what lay ahead. It did nothing to distract from the heat. At noon, the sun became an insufferable enemy, especially while we were fully exposed and not under the protection of the church parasols. Even Phoebe complained.

After several days, I decided I'd been right about the canoe pilots and their practical choice of nudity. The pilots, just as I'd first determined, were rational and just. After all, we were born into this world without a stitch on our backs. So, despite the sins of Adam and Eve, even women should be allowed to wear clothes that didn't suffocate us. Or, maybe not wear clothes at all. When I thought no one was looking, I'd started to fold up my skirt — in order to air out my legs — all the way to my thighs. Eventually, I didn't care if anyone saw my legs, including old man Pierce with his disapproving glares. That old man seemed to disapprove of nearly everything we did, telling us more than once what fools we were for making the journey alone. I was too hot to care what he thought of my exposed calves. Phoebe and Beatrice soon took up the practice. At least Eugene seemed to find it entertaining.

After three days and three nights down the Chagres River, we reached Cruses. Along the way we'd stopped and stayed in local villages, where we'd boiled coffee and listened to the native songs and hoots. The children had been curious about us and had kept us company, feeding us dishes of sugary fruits and corn pudding. All had been delicious. My favorite was the corn pudding. Beatrice had loved it, too, vowing to learn how to cook it someday for Aaron and the brood she imagined having.

In one village, a little boy with hair the color of soot had led me and Phoebe behind a bush to show us a three-foot-long lizard. I'd steeled myself against screaming and feigned curiosity. The child had called it an *iggwanna*. It was a greenish bronze with scaly skin and possessed four stubby legs. Lizards were horrible creatures but seemed harmless. The snakes dangling like slick hooks from the tree branches seemed the viler of the two species.

When we finally reached Cruces, I was surprised to learn we were still twenty miles from the Pacific Ocean, where we'd hopefully board another steamer that would take us up the coast of California to San Francisco. The Pierces told us it was rumored that men had waited months to gain passage on the steamers. I didn't care to believe this unthinkable rumor. Our passage had been paid for ahead of time, so I expected we would be able to board straight away.

We decided against the hotel in town because they were known to be teeming with vermin. Many of the men chose instead to pay twenty-five cents for a hammock on the hotel's veranda. As women, of course, we could not risk our safety by sleeping in hammocks. Thankfully, the Pierces escorted us to an encampment and found us shelter in a tent. They set up one for themselves next to ours.

But the tent was an oven. Phoebe and Beatrice fell right asleep despite the heat, but I was kept up by a sharp stone poking me in the spine. Also, one of the Pierces was snoring for all of creation to hear.

Though my eyes were closed, I was still wide awake when our tent flap parted open. Then I heard a man's rough breathing. He reeked of rum.

Beatrice lay to my left, and I felt the man peeling the blanket off her shoulders. Rather than sitting up and shouting for him to leave our tent, I lay paralyzed, my eyes shut even more tightly than before.

Then in an instant, I heard the flap tossed open again and another man entering. Would we be violated by two strangers? I started to tremble and cried with my eyes closed.

I dared not look but felt the wind and heard grunting, as one man pulled the other outside the tent. Then shuffling and shouting. Followed by the distinct sound of flesh meeting flesh and several oaths and swears.

Beatrice woke and sat straight up. "Effie? Do you hear?"

I pretended I'd been in a deep slumber and mumbled that she should go back to sleep.

"Should you see what's got the men swearing?"

"Probably just arguing over who's the big-

41

gest toad in the puddle, as men are inclined to do."

After a few minutes, the sounds stopped. Beatrice fell back asleep. Phoebe had slept through the entire ordeal. But I couldn't sleep, nor could I stop weeping. What just happened was a worst fear coming to life. And I'd done nothing.

Over coffee the next morning, Eugene told us how one unsavory sot had entered our tent.

Beatrice drew in her breath.

"I pulled him out," Eugene exclaimed, "and beat him blue. Broke his nose. Bloodied his lip."

I feigned shock while Beatrice thanked him over and over for his protection, going so far as to embrace the man for his "valiant" efforts. Even if she weren't a married woman, she should not be embracing strange gentlemen. I'd advise her of this later.

But I'd never tell her I heard everything and had done nothing. If the stranger had tried to violate her, would I have just lain there with my eyes shut? Would I have even had the courage to scream?

Later that day, we found out how we'd be traveling the last leg of the isthmus. By mule. Before I could temper myself, my resentment boiled over.

"I've never ridden a mule before," I said to Beatrice.

"You'll get your chance today," she snipped.

Phoebe's eyes lit up with excitement. "This will be even better than the river."

"Mules are stubborn. And they bite," I said. "Remember when Mr. King was bitten by a mule?"

When we were children, Mr. King was our butcher. One day, as he sliced bacon with his right hand behind the counter, I noticed his left wrapped in a bandage. I'd presumed he'd cut himself butchering an animal. In fact, he'd been bitten by a mule. If logic prevailed, mules were more dangerous than knives.

But there was no other way. We couldn't afford horses, which is what the Pierces sped off on. One young Argonaut, hearing my complaints about mules, was quick to defend the creatures. He said mules weren't stubborn. "They're just not as impetuous as their mothers. You see, ma'am, they care more for their own lives and can sense danger more than a horse or donkey." The man, with his soft eyes and long eyelashes, looked a little like the beast he was praising.

"Just treat them kindly," he added. "Be gentle and agreeable, and your mules will aim to get you where you need to be."

Phoebe had listened and was now even more enthused to ride a mule. She remained so until hers died about halfway through our journey. Hers was not the only dead mule on route to Panama City. Rotting corpses of mules lay everywhere, big black cormorants roosting on their bloated bellies. Phoebe cried and blamed herself for the death of "Oscar," what she'd named the poor beast. I tried to comfort her, explaining how they were being ridden to death by the hundreds of gold-starved fools and all their weighty trunks trying to get to California.

This didn't help Phoebe's gloomy mood. All it did was cause Beatrice to grow angry with me for insulting Aaron, which was not my intention. Of course, I believed her husband to be a naïve dupe, but I wouldn't have said this aloud.

Worse than the dead mules and the bickering with my cousin was the mud. It rained nearly the entire twenty-mile journey, and we slogged forward with much effort. With the obstinate nature of the pack animal, regardless of how kind we'd been, every half hour or so we would have to walk, the mud up to our thighs in places, tugging and cajoling the animals forward. We watched as other travelers beat and swore at the poor beasts, one angry man with a big beard shooting his mule between the eyes. We all wept upon seeing that. And now our faces were streaked with tears and sludge.

Several miles later, we saw the worst sight of all. A dead horse. We couldn't help but wonder if it had belonged to one of the Pierces.

"Serves them right," Phoebe said.

Beatrice wiped mud from her eyes and squinted at the dead animal in the distance. "Eugene Pierce saved our lives last night! You shouldn't be saying such a thing."

"They rode off as if at the races," Phoebe stated. "If they had any concern for our welfare, they would have accompanied us all the way to Panama City."

"We're not their responsibility," I said. "We're on our own."

Others around us struggled with their own mules. All were men. Men who surely viewed us as trespassers on their great adventure. They wouldn't be helping us today or even tomorrow.

"We're not on our own," Beatrice said. "We just have to reach Aaron. He'll take care of us."

I tugged at my mule, and it finally took a few steps forward. And then a few more after that. We slowly made our way to the city, and it seemed a miracle we reached it at all. The only good thing about the terrible trek was that we now barely resembled women. Our braids had disassembled. Our skirts and bonnets appeared to have been cast in muck, our faces barely visible. If we weren't allowed a bath soon, we would have to leap into the sea to get clean. Or maybe we should just maintain this layer of grime. Maybe it was the only thing that could protect us.

THREE

For four days we waited along with hundreds of others in sweltering Panama City. If patience really were a virtue, as my mother had taught us, then I was indeed more virtuous than my sister and cousin. Patience had evaded Beatrice and Phoebe, albeit for differing reasons. Beatrice was anxious to be reunited with her husband. Phoebe just wanted to get on with things.

We were able to stay in the United States Hotel in Panama City and took most of our meals in the hotel's eating house. We hadn't seen the Pierces since they'd galloped off on horses, so we were on our own. I tried to prevent Beatrice and Phoebe from venturing out, but they were restless. And I had to confess I was, too. So, on several occasions, we'd gone to town. From afar, we'd witnessed a cock fight. It startled me that a priest had owned the losing rooster. I liked the way people dressed here. The men donned white slippers and linen pants, their light straw hats practical, shading their heads but also airy enough to sift out the heat. Everywhere, men and even some women smoked cigars. Phoebe had suggested we try a cigar. An outrageous and unbecoming idea, I gave her a tongue-lashing. Later, I wondered what other vices she might consider once we reached California and worried myself out of sleep thinking on it.

Since everyone we met complained about how long the wait had been for them, I supposed we were lucky to wait only four days to board the steamer to California. Though I was anxious for our journey to end, I dreaded having to tell Beatrice and Phoebe about my uncle. He had likely already died. My grief over this I kept secret. I didn't ever want to tell my cousin. And my dread at having to do so overcame any great urge I had for our travels to conclude. Unlike Beatrice and Phoebe, I was actually glad the steamer would be stopping in Acapulco and then Mazatlán for coal. Despite having to pick up even more passengers in San Diego on the already crowded ship, I was glad that the stop would extend this last leg of our journey, as miserable as it was likely to be, to at least twenty-one days.

I tried to focus on fortune rather than misfortune. One blessing was that my uncle planned our journey in advance. As I predicted, this was why we were able to board a steamer so soon.

The small steamer was built to hold eighty passengers, unlike the larger one we'd traveled on to reach Chagres. We soon discovered that despite the capacity limit, four hundred souls would be traveling with us. And all cabins, both steerage and staterooms, were full. I hurried to speak to the captain and explain that we, as women, be allowed shelter. Harried and impatient, he just shook his head. Thankfully, one of the crew members provided us a tent, which we erected on deck. It wasn't ideal, but other passengers who were forced to sleep on the deck simply chalked out a border to claim their space. Then they slept out in the cold air inside the space, with only a few blankets, their hats over their faces, and their belongings at their feet.

How desperate these men were to suffer so over dreams of gold. I was determined to get back to Boston and couldn't begin to understand why those around us were here by choice. And as addle headed as my cousin was, her reasons for going to California were far more practical than the

Argonauts'.

The Pacific looked colder than the Atlantic. Its waves didn't roll in a regimented manner. Instead, they cut and stabbed their way across the horizon. It was a cold boil full of whales, sharks, and dolphins. When we first saw a whale, I, along with others, gaped and gasped at the majesty. One man, so thin he always had his hands in his pockets to hold up his trousers, wept at the sight. Whales indeed seemed one of God's glories. So were the sunsets. I had seen the sunrise on the ocean my whole life and marveled each time. Here, on this steamer's deck, we three would stare out at the horizon as the sun sank, a bright yolk spilling across the water.

After a few days, I decided this voyage with its whales and sunsets was preferable to what waited for us in San Francisco. At night, I would contemplate and rehearse in my head how I would phrase the dire news of my uncle's death to Beatrice and Phoebe. No rearrangement of words seemed to help. The news was bleak no matter how I parsed my phrases.

Maybe exhaustion had expelled my criticism, but I'd, as of late, adopted my uncle's optimism about Aaron Criswick. This dammed up some of the worry. I tried to imagine Aaron, clothed in a clean suit and a dapper hat, meeting our steamer at the docks. I pictured him telling us about all the gold, even if it were a small amount, that he'd found. I envisioned borrowing money from him. Phoebe and I could add this loan to the coins we'd sewn in our dresses. It might be enough to pay for our passage back to Boston on a wagon train. Once home, I would pursue school teaching. I knew exactly who we would board with — a nice widow who boarded other single women for a fair rent. Phoebe and I would resume our lives and be surrounded by friends. I would then, with my future wages, pay Aaron and Beatrice back.

When we reached the temperate San Diego, at least a hundred men fought and shoved each other for the thirty spaces the captain was offering. One of the men who'd made it aboard, a pale and gangly fellow with an Adam's apple the size of a fist, chalked out a place on deck near our tent. Most the men ignored us, but Mr. Charley, as he was called, treated us the same as he did the men. Saying good morning and good night and asking on our sleep and telling us stories about San Diego. He'd described it as a "mud town" and a "miserable seaport." And he'd complained that

California had only one season, rather than four. But he'd said the women there sure could dance. They waltzed like a dream, he'd said. He'd also taught us a few steps from the Spanish dancing and polkas he'd learned. It helped pass the time, and we thought well on Mr. Charley.

We were a week from reaching San Francisco when he caught a fever and couldn't keep down his meals. He'd been sleeping on the deck without shelter. The cold nights seemed to weaken him further. Phoebe begged me to allow him to sleep in our tent, but I couldn't allow it. Within two days, he died. Death had ceased to surprise me. But we three were teary and clinging to each other when they wrapped poor Mr. Charley in a canvas, weighted it with coal, said a prayer, yelled *"Launcho!"* and then shoved him off the side. We watched his body slide into the deep gray waters. I was too upset and guilty to even pray.

Other than that dismal day, our voyage was uneventful. The food was stale. The nights were frigid, and we hadn't been harassed by any of the men, who were likely too cold and miserable to start trouble. We grew accustomed to sleeping on the hard deck and to the grumblings of the other passengers. Soon, we were one day out from

San Francisco. I still dreaded the unsettling news I would have to share once on land. By now, however, I was anxious to unburden myself of the secret I'd alone carried for the entire journey, a secret weighing more than my trunk.

My uncle's death was sure to unsettle my cousin and Phoebe, too. But they would persevere. They'd traveled the isthmus and were still in one piece. If they could do that, they could survive the heartache of losing my uncle. We would all be well. Surely we would. We'd survived what most women wouldn't have dared.

The next morning brought a wet, thick fog and a drizzle. San Francisco's port was invisible until we were nearly inside it. I admired the captain for his piloting skills, as the bay was strewn with ships. Beatrice screamed when one seemed to materialize before our eyes just a few feet away from the steamer. It was a miracle we didn't collide.

Now I knew why so many ships were scattered about. For no sooner was our anchor down than a rebellious fever hit the crew. The captain was shouting orders at them, orders that were ignored. The gold region too strong a temptation, almost all the crew suddenly refused duty. The few who remained loyal to their employer attempted to handcuff the others, but we watched them writhe free and escape on the skiffs. Now I understood why the captain had such a cantankerous nature. His men were contagious with the virus of greed and seemed as if they were coming out of their skins with the craving to go ashore and find their fortunes.

The ships and steamers surrounding us must have been abandoned due to the lack of men willing to work on them.

One of the few remaining crew members, older than the rest, provided us safe passage on a pontoon.

The waters in the bay were jagged and looked like gloomy leaden clouds. As we rode through the choppy waters, we dared not reach out to touch the somber shark-filled bay. I could feel the cold rising up off the waves, as if the ocean were sheathed in ice. I wondered what was worse, this icy mosaic of sharks or the hot and steamy Chagres and its hoary crocodiles.

Beatrice had written Aaron when we'd stopped in Monterey. In the letter, she detailed in her tidy script our travels, expected arrival date, the name of our steamer, and a request for him to meet us at the docks.

She was sitting up high in the pontoon, beaming, and searching the shores. "If it weren't for the fog, I'd be able to find his face from a distance. I would be able to recognize my greatest love from a fathom, even in a crowd of a thousand men."

I doubted Beatrice's eyesight was that keen. "I am sure *we* shall be easier to pick out of the crowd."

The fog frayed into a thick mist as we moved closer to the docks, and we could make out a group waiting for the steamer's occupants.

"Are they all men?" Beatrice asked.

"Of course they are," I said. "I've come to believe we're the only women on earth."

The closer the pontoon got to land, the closer we three huddled together. "They're staring," Phoebe said.

"You're the one staring," I told her. "Look away."

She, as always, refused my wishes. "I told you I plan on seeing as much of this strange place as I can."

"Do you see my Aaron?" Beatrice was half standing in the pontoon, threatening to tip us over.

I scanned the crowd of what looked to me like filthy scoundrels, their wild hair the color of mushroom rot and unkempt under brimmed hats. Most of the men looked as though they hadn't bathed in months. We couldn't look much better. Still, I couldn't help my disdain.

Beatrice's eyes were trained on the crowd, her gaze darting back and forth.

"You're certain you gave him the correct date?" I asked her.

"Of course I gave him the correct date," she said.

"What if the letter didn't reach him?"

"Is that him?" Phoebe pointed. I pushed her arm down.

"Pull your cloak over your head," I warned. "I don't like the way they're look-ing at us."

"I like the way the cool air feels on my face," my sister said, her braids wheeling about.

The pontoon pilot was now tying us to the dock, and several men had gathered there, standing on the planks and looking down at us. Seagulls were busy pecking all around them. And a flock flew overhead, all squawking.

The men shoved at each other to have the chance to assist us off the boat. Beatrice first, Phoebe next, and finally me. I tugged my cloak tightly around my shoulders and looked around. The men's eyes, fixed on us, were wide with wonder, as if they'd never seen a woman before in their whole lives. Not even their mothers and sisters. It was the same look people wore at a circus or theatre spectacle.

We hadn't walked but a foot when the proposals started. One after the other asking for marriage without even introducing themselves. This was far different from the men aboard the steamers and those we'd met in Panama. I could only guess that once they'd arrived and got about the business of finding gold, they remembered how much better the world was with women around.

Phoebe was laughing at each proposal, which seemed as appropriate a response as any. I just kept looking down at my boots, and Beatrice haughtily announced how she was already a married women. A few of the older and more gentlemanly types shoved proposers away from us, and I was grateful.

One of these, a man in tailored blue trousers and a flat black hat, stepped forward. He had bushy hair the color of an ostrich and a matching moustache that lapped over his top lip.

"Which of you is Mrs. Criswick?"

Beatrice stepped forward and proudly introduced herself. I stayed close.

The man cleared his throat and introduced himself as Rowland McCorkle.

"It is a pleasure to meet you, Mr. Mc-Corkle." My cousin curtseyed, as if she were at a fancy ball. Phoebe did the same.

"My apologies, ma'am. I'm afraid being the messenger of bad news is one of my jobs as the undertaker in this godforsaken place."

I'd heard *undertaker.* I'd heard it clearly. As clearly as the fog horns sounding off all around us.

But Beatrice either hadn't heard or chose to disregard the man's profession.

"Do you know my husband?" Her voice was squeaky and cheerful.

With a voice as even as a seam, he took a breath before saying, "I am sorry to tell you he passed on to the Lord two nights ago."

Perhaps the world stopped just then. At least it felt like it might have.

But my cousin took no notice. "I am sorry, good sir," she said. "I believe you must have the wrong person."

McCorkle gently handed Beatrice a letter. Clutching the envelope with both hands, she turned to look at me. "He has the wrong person."

Neither I nor Phoebe told her otherwise.

Beatrice tore open the wax seal, unfolded the letter, and began to read it silently, managing to ignore the foghorns and the screeching seagulls, the clatter of men, ships, and water slapping against the docks. Meanwhile, the horde of ill-mannered men continued shouting proposals. They seemed not to care about the news we'd just received. Perhaps they saw the newly widowed Beatrice as a fortunate outcome for their prospects.

Outraged, I couldn't help but turn on them. "Leave us be!" I shouted. "Just leave us alone!"

Before long, her face pale and her wide blue eyes pooling, Beatrice handed me the letter. As she did, she grasped my hands. Her own were trembling and ice cold.

My cousin disappeared on the dock as if swallowed by the fog. Phoebe ran after her. When I squinted toward them, I could see their dream-like silhouettes.

I had to read the letter to know for sure. Perhaps Beatrice was right. Maybe the undertaker had the wrong person. But it was Aaron Criswick's script. His loops unrefined, the slants disjointed. He wrote that he was ill and planned to live. The letter, in case he died instead, was written as a farewell and a promise to meet my cousin someday in heaven. He also said that what little money he had managed to earn was left with his friend, Mr. Malcolm Everhart, and that Mr. Everhart had been instructed to give it to Beatrice on her arrival. The letter then rhapsodized about Beatrice's beauty, some claptrap about her eyes and hair in the sunlight, not at all useful to our current situation. The letter ended with, *I am sorry about your father.*

I could hear Beatrice's sobbing over the sound of the Argonauts milling around us. I could hear her over the seagulls, too.

I didn't know if she had read all the pages or if she'd even understood what Aaron's salutation meant. Did she know now that her father was gone, too?

I had the urge to toss the letter into the bay. But I could never do that to my cousin. She would want to read that letter again and again. I would have to explain sooner than later what he meant about being sorry for her father. I had never uttered a curse word in my life and didn't intend to do so now. Still, this moment seemed enough to spur a barrel of oaths and swears.

I felt a kinship with the poor mules in Cruces tasked with carrying the heaviest loads. But why should I pity myself? My cousin's husband was dead. For many, this would be a calamity due to loss of security. But Beatrice had married solely because she adored Aaron Criswick. And he'd adored her.

In the time it took me to read the letter and for my cousin and Phoebe to return, the fog and mist had cleared somewhat, and I could see a skull-shaped patch of blue. I wanted to believe that this bit of sky breaking from the doomful gray symbolized hope in our desperation, but I couldn't trust such an omen.

By now, they'd lugged our belongings off the steamer. With nowhere to go and no one to meet us, we stood next to the trunks, our cloaks gathered tightly around us to fend off the damp wind.

"What shall we do, Effie?" Phoebe asked. Beatrice was looking to me as well.

I breathed deeply because the unknown was as deep as the bay around us. We couldn't just stand here and wait for the fog to swallow us whole.

"We ask some of these young Argonauts to bring our trunks to the undertaker," I said with a confidence I didn't possess. "We see to it that Mr. Aaron Criswick has a proper Christian burial. Then we shall find this Mr. Everhart, retrieve any money left to Beatrice, and ask him where we should stay."

"Who's Mr. Everhart?" Phoebe asked.

"He was mentioned in the letter," I explained. "Aaron's gone. As is our uncle. We have no choice but to seek out a stranger."

Phoebe's mouth dropped open. "What are you saying about our uncle? Our uncle is in Boston."

Beatrice's cloak hood had fallen away from her round grieving face. "Effie?" she said.

I had no choice but to say what was true. "He, too, has passed, Cousin. Or has nearly passed. He wrote me a letter before we reached Chagres that explained he was dying. He knew before we left but felt confident that Aaron Criswick would care for us. He'd written him the news as well. Made me promise not to tell you until we reached California."

Beatrice fell to her knees. But, as badly as I felt for her, we had no time to entertain her grief. "Get up," I said firmly, as if speaking to a young child.

Phoebe had also started to cry.

But I didn't have time to wallow or carry on. I had to find someone to carry our trunks.

FOUR

I had never seen so many men. Dirty men. Dapper men. Old men. Young men. French. English. Irish. Italian. Mexican. South American. Indian. Chinese. I even noticed one man in a dress. I only knew he was a man due to his mutton chops. Here all the nations of the world were represented and intermixed. They seemed confused and comical, some sleeping on boxes or bales, others wandering hither and thither.

Our wagon driver had only one eye, spider-webbed red, and a black patch over where the other had been. He'd introduced himself as Willy Hand. He said, and I do not josh, "They call me Willy Hand. Let me give you a hand." If the situation hadn't been so dreadful, I would have found amusement in his greeting.

He was kind enough to offer his services without payment.

"Just nice to be in the company of the

fairer sex," he told us when I offered to pay. "Sure do miss my Nancy and the little ones. Feels sometimes I ain't never gonna see 'em again."

As we clopped out on San Francisco's version of streets, torn-up mud ruts tracked with wagon wheels, horse hoofs, and boot prints, I warned Beatrice and Phoebe not to look any of the men in the eyes.

Phoebe, who never would listen, refused, so had three more proposals shouted at her within ten minutes.

Mr. Hand seemed deft with the wagon, as I saw others stuck in the mud as we slogged along toward the undertaker. It appeared he knew the route well and which parts of the road to avoid. Beatrice by now had at least stopped wailing. I feared, however, that she'd slipped into a catatonic state, as she had also stopped talking.

This place couldn't be imagined, and I had tried to imagine it on many occasions. It couldn't even be called a city. The barely-finished buildings, still smelling of timber, were raucous with conversations. I heard shouting from saloons, eating houses, and merchants. Men were climbing from tents and lean-tos. I saw one man sleeping right out in the open on the side of the muddy road, his long beard a sponge for muck and whatever meal he'd eaten prior to his nap. Some with the croup were coughing and spitting for all the world to see. Others seemed in an unruly, drunken state. Boisterous and busy, this nub of a city seemed about to burst.

That we should have to endure such quarters was unfathomable. I wondered if a boarding house for women even existed.

Phoebe had pointed out several ships that had been dragged onto land, and Mr. Hand explained how some of the Argonauts found living quarters inside. Barely missing our wagon, one man tossed the contents of his chamber pot out a portside window.

I'd heard it was muddy here, though I hadn't feared the mud because of our trek with the mules in Panama. But this was indeed worse. Rather than sidewalks, a few pallets had been strewn here and there, and I saw men leaping from one to the next.

Mr. McCorkle, the undertaker, was located in a canvas wood-framed tent. Outside the tent stood several vertically propped empty caskets. While climbing down from the wagon, Beatrice gripped my arm. So firm was her grasp, I feared she'd drag us both to the ground. But I managed to hold her up and walk at the same time.

We found Mr. McCorkle inside, sitting at

a neat and compact secretary. On its surface was a crisp sheet of paper, a pot of ink, and a quill. The undertaker had competent navy-blue eyes and what appeared to be a permanent pout and scowl.

"We have come for Mrs. Criswick's husband." My sister and cousin clung to me on either side.

He paused, as if considering his words. "Afraid he's already been buried, ma'am."

Beatrice cried out. I understood she was overwhelmed with emotion, but the brazen display of it still embarrassed me.

"You see," he said, standing from his desk, "with typhoid fever, immediate burial is the best practice, lest it spread to others."

Beatrice nearly fell into the rickety chair he'd brought over to her. "Where?" she asked. "Where is my husband?"

"Powell Street. We didn't get permission to bury the dearly departed there, but after the first funeral, another followed and so on. So the dead have taken over the grounds. Seems the only power they have left."

Her eyes darted about. I didn't know what she might be looking for. "Did anyone attend his funeral?"

"Only one fella. Malcolm Everhart. Everhart also paid for the burial. Both the cost and his proper respects."

Beatrice stood and straightened her skirts, though it didn't help her bedraggled appearance. "Where's Powell Street? We'll need to go there at once."

I disagreed. "We need to speak with Mr. Everhart before we go traipsing about this honeycomb of drunken fools."

"I want to see Aaron," Beatrice said. "I want to talk to him."

We didn't have time to converse with the dead. "Mr. McCorkle, would you know where we could locate Mr. Everhart?"

"Tends to spend time at Sweetwaters, but I wouldn't recommend you ladies going there."

"I wouldn't recommend we go there, either," I said. "But we've arrived here without a benefactor or any place to lodge, so we must speak with Mr. Everhart and solve at least one of those problems."

Mr. McCorkle raised his bushy white brows. "Head down to the Barbary Coast. Can't miss it. It'll be the busiest saloon on the block. Best entertainers in the city, they say."

Phoebe's eyes ignited. "We're going to a saloon!"

I glared at my sister. "How far is this coast?"

"Not a coast, really. It's a neighborhood of sorts, or wants to be one. Walking distance. But I wouldn't recommend you ladies walking."

"No, I suppose you wouldn't," I said.

"Is it near Powell Street?" Beatrice asked.

"Whether near or far," I said to her, "we will have to go find Mr. Everhart first. Perhaps he can take us to Aaron's grave. He was a friend of his. Perhaps he'll be your friend, too. And you will need to collect what Aaron left to you. Maybe it's enough to get us home."

The undertaker drew out directions to Sweetwaters with his sharp-tipped quill. He had perfect script. Its neatness seemed to stand out more in this messy world. McCorkle also allowed us to leave our trunks with him until we made arrangements for lodging. I thanked him, as did my sister.

Beatrice just stood near the entrance staring out at the street.

Sweetwaters was at least a three-mile walk, and Mr. Hand was nowhere in sight. No matter. We'd walked greater distances than three miles. I didn't pause before setting out. Beatrice tried to latch onto my arm again, but I shook her off. She would have to straighten her spine and plunge forward. We didn't have time to contemplate our dilemma of being three young women alone in a city rife with irrational, hard-drinking, and delusional scoundrels.

I noticed that both dwellings and places of business were either canvas tents or miserable rough-board shanties. It seemed only gambling saloons, hotels, restaurants, and stores had even a semblance of comfort or hint of elegance. The streets were un-graded, ill formed, and gooey with watery gorges deep enough in places to suck off one's shoes. I even saw a horse pathetically winching about after being mired in a gulf of unforgiving mud.

Many languages hit my ear. The voices were scheming, chattering, working, buying and selling, speculating. I heard laughs of reckless joy and the tones of fortunes being won and lost inside the saloons we passed.

We eventually reached Sweetwaters. We'd almost had to drag Beatrice, who'd wept the entire way. We'd forced her to keep walking, as she would have likely preferred to lie down in the middle of the muddy street and wail.

From outside the saloon, I smelled the bitter odor of spilled spirits. I also listened to a cacophony of voices, music, and shout-ing. This was no place for a woman. Not the inside of this saloon, and not this city.

Still, I had no choice but to go inside. We needed help. And this man, Malcolm Everhart, might be our only chance at untangling our current predicament.

Phoebe was pinching her cheeks to give them color, and I slapped her hands down. At this moment, I would have preferred we'd been dressed as men.

"Maybe," I suggested, "we should wait for someone to emerge and then ask him to fetch Mr. Everhart."

Two men now spilled out of the saloon, one tackling the other at our feet. Like wet dogs, they rolled out onto the mud, striking each other and wrestling about. Mud splattered on our skirts, and I was of the mind to clunk both men over the heads with a spittoon I'd spotted near the entrance.

Phoebe had used the distraction to defy me and head inside. We followed. The candle chandeliers were bright and music sprang from an upright piano near the staircase. Hazy with tobacco smoke, the room reeked of brandy fumes. Bags of gold dust exchanged hands on the turn of a card, and everywhere tables were heaped with lumps of gold and silver coins. Dozens of tables, each with a crowd of eager bettors around it, surrounded us. The whole room was crowded with men, and we had to elbow our way through to reach the bar top. A few of the men were so preoccupied with the card game they were playing, they didn't seem to detect our presence. But most did. I was hoping my stern glares would keep them at bay.

We saw women, too. More than one. They hovered over the tables or even perched near the gamblers. One woman in silky finery sat on one man's lap. Another, no older than myself but with lines of living around each painted eye, was laying cards down on the table and appeared to be in charge of the game. An older woman tended the bar.

I mumbled a prayer, asking for courage. I hoped Phoebe was praying, too.

"You ladies lost?" The bartender was probably around fifty years of age, a grayish-blonde bun piled into a nest on her head, her garment a black and pleated stiff satin. Her nose was long and thin and her lips painted dark rose red.

"We are looking for a Mr. Everhart." I spoke loudly, so she'd be able to hear me over the noise.

She tilted her head and offered an un-surprised smile.

"We were told by the undertaker we might find him here."

"Afraid Malcolm has yet to come down-stairs," she said.

It was already one o' clock in the afternoon. "He lodges here?"

She busied herself cleaning glasses and shook her head. I didn't pursue it further. "My name is Euphemia Frost. This is my sister, Phoebe. And she's my cousin, Mrs. Aaron Criswick. We have just arrived and learned her husband has died. God rest his soul. Mr. Everhart knew him and has his belongings."

"I am sorry about your solemn news." She set down a glass on a stack of others and came out from behind the bar. "Flower — um, Mr. Criswick — was a kind soul."

Beatrice's eyes welled up again.

"Generous to the bone, he was," the woman said. "Too generous."

"You knew him?" Beatrice asked.

The woman embraced my cousin, which seemed too forward. But Beatrice nearly collapsed in her arms, hooking her chin on the woman's shoulder. The woman patted my cousin's back as a mother would her daughter.

"There, there. Poor darling."

Beatrice seemed to take great comfort in the woman's affection, and I tapped my foot waiting for the dramatic moment to end. Certainly, I felt sympathy for my cousin's deep sorrows, but I knew it would get worse if she couldn't square her shoulders and at least attempt to dry her tears. It was a good five minutes of sobbing and relaying to this stranger about how her father had perished, too, and how we were alone here. I didn't need to hear our predicament spoken aloud. Our troubles already seemed insurmountable. Hearing her describe them made me feel like I'd landed in the underworld and was rowing a boat down a river in flames.

"Name's Gertie." The woman gently pulled away from my clinging cousin. "Gertie Wilson. I own this place. My husband was also taken to his maker. It was a few years back, but I miss him the same and know your grief. Though Joseph didn't have half the good heart of your Aaron, ma'am. Your husband talked of you often. You should know that."

Upon hearing those words, at least one cloud had moved its shadow from Beatrice's face. I was grateful to Gertie for that.

"Malcolm's slept too long today," she said. "I'm gonna rouse him. You ladies best stay near the piano player. He's a safe one, far as your honor's concerned. Though if any of these rascals touches you or utters one foul word, let me know."

We did as told and huddled near the piano player, a balding man with sleepy eyes, who kept his fingers on the keys and didn't look up.

"I am happy to know one person," Phoebe said over the music. "Aren't you?"

I reminded her we'd met two others, the undertaker and Mr. Hand.

"Gertie's better," Phoebe prattled loudly. "She could be a real friend. I don't want to be friends with an undertaker. Seems like bad luck."

"Where will we sleep?" my cousin asked. "Do you think we could stay here?"

"What kind of establishment do you think this is?" I asked her. "Look around. The women dealing cards and smooching up to the gamblers wear less than we do while sleeping."

Phoebe disagreed for the sake of it. "Undertaker said they were entertainers. That's what he called them."

I wanted to shake the gullible natures out of both of them. "They do more than entertain."

My cousin looked around. "I wouldn't mind staying here. Gertie's very kind. And she knew my Aaron."

I wouldn't argue but was adamant we stay

elsewhere. We couldn't possibly sleep in the same quarters with such activity taking place in the next rooms. What was Aaron doing in a place like this anyway? "We'll ask Malcolm Everhart about proper lodging for proper ladies," I said.

"But we need to save what money we have left." Phoebe was trying to appeal to my practical nature. "And Gertie Wilson might take us in out of the goodness of her heart."

Across the room, a long-haired woman with eyes as big as a lamb's wrapped her snowy-white arm around a barrel-shaped fellow with a crusted beard and dirty hands.

We would sleep in the undertaker's caskets before we lodged here.

Gertie was headed back down the planked stairs. A man tucking a black and red flannel shirt into his tan trousers followed, so tall, he had to stoop to avoid hitting his head on the beam at the foot of the stairs. I didn't know why, but I'd assumed Mr. Everhart would be as old as my uncle. But he was just a few years older than I. With a chin-length scramble of hair that was the color of the inside of a felled tree and a short beard to match, he had the brooding eyes of a falcon looking for food. Or maybe he'd just woken up.

Gertie introduced us. He ran his fingers

through his hair, his expression reminding me of a person who'd just found a sack full of stray puppies floating down a stream.

"We apologize for waking you, sir." I wasn't sorry at all. From my perspective, God-fearing men didn't burn daylight, and I couldn't help but question his character.

Gertie left us and headed behind the bar. The four of us moved toward the back of the saloon, where we could hear our voices better over the din of gamblers.

It was Phoebe who described our journey in a long fatty speech with too many details and meandering rivulets that the stranger likely had no interest in.

"And so here we are," Phoebe said, her eyes welling up some after mentioning my uncle. "Orphaned and widowed."

He nodded, turning to my cousin. "And you're Flower's wife?"

"Flower?"

"I mean, Aaron."

She nodded.

"My apologies on the nickname. We all called him Flower at the diggings. He got used to it." He turned toward the bar top. "Say, Gertie, any of that breakfast hash left?"

"I'll have Jonah warm it up," she called back.

76

"Why would you call him Flower?" Beatrice asked.

"We'd be at the claim, all of us knee deep in the water, our hands cracking from the cold, and he'd be staring out at the wild-flowers, talking about their beauty and blooms and making up rhymes and songs. He earned the name, ma'am. So you'd be Mrs. Flower." He grinned, then, those hawkish eyes now half-moons.

I considered the nickname disrespectful. "Her name is Mrs. Criswick."

"He can call me Mrs. Flower or even Bee. Aaron used to call me Bee. I don't mind."

"Well, you may refer to me as Miss Frost." I had no business being so haughty, but the informality of this man amongst the fairer sex was unconventional and against the manners I'd been reared with, manners I planned to keep intact.

He scratched his beard and peered at me. I immediately regretted my bristly behavior.

"Well, Miss Frost, please call me Malcolm," he said. "What can I help you with?"

I explained what the undertaker had said. "So we've come to collect Mr. Criswick's remaining possessions."

Beatrice reached out and touched his arm. "I am also very grateful you paid for his burial. And for being there to send him home to his Savior."

"Flower was my pard." The look returned, the one suggesting that troubles prowled around his thoughts. "Made me laugh. Even in the worst of times."

Beatrice's eyes brimmed with those words.

"Did he leave her anything of value?" I asked.

"I have his hat and the letters Mrs. Flower sent him. Afraid to tell you, he wasn't all that skilled at finding gold. Easily distracted. The few times he did have luck, he gave all his money away to those even unluckier than himself, of which there are many." He looked at my cousin. "He did manage to find a few ounces before he took ill, the value of which was one hundred and seventy-five dollars."

"That's at least something." Phoebe's optimism always found a detail to float off on.

"The bad news is that he went and invested in a share of a claim on the Feather River. We were going to head up there once Mrs. Flower arrived. Then he died. Didn't want to leave the city until I could pay for his share. Just need Mrs. Flower to name the price. Don't mind paying more, considering your situation."

As we were all completely ignorant of how

any of this business worked, I didn't want Beatrice making a rash decision, as she was inclined to do. "How many shares are there?" I asked Malcolm. "Is it just the two?"

He shook his head. "Five of us went in on it. Some of the claims up that way are paying off, so we figured it'd be worth a try to buy us one."

"I suppose if you could just pay me the amount he put in, we'll be even," Beatrice said. "Is that fair?"

"We know nothing about claims or their value," I argued. "We could get far more for it. We will need to discuss and come up with the amount tomorrow."

Beatrice glared at me. "Malcolm was kindly enough to wait for me. Kindly enough to even offer to buy Aaron's share for more than what my husband paid. He could have just left, Effie. And I'd have nothing."

My stomach growled loudly. "We will consider and discuss. For now," I said with a confidence I entirely lacked, "we need lodging. We will be returning to Boston as soon as we discover a way, but we need shelter tonight."

"Shelter will likely cost you, at least the kind of shelter you're looking for. As you're all from the land of steady habits, you'd be better off accepting a proposal. Not all the fellas here are heathens. Some are godly and educated. Fella over there owns a farm back home and can speak French and recite yards of poetry."

"I don't care if he can recite every word of Shakespeare or speak every language that came about after God destroyed the Tower of Babel," I said. "We will not be marrying anyone."

I could tell he wanted to say something. Before he did, Gertie came over with a basket of buttered bread and four plates of hash and eggs. The dish smelled as if it had been prepared on heaven's stove. The last time we'd eaten was the night before on the steamer. Except for Phoebe, who set upon the food with vigor, Beatrice and I managed to maintain our good manners and behaved as if we would barely sample the food before us. In truth, I planned to clean my plate.

We barely spoke while eating, and I felt less cantankerous after a few bites. Still, I wouldn't apologize for my petulance. How dare he suggest our only option was to marry a farmer who could recite poetry! And what of Aaron's share of the claim? How much was it really worth? I would not let Malcolm Everhart or anyone else take advantage of our situation.

Malcolm wiped the food from his mouth with his kerchief. "So, as I said, marrying up is likely your best choice in these parts."

I swallowed the last of my hash and was still hungry. "We have no intention of marrying an Argonaut. I do not care how many farms they own or how godly and educated they are. They clearly don't have any sense since they were foolish enough to come here. Our intention is to get back home, sir. To Boston. Meanwhile, we'll have to find somewhere to rest. Before nightfall."

At this, Beatrice burst into tears.

"Are you choosy about where you sleep?" he asked over the noise in the saloon and my cousin's crying.

For the past twenty-two days, we'd been sleeping in a tent on the deck of a steamer. "As long as it's not in an establishment similar to this one," I said.

"A bath would do us good." Phoebe didn't even blush, though the statement required a head to toe glow. "Do you know of somewhere we could bathe?"

"Gertie might let you have a soak here if you're not too high and mighty."

I was offended. "We are neither high nor mighty."

Phoebe agreed. "But we sure need a

scrubbing."

He rose from the table and went to ask Gertie. I turned to my sister and saw that she was licking her plate.

"Stop that," I said. "You were not raised to lick your plate like an animal. And you are not allowed to discuss a topic like bathing with a man."

I was mortified she'd brought it up, even more so that Malcolm had behaved as if it were a common practice to discuss such indelicate things with a woman.

"If I hadn't mentioned it," Phoebe countered, "we'd lose our chance. And you probably want a hot bath more than either of us."

She was right. I would need to temper my tendency to be appalled and mortified. If I tried to preserve such traits, I'd never survive this place. And then I'd never be able to go home. I would have to learn to accept this new land for what it was — dirty and lacking etiquette of any sort. In truth, I would be grateful to bathe anywhere. And perhaps the accommodations Malcolm spoke of would be pleasant and private, a chance for me to collect my thoughts and plan our next days. I touched the side of my face just then and realized I likely resembled a grubby vagrant. Phoebe certainly did. And

Beatrice . . . well, she was so filthy, her tears looked more like muddy streams.

She'd stopped crying for now and was sniffling and wiping her nose with her wrist.

"He's a fine looking man," Phoebe said. "Maybe I'll marry Malcolm Everhart."

"You'll do no such thing," I said.

She looked over to him. "He's handsome and strong, and a good and loyal friend."

"You know nothing about him," I told her.

She glanced around. "He's twice as handsome as the other fellows in here."

Beatrice had started to weep again, and I was somewhat grateful. It at least distracted my sister from further chatter about Malcolm Everhart's handsome face. I was hoping a bath would clean not just her body, but her mind of its feeble thoughts. She also needed to cleanse herself of the idea of marrying here. These men were rowdy and uncouth, just like the city we were in. I was as certain of this as I was of our need to go home.

FIVE

The room upstairs held one tub, and Gertie Wilson had a Chinese man fill it with boiling water. Though I'd allowed Phoebe and Beatrice to wash before me, the water was still warm by the time I had my turn. Washing our hair for the first time in weeks and scrubbing our nails of filth was a luxury. Our clean frocks and hairbrushes were still in our trunks at the undertaker's, so we were forced to wear our soiled dresses. I had the urge to launder my own in the bathtub. But I'd surely freeze in the cool winds of this city, and the dampness of the air would prevent my dress from drying quickly, if it dried at all.

But Gertie Wilson, whose hospitality I would always be grateful for, had a spare hair brush, and we helped each other comb out the many knots. Our eyes watered with the amount of tangles we'd freed. Phoebe's curls were the most difficult to tame. Afterwards, we braided and pinned our locks back into their modest buns. Well, Phoebe and I did most the brushing and braiding and pinning. Beatrice seemed as stunned as a rabbit about to be mowed over by a carriage. I was happy she hadn't drowned herself in the bathtub.

The upstairs hallway was as noisy as the saloon. Only the sounds were not meant for Christian ears. The grunts, the shouts, a woman squealing. Phoebe tried to gossip about it, but I chose to ignore the squalid noises and pretend the world was ordinary. This became difficult when we passed one room with the door partially open. I couldn't deny what I'd seen. A woman bent over, her bare rump hoisted in the air, and a man heaving behind her. I shoved my sister down the hallway, but I think she caught a glimpse despite my efforts.

Back downstairs, Malcolm was speaking with a young mustached man sporting a white bowler hat. The man's smooth skin matched the hat, as if he'd spent little time outside. This differed from the other fellows, who were sun struck, lined, and ruddy from the outdoors. He wasn't tall or short, and his pearly fingers wrapped around a glass cane.

I dared not interrupt the conversation. But

Malcolm noticed us. So did the pale stranger.

Soon enough, Malcolm was at our sides. "You ladies ready?" He seemed anxious to squire us away from the place.

"Indeed," I said.

"Who's that man?" Phoebe's curiosity seemed a potent danger in a place like this.

"Mr. Russell Oxley. Wants a share of the claim in exchange for provisions. Problem is he doesn't actually want to work the diggings, which means we'd have to work it for him and hand over a cut of what we find."

We left then. Malcolm had arranged for a wagon to take us to Powell Street, so that Beatrice could say goodbye to her beloved. We stood aside as she made her way down to the graveyard after Malcolm had pointed out Aaron's fresh plot. It stunned me that Aaron would lie here for eternity. The clouds had combined to form a mist, and the dreariness of the city could not be ignored. It was lonely and cold here. Merely a clatter of seagulls mixed with random shouts in languages Aaron wouldn't understand. Aaron, despite his foolishness and unsuitability as a husband, was a good and decent soul and deserved to be buried back in Boston.

My cousin, her trembling back to us,

stood by his grave for the longest time. I tried to be patient, but we needed to leave. I understood this would probably be the last time she'd be allowed to pay her respects to her husband. I also understood that we could become ill out here in this cold and damp air, which carried diseases from all over the world in its gusts. And I wouldn't allow us to die here. I refused to make San Francisco *our* permanent home.

Phoebe, hiking up her skirts, set out to fetch our cousin from the side of Aaron's grave, which didn't even have a marker. I could hear Beatrice and Phoebe saying the Lord's Prayer from where I stood. I joined in. *Forgive us our trespasses. Deliver us from evil.*

Our *Amen* was barely audible in the wind.

We climbed back in the wagon. Beatrice buried her wet face on my sleeve.

"I arranged for someone to bring your trunks over from the undertaker's," Malcolm said.

I thanked him but was suspicious of his help. I didn't want to be obligated to anyone. Still, I'd been worrying about how we'd retrieve them.

We rode the few miles up and down the hilly roads to where we could finally rest. I was hoping no one noticed my profound disappointment upon seeing the shelter.

I'd seen these makeshift huts when we'd first arrived — no more than wood scraps and pallets nailed together in a slipshod manner. Some, ours included, had mud packed on the roofs and an iron gate. A dark-green wool blanket had been hung up as a version of a door. The blanket might stave off the rain and wind, but it wouldn't protect us from scoundrels or thieves.

I expected Malcolm to apologize for the accommodations and was prepared to tell him I understood. How I knew we were inside a grim situation and that beggars could not be choosers. How I was grateful, nevertheless, to have a roof over my head.

But he didn't apologize.

"Flower slept here. I spend most nights at Sweetwaters so don't have much use." He turned to Beatrice. "It should give you some comfort to know he'd only head to Sweet-waters for food and drink and only had eyes for you."

"I should think so," I said. "I should think any decent man would avoid the entertain-ers here."

He looked at the ground and shoved his hands in his pockets.

I noticed a cow bell hanging in front of the blanket. This was, I suppose, San Francisco's version of an alarm. "I don't see how that helps. It will only serve to wake us before being molested or robbed. I'd rather be asleep during the ordeal."

Again, I expected an apology, but none was forthcoming.

"Tried to make it comfortable for you ladies." He ran a wide hand through his hair. "But I'm afraid straw mattresses are dangerous here, what with the fires, so you'll have to take to the ground. Blankets pad it a little and make it a little softer on your bones."

"Fires?" Phoebe asked.

"You must've seen the blackened buildings near the undertaker's. Town keeps burning down."

Every structure here seemed to be in a stage of this or that, so I didn't think much of the buildings near the undertaker's. The entire city reminded me of our room back in Boston when Phoebe and I set out to make a dress. Fabric and needles and patterns and threads spread everywhere.

Beatrice had barely spoken in the last hour. But she chose to now: "We are grateful. Extremely so. Thank you Mr. Everhart."

"Please call me Malcolm, ma'am." His grin opened up like a gate, and I quickly looked away. "I've left your husband's hat and letters in there, along with the pistol he left behind."

Beatrice parted the blanket and disappeared inside.

Phoebe was marveling at a group of Chinese men building a structure across from ours.

"Once we've returned to Boston," I said, "we will repay you for your troubles."

"No need for that, ma'am. You three returning to Boston on a steamer? The way you came? Or will you be headed around the Cape?"

We had no funds for either method of travel. But I wasn't going to reveal our desperation. "We will likely travel overland, as we've all tired of the sea."

"How you fixing to do that?"

"Would you know of any wagon trains that will allow us passage back East?"

"Most of those trains are traveling in the other direction," he said. "Everyone's coming here, Miss Frost, not going."

I wanted to deny the expression of pity on his face but could not. I'd never experienced such a gaze, even after our parents had died. It was unnerving. I'd never been pathetic. My father had relied on me to bring order and sense. Phoebe was the child who'd been called "a delight." But it was I who ensured we ate our meals on time and that the house was tidy and our schoolwork complete. "Are there any female miners?" I asked.

He smiled at this.

"I have not said anything funny."

"Effie!" Phoebe said. "You are not thinking of such a thing! We can marry any miner we please here. And they can find the gold for us!"

"I will not be obliged to a one-toothed Argonaut daft enough to come to this godforsaken place."

"We might all be daft or we might not," Malcolm said. "Some of us have found nuggets big as your head. And some of us have more than one tooth."

"I did not mean to insult you." I would need to learn to bite my tongue.

"You didn't insult me. I didn't come out here to find gold. Long as I was here, though, I decided to give it a try."

It was Phoebe who'd asked why he'd come, not me. I didn't think it my business, nor did I care.

"That's a story I prefer not to tell." He got that brooding look again. "But it's true that some have found enough gold to be called a fortune. Some find nothing. That's the truth, too. And many gamble away everything they find."

91

"How would I go about finding these gold nuggets?" I asked. "Beatrice has a share of your claim, yes? If I can find enough of the gold, we will have funds to see us comfortably back to Boston, where my sister can marry a proper and educated gentleman."

"Some of us here are educated, ma'am."

I ignored him. "I do not need a fortune. I need only to find enough to get us home."

"Haven't ever seen a female miner."

"I wouldn't think it's any more disgraceful than how the women at Sweetwaters are earning their keep."

"Women like you three tend to marry up."

"I don't plan on marrying up or down. How shall I go about finding these nuggets on my cousin's share of the claim?"

"Too many of us are working the claim already. The only reason I'd ever bring a woman would be to cook, clean, and wash our shirts."

I felt my face grow warm, and I nearly lashed out at him. But I was able to stop myself. From inside the shelter, I could hear Beatrice crying. I had to remain calm for her and Phoebe. I couldn't make an enemy out of the only person who might be able to help us. Besides, I knew how to prepare basic meals. Admittedly, they were neither tasty nor filling. "I can cook, but I prefer to find nuggets."

"Don't need a woman with arms as skinny as a rope working the claim. And I don't want you coming up to cook for us, either."

I looked at my arms. He was wrong about me. I may have been petite, but I was strong. Stronger than lots of boys. When I was younger, I could lift Phoebe six inches off the ground with barely any effort. "You just said you need a cook."

"No, I didn't. I was making a point."

"I can clean and wash, too," I said.

He seemed flustered. "We can manage that on our own."

"If you go off to cook for these men," Phoebe asked, "what will happen to us?"

"I'll be back every night."

"Nope," he said. "We're headed all the way up to the North Fork on the Feather River, so all three of you would have to come, and you'd be there for the entire winter. And the winters are harsh. But you're not coming. Not you, your sister, or Flower's wife. Got enough worries without having to be burdened by you."

Spending an entire winter in a strange land with even stranger men seemed a terrible idea. But staying here seemed worse. "When will we be leaving?"

"We're leaving in the morning. And we're

doing so without you. You need to tell me how much Mrs. Flower wants for her share. I'll pay you now and be done with this."

I took a deep breath. I was determined to find several nuggets to pay for our passage back to Boston. While I figured out how to do this, we'd have to do the work of servants. Otherwise, we'd be stuck here in this city of stagnant water, sin, fire, and wretched-smelling saloons.

"I am an excellent cook," I said with conviction. "And Beatrice knows how to launder. My sister Phoebe cleans better than most. She's very tidy by nature."

Phoebe didn't make a sound or a face, but we both knew I'd just told the biggest fib of my life. Beatrice had never in all her days washed a garment. And Phoebe left a mess wherever she went. And the food I'd prepared in my life required a strong set of molars.

He sized me up, growled a bit, and then seemed to grasp that we would be going up to the claim whether he liked it or not.

"I'm headed out tomorrow," he said. "I'll probably regret this. I already do. And you'll regret it, too. The journey's long and hard. And when we get there, there's a chance we won't find enough dust to fill half a poke."

"Since Beatrice owns a share, I'm presuming we'll be exchanging our work for a percentage of what you find, correct?"

"I expect that's fair."

I nodded tersely. "Then we shall take you up on your offer, Mr. Everhart."

He rubbed his chin and looked up to the sky.

"But I expect that we will be treated like ladies." I looked across the road and saw a squatting man in a straw hat defecating.

Malcolm glanced over his shoulder and must have seen it, too. "I don't want to be yoked to the burden of you three being in my charge."

"I have never in my life been a burden."

"You can stay here or you can come with. Your choice."

"We will be ready in the morning," I told him. "You'll be glad for it."

"I'm sorry for it now. And I'll be sorry for it later. But you don't give a man much room to say no."

After we'd arranged the details, and he'd left, I climbed inside the drafty lean-to and lay next to Beatrice, whose eyes were fixed in a watery stare.

Phoebe lay on my other side. "We might be better off marrying, Effie, rather than going off to live in the woods with miners. Don't you think?"

For the first time in my life, Phoebe sounded practical. Wise, in fact. However, hers was a solution for the here and now. I believed we needed to think of our future happiness and well-being. But happiness could only be found in Boston. "Marrying from a place of financial desperation would only result in disaster. One needs to be choosy in these matters."

"I shall never marry again," Beatrice proclaimed before starting to cry again.

"You will need to learn how to do laundry," I told her. "I will be cooking, and Phoebe will be cleaning."

Beatrice's wailing filled up the night, but I was certain the wild sounds of the street drowned out her noisy mourning.

Six

Just after sunrise, the fog thick as cream, Malcolm Everhart sent a wagon for us. We'd changed into our clean frocks. Mine was dark blue and neatly stitched, as I had taken my time sewing it. We wrapped ourselves in our wool cloaks to ward off the bracing wind. For the journey to the Feather River, we'd packed just one other dress each since we'd been told we could only bring a single trunk for all three of us.

Phoebe insisted on packing her favorite frock. We'd bickered because it was marigold yellow and would easily stain. But she wouldn't listen. She never had listened to me and likely never would.

Along with the clothing, we managed to fit in a few other items, including my mother's cameo locket; extra undergarments; Mr. Criswick's letters; our brushes, ribbons, and hairpins; some essential toiletries; sewing supplies; a small sack of seashells Phoebe had collected in Panama City; as well as the Colt pistol, holster, and bullets Aaron had left behind, which none of us knew how to use. We left the rest of what we'd lugged across Panama behind in the lean-to. We'd probably never see any of our belongings again, and I regretted bringing any of them in the first place.

Our wagon took us to the river banks. We'd be traveling by boat up to Sacramento City before we set out on land toward the claim. When we arrived at the docks, Malcolm and one other young man, his weather-thrashed hat pulled low enough to shade his face, were busy loading provisions onto the boat.

"Flower's wife," Malcolm said, as we approached. "And her cousins."

Beatrice straightened and seemed pleased at being introduced first.

"I'm Duffy Fields." Duffy's shoulders were wider than an oxen yoke. And he never stopped working while we introduced ourselves, nor while he offered up his condolences for "Flower."

I would have insisted they call Aaron by his real name, but Beatrice seemed taken with her husband's nickname.

Phoebe noticed a monarch fluttering behind Duffy and pointed to it. "It's like a flying tiger with wings! We'll be seeing all sorts of new and pretty things, I expect."

Duffy's grin took up the whole of his square jaw, and his freckles seemed to jig across his cheeks and nose. Most men would have thought my sister childish, but Duffy seemed to share in her delight. I noticed him now humming a hymn while lugging a crate up onto the boat's deck. Maybe he was a religious man. Or maybe hymns were the only songs he knew.

Malcolm told us two more fellows, waiting on the provisions that would see us through the winter, were back at the claim. "Can't leave it for longer than a week. A week passes, and it's fair game again for any passing miner who wants it."

I refused to be useless so pitched in along with Phoebe to help load the boat. We began lifting and carrying some of the lightest crates, and the men seemed grateful. My cousin just stood under a cottonwood and fanned herself with a small plump hand. I noticed her wedding ring catching the morning light. I wondered if she'd ever take it off. Near her, resting on a tree stump was the man we'd seen Malcolm speaking with at Sweetwaters. Malcolm must've taken him up on his offer. Mr. Oxley must've thought himself a king the way he sat there, legs spread, his willow-soft hands wrapped around the cane, as if holding a scepter. Why was he still wearing that silly white hat? Malcolm must've noticed my disdain so explained how Russell Oxley had just arrived, by means of the Cape, to San Francisco the week before. Seemed to me that was all the more reason to want to prove himself worthy.

Others were loading their provisions on the boat, as well, as several parties would be headed down the river with us. It took a few hours before we were ready to leave. All the men except Russell Oxley allowed us, as the only women, to board before them. Casting chivalry aside, he stepped in front of us, then plopped himself on the bench with the most shade. Without looking up, he opened a slim book and read with squinty blue eyes.

"He's pitched in quite a sum for our provisions," Duffy told us, once we'd set off down the river. "Blue-nosed college boy from New York. Out for an adventure paid for by his father."

I'd known several wealthy, young men who attended university. They wouldn't have dared sit while other men worked around them. Still, those same men didn't give a second thought to lounging about as harried servants busied themselves with household chores. This Oxley fellow must have viewed us as servants.

Even so, I hoped he had more books in his trunk. Despite his loathsome nature, I would be very pleased to read a good story.

The day heated up quickly, and I tried not to worry about my sister, who'd abandoned all decorum and decided to converse openly with the men. She flitted about while Beatrice sat, her hands folded in her lap, her gaze locked on the river water. By noon, we'd removed our cloaks and had to repeatedly pat our faces and brows with handkerchiefs. I comforted myself by comparing the mild heat here to the staggering swelter of the Chagres.

But the heat was the least of our worries because, before long, I doubted our boat's seaworthiness. Tipping this way and that, crates, trunks, and pallets slid across the deck. I was grateful that this river wasn't teeming with crocodiles. Still, if we capsized, we could drown. More and more, I considered our thick frocks a burden. If we tipped over and spilled out into the river, the folds of our skirts would soak up the water and drag us under. We'd sink like a sack of bricks. I was sure of it. Beatrice, in her current state, would probably welcome the occasion.

The boat's rocking, however, couldn't be blamed on the river. The captain, evidently, had been drinking gin slings and whiskey punch the whole night before and was corned and half seas over. After some singing and loud curses, Malcolm and Duffy had gone to inspect the matter of the boat's listing. We watched them wrestle the captain down on the deck and pry a jug of spirits from his hairy-knuckled fist. The captain, his drunkard face flushed and lathered, spat out curses and swung wildly at the air. Finally, with great effort, Malcolm and Duffy strung the man up in a fish net. To my surprise and Phoebe's amusement, the captain — still bundled up in the fish net — fell asleep a few minutes later. I didn't know how a man could sleep bent up in a fish net, but I was relieved to learn that Malcolm knew how to steer a boat.

After the ruckus, except for the sloshing of the river on the hull and the whispers of cottonwood trees, it grew quiet. Perhaps this is why Beatrice reverted back to her mournful thoughts. Soon, she was seized with emotion again. Phoebe sat to her left, I to her right. We propped her up with our shoulders and tried our best to ease her grief. But no word, pat, or embrace could sooth her.

"Wasn't he the kindest man?" she said between a choke of sobs. "The best man? Why would the Lord take him home so soon? Why him? Why me? Why Father, too? Why would both be taken at once?"

She wasn't the first to ask God such a question. I'd asked the Almighty myself. Why had my parents and brothers died? It didn't make sense then. Made less sense now. It would never make sense to me as long as I lived.

Phoebe now embraced our cousin while she cried. "You know," Phoebe said, "when Mama died, and then the boys, and then finally Papa, I would imagine them all together in heaven. I imagine dear uncle now, too. Maybe try to do that."

Beatrice shut her eyes and seemed to find some comfort. I recalled trying to imagine the same thing, which is what our pastor had advised. It hadn't helped. I could only picture a heaven that resembled Boston. It rained. It snowed. Everyone lived in a house. My brothers still went to school. I was incapable of imagining them in the heaven that had been described to me. The jasper wall. The mansions. The everlasting peace and joy. The streets paved with gold.

Why would the dead need streets paved with gold? My brothers needed trees to climb. Creeks to swim in. Books to read. Cake to eat.

Why did anyone need gold? What use did it have?

I hoped that picturing Aaron and my uncle in heaven would ease Beatrice's sorrows. But I doubted any of us could imagine heaven. If we were capable of doing so, at the first sign of suffering — even something as small as a bee sting — we'd take our own lives.

I'd never admit to anyone how, in the months following my family's deaths, I'd pondered whether heaven existed at all. How it seemed as far-fetched as the advertisements trying to lure people to California with similar promises. I had to ask for the savior's forgiveness in a silent prayer as I wondered now if heaven was like California: a muddy clump of gamblers, oaths, whoremongering, and greed.

I needed to keep these thoughts to myself. If I voiced them, Beatrice might never stop crying. Her tears had now soaked through my sleeve, and my arm was wet. She'd been carrying on for so long, I feared she might faint. Eventually, after far too much time, she stilled and slept, her head in my lap.

I dared not move and was grateful to Phoebe, who brought me a tin cup of water.

"Thank you. I was thirsty." I sipped the water, lest I wake my cousin with overzealous gulping.

"You hungry?" Phoebe asked.

"Not yet," I said.

"You think she'll ever be herself again?"

"She's herself now."

Phoebe shook her head. "She's never acted like this before."

"She's never had troubles before," I said.

"That's true, I suppose. Don't you think she should get used to trouble? Probably more to come." Phoebe glanced over at Oxley, who was still reading from a small hardbacked book. "Is he really reading or just staring at the words? I haven't seen him turn the page once."

"You shouldn't be looking at him at all."

"I don't think he's reading. When you read, you turn pages. And he hasn't turned one."

I didn't care about Oxley's reading habits. I only hoped he had more books with him. I wished I could get a hold of one of his books right now. It would certainly help pass the time. Still, I was grateful for the peace and quiet Beatrice's nap afforded us. It was an hour before she stirred and sat up, her lips dry and cracked, her eyes pink and puffy. "Where are we, Effie?"

"On another river," I said. "Headed to the Everhart bar. We've been hired to cook, and clean, and launder for several miners. I already told you this."

She started sobbing again, even louder than before.

Nothing I could say helped, and my legs were tingling from sitting in the same position for so long. Beatrice didn't act like she noticed when I lifted her head off my lap, set it on the bench and stood to stretch. She just curled up and sobbed more. Her nose was running, and she didn't seem to care about that, either.

I needed to move about. I left Phoebe and Beatrice and walked around the deck. I soon spotted Mr. Oxley leaning over the rail and spitting up his lunch. He leaned a little too far, and his hat fell off his head of slippery dark hair and twirled off into the water. He cursed, and I watched it float away. It looked like a white turtle.

When I returned, Beatrice was still in her state of relentless lament. Even Phoebe had stopped trying to comfort her. We just talked over the noise. My sister pointed out trees and the fish in the river, some large, some small. Then she rose and wandered around. I could hear her telling the story of our journey to some of the other travelers. Every time she retold it, the crocodiles grew larger, the lizards longer. I watched as she waved her arms about, animating each leg of our odyssey.

Beatrice ran out of tears by the time we reached Sacramento City.

"I don't understand why they call this place a city," I said as we disembarked. "Boston's a city."

Phoebe looked around. "I suppose in California you can call a place whatever you want."

If she was right, then I would label Sacramento a rubbish dump. Comprised of only a few proper wooden houses, it mostly had a patchwork of stained tents, some big, some small.

Phoebe squinted at the surroundings. "Duffy told me that almost every other tent's a gambling house."

He'd exaggerated only slightly. Many of the tents served as gambling halls but not every other one. I was shocked at the many men all too eager to toss away their hard-earned money on cards and wagers. On second thought, maybe their money wasn't hard earned, and that's why they treated it like it grew in their gardens.

But I had no business thinking this because what did I know about finding gold? I didn't know what any of the tools were for or what a claim even looked like. I didn't know if the work was backbreaking or if the miners, as if on an Easter egg hunt, wandered about and plucked the shiny bits of rock from the ground. I did know that whatever work it might require, either backbreaking or easy, I was willing to do it. If *Flower* Criswick could find gold, then I could, too. I could find more than he could. And then we could go home, because staying in this wild country full of wild men and wild ways was preposterous.

The banks of the river were piled high with goods and provisions. Oxley had promised to purchase the rest of our supplies before we set off. I learned that once we had everything we needed, we'd be headed out to the claim on mules. I would have died happy to never see another mule. But here we were forced to rely on the beasts again.

I was astonished at the price of basic items in Sacramento. Flour was fourteen dollars a bag. My goodness! If my thrifty father were still alive, his hair would likely fall out hearing about such prices.

Malcolm had kindly arranged for us three women to stay in our own tent while the men sauntered about the lively place. When Beatrice and Phoebe were settled inside, Beatrice again reading her precious letters from Aaron, and Phoebe tracing her finger across a Bible page, I left to find us food. A Mexican woman sold me some beans, a bit of beef, and what she'd called *tor-tee-uhs* for three dollars. I had to resist haggling about the price. Lord have mercy, I could have fed us all for a week on that price back home.

I thanked her, instead, and wound my way back through the town toward our shelter, avoiding the glances and gazes and a few lewd shouts from the rogues I'd passed along the way.

When I drew back the flap of our tent, I felt my face flush with anger.

Phoebe was gone.

Beatrice lay on her side, her shoulders shaking, overtaken again by her grief. But I couldn't muster compassion for her. She should have done anything to keep Phoebe safe. She was older than Phoebe. Why couldn't she shake off her woe for five minutes to look after her younger cousin?

"I didn't hear her leave," Beatrice said.

I kicked at her blankets and breathed out of my nose like a bull. It was all I could do to keep from shouting at my tear-streaked cousin's face.

"Maybe she needed to use the privy," Beatrice offered.

She was wrong. She knew she was wrong. My sister was pig headed and sneaky. She'd begged me to roam around the scandalous roads with her, so we could have "fables and tales about our adventures." I'd refused. So she'd set off on her own.

Fastening the holster around my waist and snatching up Aaron's pistol, without an inkling on how to fire it, I set out to find my rash sister. It was late afternoon, the dirt roads dense with drunkards, some barely able to walk straight. Even with my sunbonnet latched tightly under my chin, hoots, hollers, and uncouth proposals whizzed about me from all directions. The only thing that kept my mind off the terrible situation was planning a punishment for Phoebe. I would punch her in the arm until it was blue. I would make her sweep the tent. I would tie her up with laces and hair ribbons. Maybe Malcolm would lend me some rope.

When one scraggly man started stumbling toward me from across the road, I ducked inside the first gambling house on our row. Whether that would be any safer, I didn't know. But lo and behold, there was Phoebe, standing in the back, as if watching a Fourth of July parade. The brightness of her yellow braids and marigold frock cut through the clotted smoke. She'd removed her bonnet and was watching, obviously amused and completely unaware of how treacherous this place was.

I wove in and out of gambling tables, ignoring the stares, and made my way over to her.

When she didn't apologize, I was shocked. "What game are they playing?" she asked me, as if I would know.

"I told you not to leave the tent."

"I offered up all my prayers for the night and felt the protection of my savior. See," she said, twirling about, "nothing's happened so far."

"You'll need a lot more prayers to be safe from me." She grinned at this, and I wanted to throttle her. "We are leaving now," I added.

"Watch that gentleman there, Effie. I saw him lose seventy whole dollars in one flip of a card."

I tried grabbing her arm and pulling her, but she twisted out of my grip.

"Watch him, Effie. He won fifty of his dollars back. It's like magic."

"There's nothing magic about it." I

watched a young woman with heart-shaped lips and silky blue-black hair deal the cards to him. She spoke French, her painted eyelids heavy and exotic.

"I keep hearing them shout *mon-tee,*" my sister said. "So maybe that's what it's called. Wish we could play."

"You wish we could play? You wish we could just toss away what few coins we have? If that's so, you wish us all to starve and be damned to this place for eternity!"

"No, silly, I'd just like to play. Without the money. It looks entertaining. We can learn and play this instead of whist. We'll make bets with straws or buttons."

We would not pretend to gamble. Not now. Not ever. But something got me curious about the game. The French woman was pulling two cards, one from the bottom and one from the top. The players at her table seemed to be betting on whether the next card in the deck would match the suit. At another table, from what I could observe, the men were trying to get as close to a total of twenty-one in their hand without going over. It seemed to me that the men were in a trance, the gambling having a grip on them they couldn't control. Had they forgotten that money was actual and real? That its sole purpose was to purchase the necessary things in life like food, shelter, and clothing?

Instead, they seemed to be treating money as if it were scrap. And the pretty French woman kept acquiring their bills after they lost and storing them in a silver box. I had only been watching her for a short time. Though she had to pay those who won, she appeared to be collecting hundreds of dollars for herself. She was certainly earning more than those playing the cards. I decided she was the only person in the room with any sense.

Finally, I was able to convince Phoebe to leave by expressing concern about Beatrice being alone. As we'd both given up on trying to cheer or humor our cousin, my sister was probably hungry, as I'd also told her about the dinner I'd bought for us. Now dusk, we walked back to our tent, which was warm and stuffy. Beatrice still hadn't eaten her portion of the meal. I worried she'd never eat again. She lay on the blankets with her eyes closed, but I didn't think she was asleep.

Phoebe's appetite was as strong as ever. I had to scold her about leaving some for Beatrice in case she felt like eating later. Phoebe relished the food, and I was hungry enough not to mind the beef, which was tough as a rope. I wasn't sure if I liked the beans or not. Unlike the beans we ate in Boston, these were unsweetened, peppery, and lacked molasses. The *tor-tee-uhs* were cold and stiff, but I enjoyed them enough to want more. They were warm when I'd purchased them, so it was my fault — no, it was Phoebe's fault — they'd grown cold.

We were almost finished with the meal when we heard a man screaming. Phoebe poked her head outside. I joined her. One man was tied to a wooden post, and another was set on lashing him with a horsewhip. I yanked my sister back inside. The man's screams pierced the air, and we all covered our ears in a failed attempt to block out the noise.

In the morning, we learned that the man tied to the post had been accused of stealing some bread, and several vigilantes had ordered the lashings.

"That seems a terrible punishment for such a small crime," Phoebe said. "Cruel. If we'd been starved, would we steal bread?"

I didn't know what we'd do, but I didn't want to ever be hungry enough to be forced into that choice. Justice was difficult to measure anywhere in the world but seemed harder here. Perhaps it needed to be. The land was lawless. If men just took what they wanted, small or big, any semblance of order would vanish.

Where we were headed, according to Malcolm, it was even more lawless. All we'd have is the miners' code, which said that a miner could only have one claim at a time and was forbidden from jumping someone else's claim. Also, men had to work a claim until it gave out and couldn't murder each other under any circumstances except self-defense.

"Do people still get murdered, despite this code?" I'd asked.

"Oh, sure, now and then," he'd said.

"Is that the whole code?" Phoebe had counted the rules on one hand.

"Can't steal another's pick, shovel, or pan neither," he'd said. "Can't steal anything. Also, we frown on making up tall tales about how well a claim is doing just to sell a fella provisions or take his money for a share. Most try and live by the code to keep the order of things. As much as we can keep order. But no denying it's wild country. Indians live near our cabin. We'll be going for days without seeing another soul but each other. Given enough time, you'll come to hate my face, the sound of my voice, and even the smell of my skin. And you'll blame me for any troubles that come to pass."

"I'll never blame you," Phoebe had said. "No matter what comes to pass, I'll never feel hateful toward you. Why, you saved our lives."

I'd kept quiet when he'd made his prediction. I expected he was right that we would all come to loathe each other after being cooped up in a frustrating proximity for any length of time. More so, I didn't believe that Malcolm had saved our lives. Far as I could tell, we three still had no one but each other to do any sort of saving. If anyone deserved credit for saving Phoebe, it was me. But this was a prideful thought, and I admonished myself.

Either way, no matter what Malcolm said or what troubles lay before us, I was determined that by this time next year, we'd be back in Boston where we belonged.

From behind me, my sister shrieked. Then came a thud.

She'd tumbled off her mule when the saddle, too large for the beast, slipped around toward the mule's belly during a quick trot. In a heap of skirts, her nose and forehead dusted, Phoebe appeared stunned.

Quickly dismounting, I prayed she wasn't injured.

Spitting out a mouthful of dirt, she began

to giggle like a child. Relieved, I laughed with her. Almost everyone did. Even Beatrice. Everyone but Russell Oxley, who looked bored, hot, and irritated at having to stop. I allowed myself a moment of spite by feeling satisfied that he'd lost his precious white hat. Also, I didn't see the cane anywhere. He must've left it on the boat, or maybe it had been stolen in Sacramento City.

Duffy had dismounted, too. He reached out his hand and pulled Phoebe up. Then he got to work tightening her saddle. By evening, we'd made it to the flat and grassy Marysville. The fledging village with its few merchants, boardinghouses, and tavern wasn't a town yet but yearned to be one.

A rancher Malcolm knew with short legs and a belly bigger than six jugs of water offered us shelter and a soft place to sleep. That night, the rancher's wife prepared a meal for us. We sat around a long table, and the rancher said grace. When he was through, Phoebe practically shouted an "amen."

"You think God's hard of hearing?" Oxley said to her.

She blushed. "I'm just thankful for the food and the company and an actual table." She ran her hand across it, as if the table itself were a miracle.

Duffy nodded. "I'm just as grateful. Also grateful for the company," he said, smiling at my sister.

Oxley fixed his eyes on our host. "You got a whole field of beef out there, and all you can serve up are hot oysters, toast, tomatoes, and coffee?"

Shocked by his bad manners, I thanked the family more than once for feeding us and allowing us to stay. After dinner, I'd seen Malcolm take the old rancher aside to smooth over Oxley's insolence. The food was delectable, far as I was concerned, and I would never for the rest of my life take for granted a good night's sleep in a proper shelter.

The next day, we rose at dawn and left Marysville, passing some of the most scenic country I had ever seen. Massive California oaks. The rolling buttes. And the snow-capped Sierra Nevada in the distance. After half a day, we came upon a group of Indian women wearing nothing but grass skirts. Malcolm said they were gathering flower seeds. Phoebe wanted to stop, and Malcolm allowed for it. Phoebe and I eased toward them, and they ceased their work to stare at us. Phoebe waved. A few women approached. Though I didn't speak their language, I understood the tone of their words as a greeting.

"I'm Phoebe," my sister said, pointing at herself. The women laughed. Maybe her name sounded comical to them.

The youngest of the women reached out to touch my skirt, feeling the fabric between her fingers. I admired the starling black of her hair and the glossy skin of her bare limbs. The decorative and tightly woven baskets she and the other women carried on their backs to collect the seeds seemed a marvel. I turned to Malcolm and asked for his knife.

"She's just touching your calico," he said. "No danger in that."

"I'm aware. I just need it, please." He shrugged, then dug the knife out of his pocket. I took the blade and sawed off a small square of my dress's hem, handing it to the girl. She seemed pleased.

As we rode off, Duffy told us they mixed the seeds with pounded acorns and grasshoppers to make bread.

"Grasshoppers?" Phoebe said. "Yuck."

"Everyone's got to eat," Duffy said.

Phoebe thought for a moment. "If we can eat grasshoppers, then God doesn't stand a chance should he send another plague of locusts. We'll just make some bread!"

"Ain't you shrewd?" Duffy said. "I sure like me a shrewd woman."

My sister was far from shrewd, but I didn't correct him. He'd find out in good time that my sister was as capricious as they come and that a woodland fairy had more sense.

We soon came upon a tall flat-topped hill that Malcolm called Table Mountain.

Phoebe remarked that it looked like God had taken a cake knife to its peak. That got me thinking about cake, which made me hungry. Since it would be hours before we set up camp for the night, I couldn't be thinking about cake or pies or anything else.

The farther we traveled into the foothills, the thicker the pine, oak, buckeye, and sleek Madrone trees. With the moon just beginning to rise over a bluff, we stopped to set up camp. Worn out, achy, and hungry, I still could appreciate the clean smell of green leaves. It was idyllic here, almost out of a storybook. For just a brief moment and for the first time since I'd left Boston, I thought myself fortunate for the experience. I sat on a log with Phoebe and Beatrice and tugged the bonnet from my head. The soft air felt refreshing. I would have enjoyed the moment if it weren't for the rustling I heard in the manzanita shrubs and the fact that

Beatrice had pretty much leapt into my lap.

"Oh no," she murmured. "Could it be a bear?"

Grizzlies were all around us according to Malcolm. Since we had yet to see a bear, the creature still seemed imaginary. I wanted to keep it that way. As lovely as this wild country was, the price for such beauty was danger in the form of grizzlies, poisonous snakes, and wildcats.

Malcolm was building a fire. "Don't get all quiet," he said.

"Yeah, stir up as much noise as possible," Duffy added. "Scares 'em off."

My sister started singing "Rock of Ages," and Duffy joined in, singing the harmony. He had a nice tenor voice and would have been welcome in our choir back home. Soon, Beatrice, in a shaky soprano, picked up the refrain. Before long, everyone was caught up in the hymn.

We kept up the singing, and anyone who overheard would have thought he'd stumbled across a country church. If the bear or whatever had made the sound was still lurking about, we wouldn't have heard it over our hymn. After supper, we slept like stones, even with the fear of a bear prowling about our camp.

■ ■ ■ ■

In the coming days, the travel grew more cumbersome and tiring. We rode on and on, uphill, downhill, through fir groves, and along the narrow edges of shadowy ravines. We'd come upon a few clearings where the sun would beat down on us until I thought I might go blind. Then the trail would tighten up, and we'd be cast for hours in a chilly shade from the eastern cottonwoods. On several occasions, we had to stop to tug a fallen tree from the path. Everyone pitched in but Oxley, who folded his arms over his chest and smirked while watching our efforts.

We met up with only a few other folks along the way, one a prospector who looked as though he'd been growing his beard his entire life. He was kind enough to share some much appreciated coffee. As we sipped the bitter brew, he told us a mournful story about a Frenchman and his wife who'd been murdered by Indians a few weeks back. "You shouldn't fret over it," he said to us. "Rare they'd kill a woman. Most gals are snatched up, instead, and made into chieftain wives. Don't hear of them being kilt as often as the men."

Beatrice paled.

But Phoebe seemed to find it interesting. "Wouldn't that be a turn?" she said. "Coming out here and ending up married to an Indian chief. Wouldn't that beat out any expectations you might have had for your life?"

Beatrice didn't answer. But I shook my head at Phoebe, indicating she should shush up. As for me, I didn't like the idea of marrying anyone, but would refuse to marry a man who insisted I dine on flower seeds, grasshoppers, and acorns for the rest of my life. A more bitter meal I couldn't imagine.

In the next few days, the pine trees rose so grandly, it seemed their limbs were reaching out to swat the birds from the sky. Except for a few tiny lizards wiggling to and fro between the mossy roots of ancient conifers, it felt as if we were the only living beings on earth. My theory was challenged this afternoon when we spotted a deer framed by tree leaves, motionless, gazing at us with saucer-shaped, frightened eyes. It stared at us for a good five seconds before bounding away in a blink, its white tail a blur.

My legs, back, arms, and head ached and stormed by the time we reached the last stretch of downhill travel to the Everhart

Bar on the north fork of the Feather River. The river, as if scattered with jewels, gleamed, glittered, and roared. To reach the cabin, we'd have to ride our mules down a five-mile steep hill. If our mules misstepped, we could be dashed to bits in the ravine below. But I had to trust my beast. He seemed clever at picking his way across the land and keeping his own footing. I regretted ever casting doubt on mules and vowed to forever defend them, as they had carried us and our provisions all this way without the least bit of skittishness. With my whole heart, I believed they would bring us safely down this treacherous path to the cabin, where I planned to sleep for days.

Seven

Phoebe must have cast off her high and mighty standards regarding men because she wouldn't stop chattering with the bedraggled stranger on the porch. She'd also abandoned any previous held convention when it came to proper interactions between men and women. The oily-haired miner with a half-shaven chin on our porch had arrived to our camp only an hour after sunrise.

"Haven't seen a woman for months," he'd said to Malcolm. "So I left the diggings and gambled on you allowing me an introduction."

How dare this fellow suggest Malcolm was in charge of who we could and couldn't meet! Before I'd been able to lash out with my distaste, my sister had pushed past me and headed outside.

Twirling the end of her braid around her freckled wrist, she introduced herself and asked the man if he was a good Christian. He looked stricken to me, as if he'd never seen a girl in his whole life. As she described our journey, he looked as though he were in a dream. When I went out to fetch her, a few more miners from the neighboring camp were emerging from the thick grove of cedar, fir, and pine. I was fastening my apron, and one man, watching, began to laugh. Did he doubt my ability to tie a proper bow? A moment later, I realized it was not the kind of laughing we did while joshing each other. It was the type of laugh a child has while on a swing or seesaw.

"Get back inside," I said to my sister. "And help me with breakfast."

With her fingers, she waved goodbye to the gathering crowd before obeying.

Once I shut the door, she twirled around the room. "The men outside seem very kind. And welcoming."

"They're grubby," I snapped. "They reek. Their beards are likely used as nests for the bluebirds."

"I enjoyed the conversation."

"You did all the talking."

"I suppose I did," she said. "I don't even know his name. I enjoyed our conversation all the same."

"It can't be a conversation if you didn't

converse." I was tugging a large bag of flour out from under the bedstead. "We'll make soda bread and potatoes with onions. Malcolm said we needed to eat plenty of onions, or we'd get terribly ill."

Phoebe was sweeping the floor. I appreciated that I didn't have to ask. As for Beatrice, she was still lazing on her blanket on the cabin floor, her eyes fixed on a wall, where an ant the size of a blackberry scuttled toward the beamed ceiling.

"It's morning. Rise and shine," I said to her. She didn't move.

I walked over and nudged her with my foot. When she rolled over on her back, the blanket tugged up to her chin, her eyes were swollen and her face splotchy. Crouching down, I smoothed back a few wisps of her hair that were wet, sticky, and clumped with tears. Her face, once bright and plump with rose-red lips and a narrow nose that turned up happily at its tip, appeared waxy and gray. Her full cheeks caved in. Her eyelids were as thick as some of the succulents we'd seen on our travels down the Chagres River.

"When's the last time you ate, Cousin?"

She licked her lips and said she didn't know.

My uncle had trusted me to care for her. He had trusted me, as my father had trusted him to care for me and Phoebe. And I was failing him. "You'll need to make yourself decent," I said, as gently as I could. "Men will be coming in, and you'll need to help me with the breakfast. The cleaning, too. We have nowhere else to go, and we can't let these fellows down by burning daylight."

"Nights are bad. Mornings are even worse."

"We've got blue skies and plenty to do," I said. "So rise and shine."

"When I wake, it's like I've just discovered Aaron's dead."

I remembered the way grief jumbled with time. I remembered the agony of waking up and realizing all over again my family was gone. That I would have to live another day without them.

"It smells like dirt here," she complained. "I feel as if it's in my nose."

My goodwill toward her faded some. After all, if it weren't for Beatrice, we wouldn't be here. I walked over to the small galley and laid some onions out to slice.

My sister was unpacking the provisions. "It smells like trees and river water and soil. I like it." She took a deep breath.

Beatrice moaned. "We should have never come."

I didn't want to hear this from my cousin.

128

"I hate it here," she kept on. "It's filthy. We'll never be clean. It's no place for me or for any woman. It's . . . it's barbaric."

I was cutting up an onion, my eyes watering with each layer. "We have shelter."

"Both of you stop crying," Phoebe said.

I slammed the knife down. "I do not cry! It's the onion."

"Whatever your excuse, I think it's marvelous here," Phoebe said. "Duffy told me he saw some Indians walking in the woods last night. He said they were probably out hunting."

Beatrice pulled her blanket tighter around her.

Phoebe kept on. "And he says the river has big boulders that are thousands of years old. That's nice to think on, isn't it?"

"We'll probably drown in that river," Beatrice said. "And no one will be around to save us. Not Daddy. Not Aaron."

"We'll just have to save ourselves," I said.

Phoebe laughed at me. "We've got whole camps of men who'd likely run through a fire for us. Surely, they'd jump in a river."

I wagged the knife at her. "Shush up with that."

"It's true."

Beatrice had turned on her side and was again staring at the cabin wall.

I'd had enough and demanded she help out. Grumbling and sniffling the entire time, she pulled herself up and then wearily rose from the floor. Her dress, one that had once hugged her figure, hung on her like a willow branch. She needed to eat. Maybe her gloomy thoughts would fade some after a good meal. In truth, I wasn't sure I was capable of preparing a good meal. She'd at least have some coffee.

The men had also risen early. Malcolm and Duffy. So, too, the other men who held shares, those who'd hung back to keep Everhart Bar safe from claim jumpers. We'd met them last night, but I'd been too exhausted to converse much. One man was called Cecil. He told me he had been a preacher before coming to California but would never preach again. I hadn't asked why. He was older than the others by a decade or more, had long lean limbs, and a wide purplish scar in the shape of driftwood. The scar coiled from his jaw all the way to his collar. It relieved me some that he seemed indifferent toward us as the fairer sex. I was sick to death of being fawned over and proposed to everywhere we went.

The other man was known as Big Al. I didn't understand why he was called Big Al because he was almost as small as a boy and skinny enough to use the last hole in his belt.

The best of the crew, far as I could tell, was Duffy Fields. The others, even the so-called preacher, seemed to sling their oaths and blasphemies around with abandon. But Duffy was careful to choose his words so as not to offend. I would also vouch that he was the hardest worker of the bunch, unloading the picks, shovels, food, and provisions from the mules with a jaunty work ethic and directing the others with humor and gusto to do the same.

Despite sleeping on the floor, I'd had one of the best night's sleep since we'd left Marysville. Well rested, I'd been happy to wake up in something that at least resembled a house. So tired of boats, tents, and the forest floor, I was grateful for this small cabin. Malcolm told me he'd bought it off a dead German called Josef Weber. The claim had been Weber's, too. Weber had tried to jump a nearby claim on top of the one he was already working. When the owner had warned him off, Weber had drawn an Allen's pepper box and had shot the owner in the leg. Then the owner had beaten Weber over the head with a shovel, killing him. The miners held a trial and found the owner killed Weber in self-defense. They'd buried Weber on the hill and sold everything at an auction, sending the acquired funds to Weber's family in Pennsylvania. And that was how Malcolm and company came to own the claim and cabin.

Made of logs, it had boughs of good-smelling cedar for a roof. The large door was made from cedar, too, and the walls were pine. Another corner had cupboards with a few wooden and tin dishes, also bottles, knives, forks, spoons, a few good pots, a Dutch oven, a tin frying pan, a boiler, and a coffee pot. Under the bedstead, I'd stored seven cakes of tallow and twelve bags of flour. I'd left the door wide open this morning to air the place out, as the cabin lacked any windows. The porch faced the north side of the river, and on the east end a large fireplace built from smooth river stones rose to the ceiling.

Not one of us had ever built a fire, so Duffy showed us how. Despite the warmth of the early summer, we'd need it to prepare the meals. On the west end of the cabin was a large bedstead framed into the logs of the cabin. The cords of the bedstead were strips of rawhide crisscrossing each other. We'd find some pine needles today in order to make it soft enough to sleep on.

"You can pile blankets and the buffalo

skins I brought along on the needles," Malcolm had said. "It'll make a fine bed for you three."

I had thanked him for allowing us the comfort.

The other corners had bunks for the men to sleep on. They'd slept under the stars the night before. But that arrangement would change. Malcolm said as much. Malcolm had hung his rifle above the fireplace and promised to shoot a deer for me to cook. I secretly hoped every deer in the forest would evade him because I didn't know the first thing about cooking a deer or what in the world one tasted like. Venison, he'd called it. It didn't sound appetizing. He'd also mentioned that I could cook a squirrel stew, as those were easy to hunt. Quail, too. I'd never eaten squirrel or quail in my life. Both sounded repulsive. I chastised myself for this latent choosiness. To survive, I would have to overcome any fussiness that remained from my prior life.

In front of our cabin, a mountain rose from the edge of the river. Duffy told us it would keep the cabin in the shade until ten in the morning. Though June, the fire was welcome due to the early-morning chill. Walking out on the porch, I noticed the top of the mountain still smothered in snow.

But I liked breathing in the cool, fresh air and felt calmed by the shushing of the river. With the evergreens, pine, and cedar, it smelled rich and free. I would keep these thoughts to myself, lest Phoebe get any peculiar ideas about staying here.

All in all, it was a simple but quaint cabin. It had a few roughly hewn chairs, a well-built table, and a stash of quilts and blankets that would have to be boiled but otherwise would serve us well. For now, it would have to do. And Beatrice would have to temper her objections.

I took my task of cooking seriously. I tried my best to prepare a breakfast the men wouldn't pull faces at upon tasting. When they sat down for the meal, I stood back and chewed on my thumbnail. After they took a whiff of my undertaking, they dove into the food. Maybe they were hungry enough not to complain about my soda bread, which I'd deemed flat and much too salty. Determined to master cooking, I decided to pick some blackberries later and prepare a jam to serve with supper.

After they'd eaten, all the men but Oxley went off to work what they called the "wet diggings" while we spent the morning tidying, dusting, and putting away the supplies. I'd learned from Malcolm that a claim was really only a section of the river they'd declared as their own for the time being. He'd also explained how the gold was mostly found in the river flats, banks, and gravely bars, called the diggings.

Around noon, we set out to find the creek Malcolm had told us about so we could launder some clothes and bathe. About a half-mile walk, we easily wound our way there. Guarded by a sentry of tall pine glutted with birds warbling and trilling, it seemed private enough. Phoebe sang her hymns while we scrubbed the shirts with soap and wrung them out to dry on a large granite rock in the sun. I joined the singing, but Beatrice stayed quiet. Even when we saw a few butterflies fluttering near a big orange lily-like flower, she refused to show any pleasure.

The creek water had numbed our arms and hands. The water was melted snow from the mountains around us. But I didn't care how cold it was. I was determined to bathe. So, after we laundered the shirts, we got up the nerve to remove our clothing. Even with the thick patch of trees around us, I couldn't help but flush head to toe at the very idea of being undressed outside. I'd done the same thing when we'd been on the steamer and had to pour buckets of water over each other. I'd been embarrassed, even with the blanket held up around me.

"The men are busy," Phoebe said. "No one can see us here."

I hoped she was right but nevertheless ran and dove into the creek just in case any of the strange men who'd wandered into our camp this morning were still hanging about. When I came up for air, I heard Phoebe let out a whoop as she sprinted across the bank and then plunged sideways into the water.

"Phoebe!" I said. "Someone will hear."

She only laughed and started splashing me in the face. Contrary to this, Beatrice bit by bit lowered herself into the water as if she were about to be baptized. To wash ourselves, we used the same soap we'd used on the men's shirts, and my entire body soon numbed. Beatrice's teeth were chattering. At least the bracing water might take her mind off poor Aaron and my uncle.

Phoebe paddled about, her face beaming in the sunlight. "Feels wonderful."

Beatrice ran her hand back and forth across the water, as if she were conducting a symphony. She was staring at her own arm, as if it belonged to another. "I am sorry," she said, "for bringing you here."

I hadn't expected an apology. We were here. This is where life had taken us. We had no one but each other, and I didn't want her apologies. I wanted her to laugh again.

"I hope you can forgive me, Effie. I never dreamed we'd end up in such dire straits." Beatrice dunked her head to rinse out the soap. I hoped she wasn't crying beneath the surface.

Now Phoebe was holding up a handful of baby frogs. "Duffy called them polliwogs. Isn't that word funny? *Polliwog.*"

I didn't think it ideal to be bathing in a creek full of frogs.

"What do you think of Duffy?" my sister asked.

"I think of him as a gentleman," I said. "And he works harder than most."

"Think he's handsome?"

"It's not our place to make such judgments."

"You think he might be looking for a wife? Don't you think we'd make a fine pair?"

I was stunned. She barely knew him. And he was at least ten years older. Added to this, he'd never even been to a city other than San Francisco, which in my estimation didn't count. He was from Ohio and reared to farm potatoes and squash. Phoebe should marry a man of means with education and ideas, not a farmer. Before I could tell her my thoughts, I noticed movement to the left of me in the trees. Maybe it was a bear. Did bears swim? I didn't know.

"I think he's the most handsome man here. Even more handsome than Malcolm Everhart. Duffy's the nicest, too."

"He is very kind," Beatrice said.

I was surprised Beatrice had even been listening to Phoebe's prattle.

"Quiet," I said. "Both of you. Something's over there."

We crouched in the creek and kept still and silent.

"What is it?" Phoebe whispered.

I shook my head. I didn't know. And she needed to shush up. Suddenly, I saw it moving. A flash of black trousers and a red cotton shirt. "It's Mr. Oxley," I whispered. "He's seen us in all our glory."

Beatrice blushed despite being completely immersed in the icy waters. "Is he still there?"

"I think he ran off when I spotted him," I said.

We stayed quiet and listened, our teeth chattering. When we didn't hear anything for a while, we waded quickly out of the creek and pulled on our dresses without drying first.

"We should tell Malcolm what he did."

Phoebe was shaking the water from her hair.

I supposed she was right. But it was humiliating. It seemed speaking of it aloud would humiliate us further.

"Malcolm will make sure it doesn't happen again," she said.

"No," I decided. "I will speak to Mr. Oxley, myself. Don't utter a word about this to any of the others."

Phoebe stared at me, her hands on her hips. "That arrogant dandy won't listen to you!"

"If he has any sense, he will." I wasn't sure what I was going to do or say to the varlet. But we'd come this far alone and handled our own affairs the entire way. I could stand up to Russell Oxley by myself and make him regret his vulgar actions.

EIGHT

Last night, Cecil brought back the most gold from the diggings. It pained me to see the preacher give a percentage of his dust to Oxley, who hadn't done a lick of work since we'd arrived a week before. Oxley had purchased most of our provisions, but a man worth his salt wouldn't be capable of sitting on his tail all day, then take without a smidgeon of gratitude the fruit of other men's labors. After he'd spied on us at the creek, Phoebe had more than once wanted to spit in his supper. He should count himself fortunate that I'd stopped her every time. Maybe I should have allowed the revenge, but the act seemed too boorish.

I would have to muster the courage this morning to confront the brute about his behavior and warn him not to dare repeat the act.

After the others headed off to the river, Oxley sat under a live oak on his fold-out chair. He lit a pipe and opened a book. I set out to retrieve some of the laundry we'd been drying on the line. After gathering it up, I walked toward Oxley, marshaling my gumption with each step.

Beatrice and Phoebe watched from the open door.

"Mr. Oxley, may I have a word?"

He didn't avert his eyes from his book.

"It's in regards to your indecent voyeurism. And there's no use denying your unsavory action, as I saw you with my own eyes."

He shut his book slowly, then looked up at me with a raw and rude grin. His face flared with sunburn. I hoped his skin would bubble, blister, and peel right off.

"This behavior will not be tolerated," I continued. His oily expression was working on my nerves. "You are to keep your distance from us at all times."

"I don't believe you have any control over my actions. I will go where I choose and do what I choose."

"You will, from this moment on, not dare look at any of us at any time."

Defying me, he craned his neck and pointed toward the door. "I'm looking at them right now. Your cousin is more to my taste than the other. But either will do."

"You . . . you are to look away. You are

forbidden from uttering a word about them."

He swung his icy-blue eyes back to me, and I felt as though I were the subject of an examination. After a moment, he said, "Your cousin has the shapeliness a man like me desires. Your sister has the . . . energy. But you would do as well if I became desperate enough. It would be similar to how some of these farm boys poke their sheep. A man's needs sometimes overcome good taste."

I dropped the laundry I'd been holding.

"Pick it up," he said.

Gritting my teeth, I, at first, refused. But if I didn't scoop it from the ground, we'd have to rewash everything. So I was forced to pick up the clothing, my face heating up with anger and humiliation while I gathered and shook the dirt off the socks and linens. When I turned around to head back to the cabin, I heard him chuckling.

If I allowed this moment to pass, I feared I would experience many more like it or even worse. I could tell Malcolm later, but that would put the men in a weakened state. It would either result in a fight or Oxley's banishment. Or maybe both. And if they banished Oxley, he could pack up his provisions and leave us to starve over the winter.

I swung back around and spooned my words out as I had the flour for the biscuits this morning. "You are a weak and craven ailment, Russell Oxley. If you dare spy on us again, I shall murder you. We traveled a great distance to be here. And along the way I encountered worse scoundrels. I poisoned one and pushed another off the steamer while he was making water. And, my goodness" — I looked him up and down — "you're much smaller than those men were. If I were you, I would treat us like the ladies we are. If you don't take my advice, you might choose not to eat the food I prepare."

My skirts flared as I spun on my boot heel and stomped back into the cabin without bothering to look at his expression or listen to his reply.

He didn't need to know the threat was mostly empty. Besides, I might just be capable of the lies I'd just told. Indeed, I might be able to summon a terrible nature hidden within. I just might.

NINE

Duffy found a nugget the size of his knuckle yesterday. The size of it inspired me to ask Malcolm again to allow me to work the diggings alongside the men. If I found just a few of these nuggets, we could get back to Boston and be comfortable until I started earning a wage as a schoolteacher. We'd been here over a month, and it was high time I did what I came out here to do, which was to work Beatrice's share and earn enough to see us home.

For weeks, I'd been trying to persuade him. But every time I'd asked, he'd come up with a new reason to forbid it. The work was too grueling. I wasn't stout enough. I'd slow everyone down. I'd catch the ague. I'd wear myself ragged and be worthless around the cabin. I needed more meat on my bones. On and on.

All of it nonsense.

At least Duffy had explained the process.

In truth, it did sound arduous. But it couldn't be much harder than the work we were doing now. Keeping the cabin in order, washing their clothes, and feeding the men took effort and energy. So using a pan or shallow bowl and shaking out the rock and muddy water didn't intimidate me. Seemed similar to using a sieve to sift flour. And I could learn to work a cradle, which Duffy said took the strength of two men. I was as strong as a man. Or almost as strong. I, at the very least, could lift and carry more weight than other women.

The hardest part, Duffy said, was breaking up the gravel and slate bars to reach the gold-rich veins. But I could swing an axe and cut firewood, so I could do that, too.

While everyone ate the porridge I'd made this morning, I brought the idea up with Malcolm again. "When will I be able to work the diggings?"

He ignored me as he scraped up the lumpy porridge from the bottom of his bowl.

"I came here to work the claim, and it's my right," I said.

He wouldn't look up at me.

As if she'd been mulling it over for a while, Phoebe asked, "How'd the gold get here?"

Duffy shrugged. "Guess it's been here forever. Just no one cared to dig it out or had any use for it."

"Maybe God left it for us to find," Phoebe said.

Cecil swallowed and wiped his mouth. "Geology left it here. Many years of weather, erosion, earthquakes, glaciers, etcetera, etcetera."

"Like I said," Phoebe explained, "God left it. The preacher said so. Because it's God who makes the weather and the quakes and the etcetera. I think God made the etcetera on the eighth day and got too busy to account for it in Genesis."

Duffy grinned at her. I could tell my sister made his heart beat faster. "He knew you were coming up to this cabin someday and had to leave something that was almost as pretty, so you'd have company."

She didn't blush, as she should have. "Why, everything's pretty here. The birds and the sky and flowers. Didn't really need the gold."

"None of it's as pretty as you." It seemed as if Duffy forgot we could all hear him.

Malcolm rose from the table and cleared his throat. "Time to head out."

I watched my sister collect Duffy's bowl. Her hand brushed against his. Then I heard

146

something strange. A dog barking. I hadn't heard a dog's bark since we stayed at the ranch in Marysville.

Malcolm rushed outside and sprinted toward the sound. The dog sounded hysterical. Big Al, Duffy, and Cecil followed.

The dog kept barking, and I heard Malcolm shouting. Before long, Big Al came running back, and he rushed into the cabin. "Grizzly has a dog cornered!" He grabbed the rifle from above the fireplace, then hurried back.

We three stood on the porch and listened. "Get back inside," I ordered Beatrice and Phoebe.

Beatrice did as she was told, but Phoebe wouldn't budge. "Duffy's out there. He could get mauled."

We heard a shot echoing through the forest. From the pictures I'd seen, bears seemed too large for one bullet.

Nevertheless, I ducked inside, grabbed Aaron's Colt, and strode out after the men. I'd never shot a pistol but didn't think it would be too difficult. Aim and pull the trigger. On the way, I loaded a bullet into the chamber, as Malcolm had shown me how to do. We hadn't gotten to the actual shooting part of the lesson.

When I reached the fracas, I kept my

distance. Malcolm was either the biggest fool who'd ever been born or had a fondness for dogs that dulled his good sense. Because here he was standing between a mud-caked skinny mutt and a pacing bear. The giant bear's humped shoulders, concave profile, cream-colored snout, and silver-tipped fur took my breath away. Duffy, Big Al, and Cecil were keeping their distance and looked on the verge of running. What could they do but stay away? They couldn't fight off a bear this size. No one could.

Malcolm seemed to have other ideas. He looked small compared to the bear, though he was puffing out his chest and standing at his full height. The bear didn't seem to notice or care how tall Malcolm was. It rose up on its hind legs and seemed four stories high as it slashed the air with claws as sharp and long as ice picks. Then it came back down again and took a step forward.

"Climb the tree," Duffy said.

I had a terrible thought. If Malcolm turned toward the tree, the bear would sense his fear and attack. Also, the bear might be able to climb up after him. Of course it could. One look at its claws convinced me. Why was Malcolm trying to save a dog from a bear? The dog seemed to be doing just fine warding off the beast with its high-pitched barks.

Malcolm seemed calm. He was looking off into the distance and telling the bear they could get along. He used a soothing voice that didn't seem to be soothing anyone or anything. He and the dog were backed up together against an outcropping of granite boulders and boxed in by the enormous animal.

I stood behind the bear. The pistol felt heavy and unfamiliar in my hand. How far could a bullet travel? Was I close enough to give it a try? And would the bullet help with matters, even if my aim were true? Why didn't Malcolm shoot the bear? I'd heard the rifle go off when we were back at the cabin, but the bear looked unscathed. Maybe Malcolm had shot and missed.

"Run along," I said to the bear. I used the same voice as Malcolm. Only mine was shaking. When the bear stood on its hind legs again, I couldn't think of anything else to do but fire the pistol. Instead of aiming at the bear, I cocked the pistol and shot at a tree, hoping this would distract the beast. The force of the shot knocked the pistol out of my hand and sent a stinging shock down my hand and arm.

Worse, the bear pivoted toward me. Malcolm took the opportunity to scoop up the dog and move, so as not to be trapped by the boulders.

Just as Malcolm had done, I wouldn't look the bear in the eye. I kept my voice measured and firm and waved my arms. "You just carry on with your day and get on out of here." In that moment, I imagined my death. My life a mockery. My body torn to pieces and consigned forever to this high elevation of wild contempt for society and civilization.

But the giant animal came down on all fours and shook its broad head, slobber spraying the air around it. Then it turned around. Branches broke, its large paws bending the vegetation as it crashed through and disappeared in the brush.

I took a breath, the kind one takes when coming up for air from a swim. The sky looked heavier than before, as if dropping down on me, the tree roots darker and thicker, I noticed a gray squirrel out of the corner of my eye. Then I saw nothing.

Something was licking my hand. Maybe I'd hallucinated the bear leaving, and I was now being devoured.

When I opened my eyes, I was lying on the forest floor. The filthy dog, its eyes dark and humble, was prostrate at my side.

"Lazarus," Malcolm said. "That's what I named him since he survived death. Probably belongs to a feller from another camp, but we'll care for the mutt until its owner comes looking."

I sat up and shook the soil from my hair and wiped the side of my face, spitting out a bit of dirt. Beatrice and Phoebe were leaning over me. Phoebe was fanning me with her Bible.

"Why, Effie," Phoebe said, "you've never fainted in your life."

"I've never been almost eaten by a bear."

Big Al told Malcolm I'd saved his skin, and now all the men were teasing him about it. Saying he missed a moment to keep us well fed for the whole winter and give us a rug to boot.

"Can't kill an animal like that," Malcolm said. "Don't seem right."

"It wouldn't have had a problem killing you," Cecil said.

"Lazarus is the brave one. He was ready to fight." Malcolm was patting its head, but the dog wouldn't move or take his gaze from me, even after I stood and brushed the dirt and pine needles from my skirts.

I noticed Aaron's Colt a few feet away and went to retrieve it. "I'll need to learn how to use this properly," I said to Malcolm. "Just in case you decide to save any more dogs."

"Lessons can start tomorrow." He grinned.

I rubbed my arm and hand, which still stung, and headed back toward the cabin, the dog in my shadow. I wished it would just run off. I wanted nothing to do with the bedraggled cur. The dog had been foolish enough to challenge a bear. And I was surrounded by enough fools, especially Malcolm. What sort of man would risk his life for a mangy dog?

"Malcolm was so brave to try and save that pup," Beatrice said, once we were back inside. "I can see why he and Flower were friends. Aaron loved pups. Remember, Effie, how much he loved pups?"

I had to sit down. My hands shook. My heart pounded. The dog, gazing up at me, lay at my feet.

"Listen," I said to Beatrice and Phoebe, "both of you. If something ever happens to me, you must find a way to get out of here and back to Boston."

Tears sprung from Phoebe's eyes, and she threw her arms around me.

"I lived through it," I said. "It would be degrading to die like that, to be dragged off and eaten."

Now Beatrice looked as if she too might faint.

When the men came back in, after making sure the bear was gone for good, Duffy seemed more concerned about my sister's emotions than my fainting spell. But Malcolm poured me some lukewarm coffee that had been left over from breakfast.

While everyone else was busy retelling and hashing over the exciting event, Malcolm kneeled down to pet the dog. Then he looked up at me. His eyes were the color of a harbor. Why had I just noticed that?

"That there was a narrow squeak," he said. "For you and for me and for Lazarus, here. You've got some mettle in you, Effie Frost. I'll take you out to the bar tomorrow and see if you can work your share."

TEN

All my childhood, my father had told me I was stronger than most of the other girls and even some of the boys. Smarter, too. I'd always tried to live up to his praise. But the labor at the diggings made me think he might've been mistaken, as the work was harder than any I'd ever done.

I'd had this notion that the worst part would be working in the river. But standing in the icy waters — collecting, then swishing sediment with the slim chance of finding dust — was the easiest part. If that's all I'd been required to do, the work would have been breezy. The reality of working the diggings was much harsher. First, I had to dig into the earth with picks and axes that I could barely lift. And to reach the areas where the dust was most likely to be, I had to dig in sand, gravel, rocks, and sometimes between massive boulders. Even with all this, for the past few days, we'd returned to the cabin at twilight empty handed, bone tired, our limbs numb from the water, and our backs, necks, and shoulders grieved and achy.

The summer heat of July made the work harder while using the picks and shovels on the banks, but it did nothing to warm the river water. In this ice bath, I'd stand with the rapids up to my underarms, piling rocks to build a dam, shivering and shaking until I could stand no more and, breathless, would stumble ashore. Cecil had shown me how to shove my aching legs in the hot sand to warm and sooth them. The men would shout oaths every time a finger was crushed or a blistered hand burst open against the shovel handle. I couldn't blame them. I, too, had the urge to yell out the same curses.

After three days of the work, my strength increased, but I wasn't as strong as the others. It was all I could do to help anywhere I could, holding up a board while another hammered to build a cradle, or arranging the rocks on the dam while the others lifted. Big Al had given me a pair of brown cotton trousers, a red shirt, a pair of suspenders, and some leather mining boots. They'd belonged to his brother, who was "near to about your size." His brother had died on the overland trail from a sickness that arrived in the morning and took him on to the Lord by the afternoon. "We buried him somewhere in Wyoming on the side of the trail," Big Al told me. "Maybe I can go back there someday and mark his grave."

When I first put on his brother's clothing, I could see Big Al glancing at me now and then. Perhaps it seemed his brother had come back to haunt him. I hoped he didn't regret giving me the clothing, as working the claim in my calico dress had been cumbersome.

I still wore my bonnet, but wished for one of the men's wide-brimmed hats. I didn't want my skin to become thick and lined from the hard sun's stamp.

I often considered giving up. But every time I had this notion, I'd squash it with sheer will and work even harder.

The dog Malcolm saved wouldn't leave me alone. Even though I told him to stay put at the cabin, he'd follow me out to the river every single day, and I resented having to share my lunch with him. But I'd cleaned him up in the creek and tied a swatch of calico around his neck to serve as a makeshift collar. It was only after I'd cleaned him up that I saw he had black fluffy fur, the tail of a squirrel, and was about the size of a rocking horse. Since he wouldn't leave my side, he would have to look presentable. I only wished he could help with the work rather than just watching me from the riverbank.

As the weeks went on, I began to find dust here and there with the pan Malcolm had loaned me. It took me three weeks to earn about forty dollars' worth. Cecil was talented at eye-balling the value of what we found, so we all trusted him in this regard.

I recoiled at having to share a percent with Oxley, but Duffy urged me not to fret. "You'll find more if you work hard enough," he encouraged. So I kept at it. Despite the blisters on both my palms, I refused to stop. At least I was earning my keep and helping, unlike Russell Oxley, who sashayed around the cabin grounds, smoking his pipe. When he wasn't doing that, he was gazing at himself in a small looking glass he'd brought along, trimming his moustache or combing his black hair.

Tonight, the men planned on heading over to a neighboring camp. One of the miners there played the fiddle and had a good voice. Big Al played the banjo but had to sell it after a bad night at the monte tables in San Francisco. Rumor was the neighboring miners had one to sell him, and Big Al said his fingers itched to play.

I had a hunch the men had only been invited with the expectation they'd bring along us three women. Since I would never allow us to attend such an occasion, we would not be going. Being the only women in a room full of lonesome men was unthinkable.

I suspected our neighbors might be disheartened when only Malcolm, Duffy, Cecil, Big Al, and the peevish Oxley showed up. When I'd announced we wouldn't be going, I'd expected Phoebe to argue and beg to go. But she hadn't done that. I didn't think her nature had changed. I believed she was simply tuckered out from having to do most of the cooking and cleaning herself. With me working the diggings and Beatrice's idleness, Phoebe's chores were many. It was time for Beatrice to do her share, but Phoebe excused Beatrice's lethargy. I glanced out at my cousin sitting on the stoop, her chin in her hands. I must've made a disapproving sound because my sister was quick to defend her. "She's in mourning," Phoebe said. "Hard to find energy when sorrow's got you in its jaw."

"Sorrow's jaw has nothing to do with it," I said. "She's always been lazy. This shared cabin and the responsibilities that come with living here have highlighted the trait."

"Think so?" Phoebe asked.

"Oh, I don't know." I suddenly felt sorry for speaking so harshly about my cousin. "I'm not wearing her slippers."

"Perhaps she should help more," Phoebe conceded.

"Perhaps."

After the men left around noon, riding over on a few of our mules, a blessed quiet settled in. We lazed around for the rest of the day, playing whist and warming ourselves in the sun. Around twilight, Phoebe crawled under some quilts on the bedstead, and I wriggled in next to her, as if we were young girls. Beatrice sat by the fire and stared into the flames. I was becoming comfortable and had opened one of Oxley's books when Lazarus, wanting to go outside, scratched at the door.

Irritated, I rose to open it. The dog rushed off and began to bark. When I squinted, I could see the silhouette of a man in the setting sun. He was skulking in the clearing in front of the cabin, as if trying to figure out what to do.

I turned to Beatrice and whispered, "Hand me the Colt."

She looked suspicious.

"Do it!"

She slid the pistol from my satchel and brought it over. I was thankful Malcolm had shown me the proper way to use the weapon, and I was improving with my target practice. My aim wasn't anything to brag on, but at least firing the pistol didn't nearly break my arm.

"Who's there?" I tried not to sound afraid.

The man stepped closer. Lazarus crouched down between us and growled. The stranger wore a thick kerchief around his neck and had a beard large enough to hide a hive of bees.

"I asked who you might be."

Still, he didn't answer.

"You best leave." Lazarus was baring his teeth.

"You got any coffee?" he asked.

"None that's made."

"You alone?"

I clenched the gun in my right hand.

"I don't mean to scare you, Miss."

"Who's out there?" Phoebe asked me. I told her to shush up.

The man started to walk toward the porch. His heavy footsteps crunched in the dust.

"Sir, it is too late for company."

"Not even dark yet," he said. Now that he was closer, I could make out a dark-brown jug he was holding, which he now slurped from. Wiping his mouth with the back of his dirty sleeve, he edged even closer. "I'd like to spend some time with you tonight. Fellers in my camp don't care for my company."

If his companions didn't care for his company, then I wouldn't either. I held the pistol in front of me, so he could see it. If he got any closer, I'd aim. "You must leave," I said.

"You even know how to shoot that?" He spat on the ground.

"Of course I do."

"I bet you couldn't shoot a mountain if it was right in front of your face."

Lazarus was barking now, and I turned to see that Beatrice had climbed up on the bed with Phoebe, where they cowered.

"I shall certainly shoot you," I said. I meant it, too.

"Not afraid of your dog neither." He was slurring his words. "I think I'll take one of these mules. Nothing you can do stop me."

I could stop him. I could shoot him in the head. I might miss, of course, and then what would happen? Would he force his way inside?

I kept the pistol trained on him while he untied one of our mules from a post and walked away with it. I'd let the men engage in whatever justice might ensue for the theft.

I shut the door and moved two chairs to secure it. Then I shoved our table in front of the chairs.

I glanced over to my sister and cousin, whose eyes were wide and flicking about. It seemed to me that they'd just realized we were as close to nowhere as ever there was.

"I hate it here," Beatrice said. Then she started to cry.

"It's where we are," I said.

"Why'd Aaron die?" she asked.

Phoebe sat up and in a tiff tossed the blanket aside. "Beatrice Frost Criswick," she said, "the Lord works in mysterious ways. We are here because you set your sights on having your way and landed us in the most precarious of circumstances. I am working day and night at the chores, and Effie's trying to find us enough gold to see us home. It's time you shook off the devil and helped. Your self-pity is wearing on my nerves!"

Beatrice welled up but said nothing.

Phoebe took a deep exhausted breath, lay back down, rolled over on her side, and closed her eyes.

Beatrice looked to me as a child would look at her mother. "I'll read to you," I said.

"Scoot on over."

"But that man's out there," she said. "How can Phoebe sleep? How can you read? Aren't you scared?"

The Three Musketeers lay on the bedstead. Once I was settled next to Beatrice, Lazarus jumped up and lay at our feet.

"I'm terrified," Beatrice kept on. "I can't ever sleep. I haven't slept since we arrived."

"You need to help with the chores," I said. "Wood rats got into the flour you left out yesterday. And we can't have that."

"I want to go home," she said.

I'd already opened the book to page one.

"I want to go home now."

Steadying my breathing, I adjusted my position and the lantern to see the words better.

"I just want to go home, Effie."

The big sugar pine out front murmured in the dark. And I could hear the river and even a frog croaking. I rested my hand on the top of hers. "I am trying to get you back to Boston. But you have no home there. We will need enough money to travel back and make a new home. I am determined to find enough gold to provide for both. But you mustn't complain. And you must do your share of the work. Now, let me read to you."

Her eyes watered, but she nodded.

And so I began: *On the first Monday of the month of April . . .*

We'd been sound asleep when I was startled awake by a pounding on the door. Lazarus whined rather than growled. This calmed my nerves. If the stranger had returned, the dog would be frenzied.

"Who is it?"

"Us!" Duffy said.

Phoebe, barefoot, had leapt down from the bedstead. Together, we shoved the table and chairs aside. They felt heavier than when I'd barricaded the door.

After the men were inside, Phoebe threw her arms around Duffy.

"I'm mighty glad to see you, too," he said, lifting her off her feet. "It was a fine shindig, but it would have been finer if you'd been there to dance with."

She started to cry and wouldn't let Duffy go. Phoebe rarely shed a tear, so the men noticed quickly something was amiss. Their good cheer turned to worry and scowls, so I quickly laid out how the stranger had wandered into the yard. "That's why we're missing a mule," I explained.

"A missing mule is better than what might have been," Malcolm said.

"Effie threatened to shoot him," Phoebe

164

said, "and the stranger let us be. Maybe he was lost."

"Lost or not," Malcolm said, "he can't be bothering you ladies and stealing our mules."

Duffy pounded his fist on the table. This was the first time I'd ever seen his ire raised. "Probably the fella who started a fight down at Brown's Bar. Men were talking about it tonight. Story was he didn't take well to being confined and waited until the others left for the claim to wreak havoc on their belongings and pour their dust onto the floor. Men returned, and he tried to slash at them with a knife before pulling a rifle on them. They wrestled him out and made him leave before he caused more trouble."

I drew in my breath. "The stranger was up to no good, but I don't think he had a gun."

Cecil leaned back in the chair and yawned, his boots on the table, the dark-brown hat he never took off pulled over his eyes. "Maybe he was keeping it from your view."

I didn't want to think on it anymore. Not any of it. I was tired and said so. I wished them all a good night and blew out the lantern Big Al had lit to show us his new banjo. Maybe they were still riding on a cloud of good cheer from the gathering, but

I'd had enough of this night. I climbed up in the bedstead with Lazarus and left them all standing in the dark.

Beatrice was already preparing breakfast by the time the rest of us pulled ourselves out of bed. I was impressed to see her cooking but didn't comment.

When I rolled over, I saw that Phoebe had spent the entire night on a bunk with Duffy. I flung off the quilts and almost shouted at my impulsive little sister. But I decided to speak with her later out of earshot from the others. For now, we needed to eat, and the biscuits Beatrice had made smelled better than mine or Phoebe's. The salt pork she was frying on the stove made my stomach growl.

When we sat down at the table, Big Al started telling us about the party and the gossip they'd learned.

A grass-widow was living about twenty miles from here on a creek. And she'd taken up with a miner at least thirty years younger. "The other fellas had a good laugh over this," Big Al said, "and gave the pair a shivaree, which angered the young groom, who broke out his shotgun and turned it loose on the crowd, peppering a few with bird shot. They were set on lynching the groom, hear tell, but the grass-widow begged them to spare the life of her new husband, and they banished the couple instead."

So starved for gossip of any kind, Phoebe was rapt with the story.

Beatrice had risen to clear off the dishes. I wondered what had gotten into her. "Do you think the stranger will return today?" she asked.

"I'll be here," Oxley said. "I'll look after you."

I doubted this very much. The look on Malcolm's face suggested he felt the same. The men began to debate on whether they should set off after the stranger to get our mule back.

"That's a fool's errand," I said. "We lost the mule and have no time to be searching the woods for a mule thief. Besides, if the man truly did threaten his partners with a knife and rifle, we should have little to do with him. Probably best he does have a mule, so he can be carried far away from us."

I was grateful they agreed. So, despite the headaches the men complained about from too many spirits, we'd be working the claim today.

While the other men went to fetch their gear, Malcolm lingered and pulled me aside.

"Got you something," he said, one arm behind his back.

I turned devil red at the idea of him thinking on me.

"The sun can be harsh out at the diggings and I thought you might find this handy." He brought forth what he'd been hiding. "Fella called it a Peruvian hat."

It was black with a cinch that tucked under my chin.

He cocked his head and stared at me in the hat until I looked away. "I thought it might make you look like a man, but I think it's gone and done the opposite."

I loved the hat. It'd keep the sun from my eyes and face and made me feel fine. "Thank you," I said.

"You're most welcome, Euphemia Frost."

I ran outside to gather my gear before more could be said. When I rounded the corner of the cabin, I spotted Duffy kissing my sister on the mouth.

They hadn't seen me, so I hastily grabbed my muddy boots and turned away. All day at the river, I thought on it. I should have confronted the lovebirds and put my foot down. Phoebe shouldn't have slept in his bunk, either. She'd been upset and scared, but the whole situation was far and long from how a lady should behave. If Duffy was set on my sister, then he could court her properly. It didn't matter if we were in the middle of nowhere. He shouldn't be sneaking off with my sister to steal kisses, or inviting her to sleep on his bunk.

It was my responsibility to forbid such untoward behavior.

As the day wore on, my righteousness tempered some. Maybe new traditions were being born. Besides, everyone was fond of Duffy Fields. He was the best of the men we'd met. Unlike Beatrice's Aaron, Duffy did have strong shoulders and a practical ambition. I could even forgive his gold fever. Duffy had explained his reasons. He'd lived on a farm his whole life, working sun up to sun down and making no more than twelve dollars a day. That would have been his fate, had he stayed home. At least here, he had a chance to make ten times or more than what he'd make back home. He was the youngest of eleven children, so he'd be working land that would never be his. And if he were lucky, he'd be forced to marry up with a second cousin, and he didn't think any of those girls were to his liking.

That seemed fair.

Still, he shouldn't be kissing my sister.

ELEVEN

I couldn't remember when Russell Oxley stopped shaving. When we first arrived at the cabin, his ritual had been to wake up and wander down to the brook, returning in time for breakfast with a clean chin and wet hair. From my observance, his vanity required much fawning and fiddling, and Duffy enjoyed teasing him whenever he had the chance, telling him he spent more time on his looks than any of us girls.

But I noticed this morning he'd grown a reddish-brown beard that didn't match his black hair.

At the diggings today, Duffy seemed a bit cranky. I couldn't blame him. Since Big Al had a blister on the palm of his hand the size of a silver dollar, Duffy only had me to help him maneuver the cradle. No matter my effort, I couldn't lift as much as Big Al. So Duffy was saddled with the lion's share of weight from the dirt and sand with which we'd loaded the cradle. Plus, with the summer sun today overheating our polite sensibilities, filtering the earth down into the riffle was a struggle. We were groaning, sweating, and Duffy was grumbling under his breath.

Meanwhile, Oxley, with his fold-out chair and prissy fan, watched us from the bank. He'd lately taken up the habit of going with us to the bar once or twice a week. I supposed it entertained him to watch the others toil. Or maybe he just wanted to make sure we didn't pocket any of the gold to which he felt entitled. We typically ignored him, but his laziness became intolerable today, especially after he laughed at us, then made a snide comment about how clumsy we two looked.

"Least my beard doesn't suggest I got a different daddy," Duffy said.

Oxley stood and tossed his book to the ground, not even bothering to save his place. It seemed to me he was taking greater offense at the ribbing than was warranted. "If you ever dare speak of my father again, we shall go to fisticuffs!"

"Fisticuffs? That some fancy word for dancing? 'Cause I'm not dancing with you. Even if Big Al plays my favorite tune on his banjo."

"I shall beat you blue!"

Duffy set down the cradle and swaggered toward Oxley. I couldn't hear what he said, but I saw Duffy laughing in the man's face.

Oxley shoved Duffy in the chest. Perhaps the shove was more of a nudge, because Duffy stood his ground. Tossing down his hat, his ginger hair matted in sweat, Duffy swung at Oxley's jaw. One jab and the king of idleness sprawled on the bank as if he'd been killed by the blow.

"Get up, you no-account lazy son of a . . ." Duffy held out the oath but refrained from using it.

Malcolm and Cecil had been over the hill but must've heard the disturbance because they were running toward us.

"Why's he on the ground?" Malcolm asked.

Duffy didn't seem to have the stomach for fibbing. "I knocked him down."

I didn't add any details because I wanted to get back to work. I'd caught a glimpse of color in my shovel as we'd loaded the cradle with rubble, so I was confident we'd find some actual nuggets today.

Nonplussed, Malcolm asked, "Why'd you do that?"

"Not sure." Duffy shook out his fist and rubbed on his knuckles. "I got mad and had some grudges stored up, I'm guessing."

Standing over Oxley, Malcolm said, "You think you'll be able to stand up?"

Oxley scrambled to his feet without any help. He dusted off his shirt and pants, then rubbed his jaw. "He called me a bastard."

This was untrue, and I had to say so. "He did no such thing."

"Are you one?" Malcolm asked. "Makes no difference out here. No one cares. We're all just a bunch of bastards and orphans, each one of us subject to the sky and wild urges of our neighbors. Be they the savages, the greasers, the gamblers, or even the miners salted with the rot-gut whiskey riling them up."

"I am *not* a bastard." A crimped and shadowy scowl gripped his face. "And that farm boy had no right laying a hand on me."

"Not sure what my right was," Duffy said. "Couldn't help myself."

"We need to work," Malcolm said, turning toward Oxley. "So if you can't avoid provoking others into knocking the snot out of you, you best stay back with the girls."

I wondered if he thought of me as a man now. I was happy to be a part of the crew, the team, to contribute with my efforts. To be accepted as something other than a nuisance seemed important. Yet it made me feel peculiar to have Malcolm thinking of me as a man.

Oxley slumped back in his chair and shook the sand off his book. "I will say for the final time that I am *not* a bastard." Without looking at Duffy, he added, "I demand an apology."

"You can demand all day and night," Duffy said, grinning. "Don't mean you'll be getting apologies. Might even buy you another encounter with my fist."

The other men laughed and then laughed harder when Oxley stood and, in a fit, tried to fold up his chair, fumbling, then tripping and falling when the chair caught in his trouser cuff.

I admit to laughing, too, as my pity had been scrubbed long ago for the man who'd said I was no better than a sheep in a field.

The thunder was loud enough to shake the trees. Still, it wasn't noisy enough to keep me from sleeping. Tired to my core from the labor at the claim, I couldn't keep my eyes open long enough tonight to read but a few paragraphs of Dumas.

We were all asleep before the rain set in.

A few hours later all but Phoebe woke from the clamor of the storm. It sounded as if the roof would come crashing down from the rain, and the battering wind was shrieking through every crevice in the walls. Malcolm, Duffy, and Big Al yanked on their boots and headed outside to make sure the mules were safe and to cinch up the ropes that tied them to the trees.

When they returned, rain water from their coats and hats dripping onto the floor, their faces expressed a danger, and Malcolm was motioning with his chin toward the rifle that hung above the fire. Then I saw why. Training a shotgun at their heads, the fellow from a few nights before lurked behind them.

"Just need some vittles," the man said. "Have one of your whores cook me up some supper."

Beatrice trembled under the quilts next to me, but Phoebe still hadn't stirred. My sister had always been able to sleep through noise. I shoved at her now, then shook her shoulder. She rolled over on her back, opened one eye, and looked annoyed before realizing our current peril.

"We need to make a meal," I said.

Lazarus had different thoughts. He'd been on the bedstead with us, growling deeply from his throat. In a flurry of guttural teeth-baring snarls and barks, he flew toward the stranger, latching his sharp teeth on the man's thigh. The man yelled a curse before whipping his shotgun barrel toward my dog. Stumbling from the bed, I rushed forward to protect him. Phoebe grabbed onto my nightshirt, trying to hold me back.

Before I was able to do anything, Cecil shot the man in the shoulder. I hadn't seen Cecil take out his pistol, but the deed was done. He may have been aiming for the man's head but missed. I'd ask him later. The shoulder injury seemed almost as bad. Blood seeped out of the wound, and the stranger's arm hung like a torn sleeve from his collarbone. Within seconds, the man fell to his knees, and Lazarus finally let his leg go.

I thought Beatrice might scream at the gore, but she just sighed, as if this violence were now to be expected. Phoebe didn't make any sound.

Malcolm tore the man's rifle from his hands.

Oxley, who'd been cowering this entire time in his own bunk, rose, walked over, and seemed overly curious about the blood drizzling out of the man's wound. My thought was a strange one. Phoebe had given the cabin floor a good scrubbing today. Now she'd have to do it again. Looking toward my sister, I could tell she was thinking the same thing. A man lay bleeding at our feet, and all we could consider was the extra burden of re-scrubbing a floor.

"Anyone else out there?" Malcolm demanded.

The man glared at Malcolm with a mean darkness.

Malcolm stepped out on the porch with the lantern and held it up to scan the clearing. I didn't think this would do much good. All it did was allow in a gust of wind and rain. If the man had been traveling with others, they'd surely scattered upon hearing the shot.

To stave off the man's bleeding, I used an empty flour bag. I'd planned on making a new dress with the fabric once I had enough empty ones. Such a shame to waste it on this devil.

If this had occurred in Boston, it would have been the most exciting event that had ever happened in our whole lives. The man, criminal or not, would have been rushed off to the doctor. As we didn't have any doctors around here, the man would live or he wouldn't. And that's the way it was and would be for any of us. If I were to admit the truth, I was only attempting to stop the blood loss because I didn't want to further sully our floor.

The whole state of affairs made me sad to

think on.

But I didn't think on it for long because the man wheeled up to his feet and staggered toward Malcolm.

Rather than striking out or causing harm, he teetered toward the door and opened it.

Caught in the wind, the door slammed against the interior wall. With that, the stranger shuffled out into the rain and disappeared into the night. I briefly wondered if he still had our mule.

The next day, Malcolm and Cecil rode to the neighboring camp to inform them of the incident, and the vigilante committee all agreed Cecil shot the man in self-defense. After all, the stranger had pulled a rifle on us.

But was the man's intent to murder us? Maybe he was just hungry. Still, he would have probably killed Lazarus if Cecil hadn't shot him first. In fairness, the dog had sunk its sharp teeth into the man's thigh. I wasn't at all sure the stranger deserved to be shot over a stolen mule and the attempted murder of a dog that was biting him. I said as much to Cecil.

"Not many of us deserve what we get." He ran a finger down his thick scar.

Cecil was an odd one. He rarely smiled

and seemed to have the melancholy even on the sunniest days. But the incident had passed. And matters were squared away. Malcolm and the others had scoured the forest and hadn't found the man or his body, so we had to presume he'd left for good. We had gold to find and had to get on with things. So work resumed, as we would have to rebuild the dam the rain had pummeled.

We had our gear readied when Phoebe complained about feeling ill. I worried. She'd had a sour stomach a few days in a row and was uncharacteristically leaving food on her plate. I decided to stay behind and care for her. After the men, even Oxley, headed off, I set to making a broth from some leftover bones and onions.

Phoebe obliged and ate the broth but soon thereafter tossed it up, as she had during breakfast.

Pressing my hand to her forehead, she didn't feel warm. Maybe something disagreed with her. She climbed back on our bedstead and slept most the morning while I did the sweeping and washing up, and Beatrice cleaned the galley.

Around ten in the morning, Phoebe rose from bed and said she was feeling fine.

"You should keep resting," I cautioned.

With her ill, I began to dwell on my worst fear: losing Phoebe. While I did the chores, I blinked back tears at the thought. If I had to bury Phoebe in this lonesome place, I'd never recover.

"I'm feeling myself." She was chewing on some hard biscuits we'd made the night before. "Wish I had some jam."

"I could gather some berries."

"I'll help," she offered. "Let's go find some of those fat blackberries. The juicy ones. Beatrice can stay and start on supper."

"She'll want to come along," I said.

"She'll be happy to have some time to herself."

"I don't think Beatrice will see it that way. Especially after what happened with that stranger. She never did like to be alone."

"We don't need to fret any about that man," Phoebe said. "He's probably dead."

"Perhaps."

"I'd like it to be just you and me. Like when we were girls. Beatrice will be safe here. Besides, you can leave Lazarus." Phoebe swallowed the last of the biscuit.

I agreed, tying on my apron so I could gather enough berries for a thick jam.

Beatrice only complained a little when I tied the dog to a tree to keep him from following and told her Phoebe and I were going off to pick berries. Perhaps Beatrice was growing braver. Or maybe she wanted to lie down and take a nap without me scolding her for it.

The sky was blue and cloudless. Phoebe and I wound down toward a creek through patches of manzanita, ferns, and ivy. The spicy smell of pines perfumed the air. We found a coil of blackberry bushes and picked them carefully, avoiding the thorns.

Phoebe talked of the weather and gossiped about how broody Cecil was and how strong Big Al was for such a small man. "He's like an ant," she said. "He can carry ten times his weight."

I agreed.

"You sweet on Malcolm, Effie?"

I was taken aback.

"Seems you might be. Seems he might feel the same. He got you the hat. He was thinking on you, it seems."

"It was a practical gift." I touched the brim. "Nothing romantic about giving a girl a man's hat to keep the sun from her eyes."

"Seems more romantic than most things. A suitor can give a girl picked flowers any day of the week. Then within a day or two those same flowers die. But Malcolm was thinking about you being out in the sun with only a bonnet."

"I am certainly not sweet on him. And he can't possibly be sweet on me. Beatrice is twice as pretty, and you're even more so."

"You're pretty. You just don't know it."

"Stop with all that talk," I said.

"You're the type of woman a man should marry."

"I have no interest in marrying anybody. Not here and not once we get back to Boston."

"I'd like to marry." Phoebe dropped a handful of blackberries in her apron. Then she popped one into her mouth.

"You've made that clear," I said. "And you can do so once we're home, and you're able to meet a proper gentleman with proper means."

"I've already met the man I want to marry. And I will never love another."

I knew she was talking about Duffy Fields. But she was only sixteen. She couldn't possibly know who she would love for a lifetime and who would make the ideal husband. I agreed that Duffy was the best of his kind in this wild place. But we weren't staying here. He could court her, but that didn't mean she had to marry him. No, she'd have to wait until she was older, and we were home.

"I believe," she said quickly, "Duffy was made for me. And I for him."

My sister was impractical and always had been. She was stubborn, too. Still, I'd have to make her understand how frivolous the idea was.

"Duffy has already offered his hand," she said.

I dropped all the blackberries I'd just picked and watched the dark purple fruit spill to the ground.

"Duffy said Cecil can marry us. He could put on his preacher robe for our ceremony."

"I saw you kissing." It was all I could think of to say.

"We could get married here in the forest. I know a real pretty spot."

I could not imagine my sister marrying a farmer from Ohio. My imagination completely failed when I tried to imagine her marrying this man in the woods. Would the guests consist of chipmunks, quail, and squirrels? Perhaps a bear would stop by to wish the bride and groom well. Maybe a mountain cat could be the ring bearer.

"We shouldn't have kissed, but we've been kissing all the time. That's what love does."

I felt an anger boil up. Somehow, what she'd told me was an affront to all we'd suffered. My hands had blistered and bled from the work. My knees were always bruised. My back hurt. My lips were cracked from the sun. All of it seemed for naught. My sister would toss everything away at the first prickle of her heart.

On the verge of unleashing all that anger on my thoughtless and feckless sister, I turned away. Stomping off, I crushed the blackberries I'd dropped under my boot heel and rushed back toward the cabin.

Phoebe ran after me, all the while shouting my name.

When we returned, all the bitterness I'd swallowed was replaced by a cold and panicked fear. In a heap of laundry she'd pulled down from the line, Beatrice lay prone and still on the path leading up to the cabin. Lazarus remained tied to the tree, and he was straining and barking to free himself.

"Bee!" I rushed toward her.

Phoebe had caught up, and we two, out of breath, leaned over our unconscious cousin. When I reached out to touch her face, I noticed my fingers were stained blood red from the blackberries.

TWELVE

Her skin hot as a kettle, Beatrice lay in our bedstead. Her eyes unfocused and dim, she couldn't keep down a bite of food. We placed cool rags on her forehead and prayed. It was all we could do. I felt as if I were praying to the walls.

By the time the men returned from the diggings, her fever had soared higher. And I feared for her life. "We must find a doctor."

Malcolm only had to look at Beatrice to know I was right.

"Please," I said.

"I'd need a horse to reach the nearest doctor," Malcolm said. "Even with a horse, it's a two-day ride there and two-day ride back. And that's if I can convince a doctor to head back this way."

Big Al stared at my cousin with concern. He'd seen his brother die. I guessed Beatrice's illness took him back to that day.

"We could trade a few of the mules for a

horse," Big Al suggested.

Malcolm agreed.

Big Al paced near Beatrice. "Fella I met at the shindig said he'd be up for a swap."

"I'll come with," Duffy said.

Malcolm shook his head. "It'll be better if you stay with the women. You and Big Al. Cecil can ride along with me. Maybe we can trade for one horse and borrow another."

Phoebe's face relaxed when she heard Duffy would stay.

Beatrice's fever had worsened when Malcolm and Cecil left the next morning, after I'd packed them enough sustenance to last a week. I prayed they'd be back sooner. I'd again taken up the habit of praying, the one I'd given up after all my prayers had gone unanswered back in Boston. I'd been praying so much, most my sentences ended with *amen*.

After they were well and truly out of sight, Oxley seemed emboldened. Since the day I'd threatened him, he'd avoided us as much as possible. But today he wandered over to the bedstead and stared down at my cousin. "Such a pity," he had the nerve to say.

But she'd get well. She *had* to get well. She kept mumbling in her feverish state about Aaron. About my uncle. Then she'd start having a conversation with Aaron again.

"You're still with me and Phoebe," I told her. "No sense pining after the dead. You need to picture being with the living!"

She only smiled at this, her cheeks crimson, her skin on fire.

To make matters worse, Phoebe and Duffy were no longer hiding their affection. Either his arm was draped over her shoulders or they were holding hands. He couldn't leave the cabin to fetch water without kissing her first. It made me feel ornery to watch it. If Beatrice had been well, I'd have someone to talk to, but I had no one. For now, I had to tolerate their out-in-the-open union. I couldn't scold Phoebe with Beatrice so sickly.

"I'll marry her if you agree," Duffy said to me the next day on the porch. "Once Cecil returns."

"Phoebe doesn't know the first thing about being a wife."

"The two of us together can do anything." His face was bright and cheerful. It always was. Especially when he looked at Phoebe. "Your sister's got pluck, and I've got a strong back. And I love her more than the

187

whole world. I'll always look after her. And you, too. We'll be kin. I'd be mighty proud to be your brother."

I took a swig from my coffee. It burned my tongue.

"Isn't it something? Coming all the way out here and finding the great love of your life? Aren't I the luckiest man on the face of the earth?"

I wanted to tell him we didn't need to be looked after. That I did fine on my own. And if anyone would be looking after Phoebe, it'd be me. But I'd save these words for my sister. I didn't want her marrying Duffy Fields, but I didn't want to speak harshly to the man. He was kind and true. Unrefined, yes, but too decent to lash out at. Besides, I had too much on my shoulders right now with Beatrice's fever. Would my cousin die? Just like the rest of my family?

I only hoped that Malcolm would find a doctor and bring him back to the cabin.

Malcolm had been gone for six whole days when Beatrice's fever broke. By midday, she was sitting up and looking around the cabin, as if she'd just been born. I remembered when one of my little brother's fevers had broken, too. For those few hours that winter afternoon, we'd all believed he'd get well.

By nighttime, he'd died. So, despite her cooler skin and alert eyes, I still fretted for my cousin. But with every hour that passed, she seemed healthier. By the next day, with her up and walking around, I had faith she'd survived.

If Malcolm and Cecil would only return, everything would be right as rain. Not only had their absence stalled our work at the diggings, setting us back, but they'd been gone long enough to make us all worry.

"Malcolm can take care of himself," Duffy said to me while he chopped some firewood.

"I am certain we can all care for ourselves." I took my best dress down from the clothesline and shook it out. "Any of us, no matter our mettle, would be at a disadvantage should we be attacked or overtaken. Even Hercules had his twelve labors."

"Hercules?"

"Did they not teach you about the Greeks in your schoolhouse?"

Duffy shook his head. "Only went to school three years. Enough to read and write some. Boys worked the land where I come from." He took a swing at a log and cleaved it.

"Hercules was the strongest of all gods," I said. "But he was continually tortured by his stepmother and endured much hardship.

It didn't matter how strong he was."

Duffy squinted up at me, sunshine glinting in his eyes. "Malcolm's had his share of hardships, but nothing can compare to what happened to him before."

I didn't know anything about Malcolm's past but didn't feel right gossiping with Duffy about it. I would ask Malcolm myself when he returned. "Do you think we should go looking for them?"

"We? No," he said. "You need to stay here with your kin."

"I fear something has happened."

"If anyone goes looking, it'll be me." He set the axe down.

When I went back inside, Beatrice was up and brushing her hair. Because she'd had it braided for a week, it looked like a golden staircase.

"Where's Phoebe?"

"Went off to pick some wild onions," she said. "She wanted to make some soup."

I nodded and began to tidy up. In order to ward off more sickness, I needed to beat out the blankets Beatrice had been sleeping on.

Without Phoebe's constant humming, silence settled in. I recalled fondly when Beatrice would chatter nonsensically for hours at a time. Would she ever be the same again? This thought made me more home-sick than ever.

A bird was singing. I could now hear Phoebe singing, too. When I looked outside, I saw her in the distance headed back to the cabin, her braids swinging joyfully.

I leaned against the doorway, my arms folded. What was Malcolm doing right now? Was he safe? Had he been overtaken by the man Cecil had shot? Or someone cut from the same sinister cloth? The worry chewed on me, and I turned back inside in order to distract myself with the chores. Malcolm was a fine man. And he *would* return. Nothing could keep him from coming back to us.

Duffy trotted up to the porch. He handed me the onions Phoebe had picked. "Me and Big Al are headed out to the bar. Get some work in. Phoebe's tagging along to keep us company."

I almost offered to come, too. I hadn't been to the diggings in days. But what if Malcolm returned while we were away? I'd want to be here. Besides, what if Beatrice took a turn? I shouldn't leave her.

But the river tugged at me. Ever since I found my first smattering of gold dust and stared at it glimmering in the pan, I'd felt an ongoing urge to find more. I didn't have the gold fever. Still, I knew the gold was there. And I needed it to get us home.

"We'll be back before supper," Duffy said. He was holding my sister's hand, and they were already hiking down the trail toward the diggings, talking with each other as if not another soul lived with them on the earth.

"Must have been attacked," Big Al said. "That's all I can figure."

Big Al was happiest when he was lifting something, playing his banjo, or shoveling the dirt. Having to think on complicated matters didn't suit him. So I didn't judge his conclusion. He was right. Cecil and Malcolm could very well have been attacked. By an animal, Indians, or even the man they'd shot in the shoulder. Or maybe one was thrown from his horse. I'd come to appreciate the unadventurous nature of mules.

I simply wouldn't allow myself to think the worst: that they could have taken the Big Jump, what Cecil referred to as death. I refused. Both men had a lot of living left to do, and I enjoyed Malcolm's friendship. If a problem arose around camp, we'd consult with each other and come to a solution. If I became overly worried about the weather or my sister, I'd confide my concerns to him. I liked the way he chose his words and how he thought on matters. I also liked the way he laughed at silly moments, like when Lazarus chased his tail or rolled over on his back to have his belly rubbed.

Duffy dabbed his kerchief on the corner of his mouth, wiping off some blackberry jam from his breakfast biscuit. We'd decided the night before he'd leave today for the neighboring camp. There, he'd gather a few of the men to form a search party. Everyone there thought well of Malcolm, and they respected Cecil as a former preacher. Maybe they believed knowing a preacher might give them a leg up with their prayers reaching the Almighty's ears.

Only Phoebe had protested. But she couldn't help herself. Still, even she understood something was amiss, and Duffy didn't have a choice but to try and help find our friends. That's what they were. Friends. One couldn't spend so much time with others without them becoming friends. Or enemies. One or the other. Malcolm might be my best friend. And we couldn't leave them out there alone if they'd found some trouble.

I had to turn away while Phoebe and Duffy embraced and kissed like a married couple before he mounted the mule.

"I'll be back soon," he said. "You won't even have time to miss me."

"I miss you when you go off to the diggings," Phoebe said. "I miss you when you're out chopping wood or fetching the water."

He leaned over and kissed my sister on her yellow hair. "I've got your face memorized. I see it when I shut my eyes. You should memorize mine, too. Then we don't ever have to miss each other again."

She shut her eyes. "I see you."

"Won't be gone long." He straightened, and the mule set off.

Phoebe stood where he left her and waved. Her eyes welled up some, but she was able to shake off her brooding quickly and help with the chores. I could only hope he'd find Malcolm and Cecil and bring them home.

One day passed, then another. Big Al and I worked the diggings. Phoebe and Beatrice, healthier every day, managed the chores. The vainglorious Oxley, with all his finery and fiddling with his moustache, was the messiest of us all, so we still had plenty to do. He wouldn't even take the time to stomp the dirt off his feet before entering the cabin.

194

When I returned to the cabin after working the diggings, Beatrice was frowning on the porch, her face red.

"Whatever's the matter?"

"It's Russell Oxley. I spilled some flour. He stepped in it, then deliberately walked across my clean floor."

"Did he apologize?" I knew the answer.

"He most certainly did not. I asked him to sweep up the mess himself, and he had the gall to call me lazy. Me? All that man does is sit around all day, lazing like an old kitty cat, while the rest of us work night and day."

Oxley slid out from the side of the cabin. He'd probably been making water. His sly smirk told me he'd heard our conversation.

"You're the clumsy girl who spilled the flour." He was smiling like a boy does when he teases his sister. I was hoping this squabble was no more than siblings sparring words.

Beatrice stood and shook out her skirts. Then she walked right up to the man, who was now leaning against the cabin post. "Clumsy? Lazy? Me? I'm only just recovering from my illness and working as hard as I can. You need to take out your looking glass and give it a good stare."

I wasn't sure if Beatrice had ever raised

her voice to anyone.

"Ah, Mrs. Criswick, you know I just like to poke at you. See if I can draw out your contempt and get your pretty eyes to look my way."

"You can get out of my way is what you can do," she said.

"What if I go out and find you some berries, so you can make me a pie? Would you show me mercy?"

Her hands on her hips, she told him he lived in a land of fables.

"I know you like baking those pies."

"I know you like eating my pies."

"You're clumsy and lazy," he said, winking, "but you sure can make a good pie."

"And you're insufferable! You will go pick me those berries now!"

"I sure will," he said.

I sat next to Beatrice on the steps, and Lazarus, wanting a nose-scratching, poked his head between us.

"I don't like the way he teases you," I said.

"Maybe I can teach him to pick up after himself and help out now and then. After all, I had to learn how to do that. People can change."

Maybe they could. Maybe they couldn't. People were the same inside, seemed to me, no matter what the world threw at them.

They could change their ways but not the reasons behind their ways. "You do make tasty pies," I said. "He's right about that."

THIRTEEN

The mourning doves were cooing this morning on the roof. I hated the sound and for a second considered shooting them and cooking them up for dinner. They made me lonesome, and I resented them.

It'd been over a week since Duffy left. Phoebe had started crying herself to sleep a few nights ago, moaning into her quilts that none of the men would ever return. She believed that something awful had happened. I'd tried providing comfort by telling her they were fine and how her imagination had run away from her reason. That she shouldn't dwell on the worst outcome when any number of things could be keeping them away.

But I doubted my words. The men had been gone too long.

Our routine of chores, cooking, and working the bar couldn't distract us. At night, reading aloud from Dumas did little to ease our minds. The only good thing was that Beatrice had fully recovered from her illness. She seemed a different person than the girl I'd grown up with. She'd doubled her domestic efforts and seemed to enjoy preparing the meals. Mostly, I deemed this good, but I did miss her childish giggle and the way she once saw the world through a prism of ease and simple joys. This outlook had mostly died with Aaron. She'd told me plainly that the men would never return. "We just have to live as if they were never here at all," she'd said.

I couldn't do that. To this day and for all my days, memories of the people I loved pervaded everything I saw or did. My brothers. Papa and Mama. My uncle. Even Aaron. When I ate a slice of Beatrice's pies, I would think of my brothers, how much they would have enjoyed the sweet treat. When I saw a wild rose, I could hear my mother exclaim at its velvet petals, its beauty and perfume. When I read a good story, I'd always think on my papa reading at the breakfast table though my mother thought this habit rude.

And now, when at the river, I could imagine Malcolm beside me. Sometimes I skipped rocks and could hear him counting the number of times the smooth stone bounced across the starry ripples. When I walked through the forest, and birds burst off a branch above me, I heard Duffy's laugh. Because that's how his laugh sounded. Like the flutter of a hundred wings. I even missed Cecil's somber stories.

What if Beatrice was right? What if they never returned? With winter coming soon, I feared being trapped here alone for months with Big Al and Oxley. Big Al had already started talking about joining the miners in the other camp, as it was tough to find the gold without other men to help work the claim.

If Big Al was thinking about leaving, then we should be thinking about it, too. But I didn't even remember how to get back to civilization or what we'd do when we got there. If we got lost, we could die. From weather. Or from something else.

I prayed almost every hour under my breath for their safe return. I had always been embarrassed to ask favors of anybody or anything, and praying for the safety of Malcolm, Cecil, and Duffy seemed like asking God a favor. But I had to ask. I had to beg. It had never done me any good before, but I had no one else to ask.

Today, Beatrice was out at the creek filling water jugs. Big Al was at the bar, and

Oxley was reading under the sugar pine.

In the middle of one of these prayers, I was hanging our spare dresses to dry on the rope that we'd strung between two fir branches. Lazarus's ears went up. Then he started sniffing the air. When he bounded off, I ran after him.

I barely believed what I saw. I wondered if I only wanted to believe. But as they drew closer, I knew they were real. There was Cecil riding a horse. Malcolm, gaunt, his hat pulled over his eyes, slumped on a bay behind Cecil's mare.

By now, Phoebe had stepped out on the porch. "They're home! Duffy brought them home!"

I couldn't see Duffy but didn't argue.

When they reached the yard, Malcolm crumpled from his saddle and ambled toward us, tipping his hat as if greeting two strangers in the street.

"We couldn't find a doc," Cecil said. "Not for your cousin. And not for Malcolm, here, who came down with the same ailment about two days out."

"Where's Duffy?" Phoebe was looking off into the forest behind them.

Malcolm, as if he couldn't walk another step, sat on the stoop and eyed my sister with curiosity.

"He left over a week ago to search for you," she said.

Cecil scraped the mud off his boot with a stick. "Didn't find us."

"Then he'll come back soon," she said.

"I expect so," Cecil said.

"Where have you been?" I asked.

Malcolm pulled me down next to him and leaned into me. I allowed it. "At a campoody."

"A what?"

"An Indian village, with some Maidu who took pity on me. Don't know why they would, but I'm glad for it. Am dang sorry I didn't bring back a doc."

I shook my head. "Beatrice's fever broke, and she's back to her full strength. I am sorry for all your troubles. You should have never left, as it was all for naught."

Malcolm took a deep breath, as if he'd been storing up some guilt.

"She's fit as a fiddle. Out getting water now," I told them. "While you two almost died."

"*He* almost died," Cecil said. "Disease doesn't stick to me. I figure it's because God wants to keep me around to mess with."

Phoebe was still looking out at the forest. "You never saw Duffy?" she asked.

"Did he set off by himself?" Cecil asked.

I explained how he was going to the neighboring camp to form a search party.

Malcolm scowled. "You heard any word from them boys at the camp?"

I shook my head. Phoebe wrung her hands.

Beatrice was walking back with two water jugs, one in each hand. When she saw Malcolm and Cecil, she grinned like she used to do — that charming dimpled smile that turned her cheeks into plums.

"You are both filthy and smell like savages," she proclaimed happily. "You will need to set out to the creek at once and wash yourselves before you'll be allowed inside our clean cabin."

Later, after the sun had set, it started to rain. Phoebe clung to my side with each crack of thunder. I knew she was likely imagining Duffy out there alone. It was a hard picture to shake.

"I fear something has happened to him," Phoebe whispered, as the rain pattered on the roof.

"He's strong and sure."

"What if he got lost? Or attacked by that man Cecil shot?"

I thought of a million things that could have happened but refused to express them.

Malcolm was going to head over to the neighboring camp tomorrow to ask about Duffy.

Malcolm, Cecil, Big Al, a few Maidu, and some of the neighboring miners had searched for three days. Still, they couldn't find Duffy Fields. It was as if the earth had cracked open and pulled him and his mule inside. The only fact we'd discovered was that Duffy had never made it to the neighboring camp.

This news tortured my sister, and nothing any of us could say eased her mind.

Phoebe, despite my disapproval, joined the search party. When some of the men from the neighboring camp wanted to give up, she wouldn't let them. They kept searching and searching and still couldn't find a trace.

After a few days, the Maidu went back to their village. And the miners, two farmers who considered Duffy a good man and friend, headed back to their camp on day three to ensure they didn't lose their claim. On day four, we searched for Duffy in our spare time but also resumed working the bar. Duffy had simply disappeared. I half wondered if he'd just headed back to Sacramento City. But I wouldn't speak this aloud.

He seemed to love my sister, so it didn't make sense that he'd just abandon her. Plus, his character seemed beyond such disgrace. Still, imagining him in harm's way was worse.

Phoebe spent her days searching the forest. At all hours, we could hear her out there calling his name. She'd left all the cooking and cleaning to my cousin. Beatrice didn't complain.

I had to force Phoebe to eat. So distraught, she'd lost weight, and her face appeared whittled from a brittle wood. Tonight, at the short end of twilight, she remained out in the woods, alone. Lazarus and I headed off to fetch her. I heard her calling Duffy's name, her voice tattered and fringed. Between shouts, frogs and cicadas gulped and sang. The river roared. I also heard Big Al plucking some sad song on his banjo from inside the cabin. I would have to urge him to play something livelier with Phoebe so easily provoked into melancholy.

Finally, I found her kneeling down and staring at the ground where the bear had cornered Malcolm and my dog.

"Phoebe," I said gently. "We need to head in now. It'll be dark. Can't have you out in the dark."

"Look, Effie. The daisies here have been

crushed."

"Don't you remember the bear?" Lazarus was sniffing about, as if he were recalling the encounter. "The bear flattened all sorts of bushes and flowers."

"What if it took Duffy?"

I didn't want to tell her my thoughts on this. If a bear had attacked Duffy, we would know. Cecil had told me as much. He detailed the grizzly's habit of leaving a bulky, messy mound where it buried its victims — or what was left of them. We'd found nothing like that. But I didn't want to describe the grizzly's rituals to Phoebe. If she knew, she'd wear herself out digging up every mound she came across. "I'm certain he didn't fall prey to a bear," I said.

"Then where is he, Effie?"

"He could be sick," I said. "He could have become ill like Malcolm and Bee. Maybe he needed to rest up somewhere before coming back."

She nodded.

"I don't think it's helping him or you to be out here night and day calling his name. Duffy wouldn't like it."

"He will come back." She looked up at the darkening sky, the moon — the color of a gypsy moth — already looming overhead.

I let her think he would return. I wanted

her to believe this as long as possible. I wanted to believe it myself but found it futile.

Despite the misery caused by Duffy's disappearance, we were trying to enjoy ourselves tonight. It had been nearly three weeks since he'd left us, and, today, we'd found some rich dirt. The richest yet. By using the rocker and tom, between us we'd pulled out at least three thousand in dust, gold pebbles, and nuggets. Tomorrow, we were sure to do the same, as we'd found what Cecil had called a Eureka vein. And we hadn't come close to digging it for all it was worth. Malcolm speculated that we might be pulling out the same amount or more every day for the entire week, so we all felt fat and rich.

Beatrice had baked a gooseberry pie for the occasion. And Cecil and Big Al were taking slugs from a jug of whiskey. Malcolm had a drink, as well but didn't overly imbibe like the others. Cecil's speech was slurring before long, and he started talking more than usual.

"You could sell these pies, Missus Flower. Best durn pie I've had in California." Diving into his second slice, he continued, "Maybe the best pie I've had in my life."

I was still surprised that Beatrice had turned out to be such a fine cook. She seemed to have a knack for it. Whether it was the distraction of cooking or her ability to control her thoughts, my cousin's grief over Aaron and my uncle seemed quashed. I was glad for that because Phoebe's gloom filled the room, and there wasn't space for anyone else's. Gone was my sister's bright cat-like grin and flicker. Tonight, when she thought I wasn't looking, she took a drink of the whiskey. I saw her do it but didn't scold her. The twisted look on her face suggested she didn't like the taste, so I didn't worry about her taking another slug.

Phoebe pointed to Cecil's scar. "How'd you get that?"

She'd asked on the scar before, but he'd always dismissed my sister's curiosity. Tonight was different. "Love and God and revenge." His eyes started to water.

I rose to bring him some coffee. He'd had enough of the whiskey. And I was in no mood to see a grown man cry. Fact was, I was never in the mood for such a display.

He refused the coffee and chugged again from his spirits. Then he told us what had happened. He was a well-respected man of God. A man who knew the Word and shared it with others. A man who baptized children, married those in love, and sent the dearly departed into their heavenly father's arms. In 1846, a woman named Nell Sherwood brought him some roses from her garden. That wasn't unusual, as his flock often brought him food and gifts. He interrupted his story by telling Beatrice that he'd never been brought a pie as tasty as the one he was eating now. Anyway, Nell started visiting the church house to pray. Not just on Sunday, but on other days, too. Mondays. Wednesdays. Thursdays. And they'd pray and talk. And then they'd stopped praying. And mostly just talked. And then the talking became kissing. And then the kissing led to "other unholy acts typically reserved for man and wife."

And so he, a "man of God," became "a soldier of Satan." Nell Sherwood was a married woman, and he knew this full and well, as her husband was a member of his flock. After a while, he thought of ending the tryst but couldn't resist Nell. "If she walked into this cabin tonight, I couldn't resist her. Even after what happened. Maybe it's especially because it *did* happen."

"What happened?" Phoebe asked.

"It was Sunday service. And Mr. Sherwood stood up in front of my congregation and announced that he would kill me. So, naturally, I asked my flock to pray for my life."

"Did they?"

"Not aloud." He smiled.

He told us how Sherwood and several other men dragged him outside, tied him on a horse, and took him to a large chestnut tree on one of the men's farms. They'd had a noose ready and strung him up. But they weren't professional hangmen, it seemed, as they left him there still kicking and alive, choking and trying with his fingers to free the rope from his neck. Still, he would have died had it not been for Nell, who'd ridden like lightning to reach him. Once she did, she took a scythe from her farm and used it to cut the rope. Problem was, the scythe sliced him from ear to collarbone.

"So Nell almost kilt me. She rode me to the next town, as the doctor in ours probably would have left me for dead. The doc sewed me up, and, when I had a bit of strength left, I headed out on a wagon train as a laborer."

I was surprised when Phoebe took another swig of whiskey. "Is that why you don't preach anymore?" she asked.

"I don't preach because I helped bury two little girls, no older than five, on the trail. One fell into a hot barrel of grease. The other angel was snake bit. I also buried a baby boy who was smiling and fat and giggling in the morning, got the cholera in the afternoon, and was dead by midnight. I couldn't find anything in the Good Book to comfort their mothers and fathers. I couldn't find anything to comfort me, neither. I'd always preached that God was a vengeful God. Only problem, vengeance often comes down meanest and ugliest on the innocent. Couldn't fathom how I'd gotten away with my dance with the devil, but those babes suffered before leaving the earth for good. For that reason, I can't cotton to worshipping such a God. He doesn't deserve my worshipping. I'll get my just desserts someday, but a man has to have principles."

Cecil slammed his fist down on the table, rage a fire in his eyes. "And I can't give a God who'd kill off babes any devotion. Not anymore. Can't justify it. Just can't. Rather burn and crackle in hell."

Phoebe thought on this before speaking. "I've been praying to God night and day to return Duffy," she said. "But maybe my savior has killed him. If that is true, I shall never pray again. I will shun the Almighty, just as you have."

I was shocked. "Phoebe!"

211

"I will, Effie." Her eyes glossed over with a seriousness I'd never seen before in my sister. "He killed our parents. Our brothers. He killed our uncle. He killed Aaron. He even killed my mule."

Malcolm said her mule was just outside.

"No!" She started to cry. "The mule in Chagres. He killed my mule. And the others, too. Mules were everywhere. Dead. And now he's killed the man I love!"

Then she rushed out of the cabin into the night, and I wanted to slam an iron pan over Cecil's head. But I ran out after her instead.

FOURTEEN

By the end of August, we'd almost pulled enough gold out of the claim to afford our trip home to Boston. The Everhart Bar was paying better than most others on the mountain. I gave all the credit to Malcolm for being clever enough to choose this section of the North Fork, as we'd heard the claims in the lower regions weren't paying nearly as well.

Beatrice, surprisingly, was also earning money from selling her pies. Some of the neighboring miners paid for them with dust or money. Others exchanged a pie for ingredients. Her pies were sought after, as miners would travel for miles to buy one. The secret, according to my cousin, was cinnamon, one of the ingredients Oxley had purchased for our stock of provisions. Her pies were scrumptious, but the miners probably enjoyed seeing my cousin as much as they enjoyed eating her pies, as she'd regained the bright skin and rosebud lips that had made her one of the prettiest girls in Boston. Her supple smile had also returned. Beatrice appeared to always be listening with interest to the words men spoke, while I knew she was likely thinking of nothing but the weather.

One of the hottest days yet, we took off from working the claim. Instead, I headed out to the creek to bathe, determined to scrape the half-moons of dirt out from under my nails. I ordered Lazarus to stay, but to no avail. He trotted at my heels, a four-legged shaggy shadow.

I was strolling, the ache in my shoulders slowing my walk. I'd been looking down, so it was too late to turn around and pretend I hadn't seen Malcolm in all his glory. He was looking right at me, as I was him.

I'd shut my eyes and thrown my hands over my face. But the gesture couldn't stop the fact that I had seen him on the creek's edge without one shred of clothing. And the image — his height, his broad shoulders, his slim waist and muscular legs — remained despite my shut eyes.

"You can look now," he said. "I'm in the water."

"I dare not." I blushed and felt foolish.

"Just soaping up my hair."

I couldn't very well just stand there with my face covered, so I drew my hands away. "I am deeply sorry. I didn't know you were here."

"Could've been worse. Could've come upon you instead."

"I suppose." I was torn on whether I should turn and go back to the cabin or keep talking to him. The water sparkled and reflected in his eyes.

"I'll be done soon, and you can have your turn. Water's too cold to stay in for long."

"How will we bathe in the winter?" It was something I worried on. The men didn't worry as much.

"We'll build a tub and heat the water on the fire. Won't be easy."

"I miss having a proper bath. When I return to Boston, I will insist upon this one luxury every single night."

A woodpecker drummed its beak against a yellow pine, and then Malcolm submerged fully into the creek. When he surfaced, he shook the water out of his hair. "Feels good. This cold creek. Don't you think?"

"Helps with the aching shoulders."

"Sure does," he said. "You can shut your eyes again if you like. I'm getting out. Helps with the ache, but it's mighty brisk."

I shut my eyes, listening as he swam

forward. I could hear the water falling from his shoulders. I could hear his breath and my own heartbeat quicken.

Stumbling forward, I reached around for a boulder to sit on. Then I felt his cool bare hand guide me. "Thank you," I said.

"My pleasure, Euphemia Frost."

I could hear him pulling on his trousers.

"You can open up your pretty eyes."

I blushed. I didn't know why he'd said that. I didn't have pretty eyes. My eyes were plain and brown. Still, I glanced up at him. He wasn't wearing a shirt. And he was grinning, a few drops of the water winding down his jaw.

I felt odd. And guilty. Bewildered. I had to aim my energies better. I should have left for the cabin immediately rather than linger here. I had embarrassed myself entirely and stooped below my nature.

Lazarus barked at a doe who ogled us from across the creek. And I was glad for it, as it broke me free from thoughts I shouldn't be having. I had no right feeling anything at all with what Phoebe was enduring. Duffy disappeared thirty-four days ago, and we'd practically turned the earth inside out looking for him.

"I'll make my way back, now, so you can have your privacy," he said.

"You are a gentleman." I averted my stare while he pulled on his shirt.

"I was once upon a time," he said. "Wouldn't call myself that now. Just a placer miner like the rest."

He wasn't like the rest, but I wouldn't say so. "Why'd you come to California? You remarked once that it wasn't for the gold."

"Came here as a soldier. Fremont brought me here."

"Why aren't you still a soldier?"

The contours on his face caught the shadows from the trees.

"Should I have not asked?"

"Nah," he said. "You need to know."

Malcolm told me that serving under Captain John C. Fremont was a blend of adventure, survival, and continual startling turns. The men were never sure what they were in for. Fremont defied orders as easily as a well-fed man turned down food just because the taste wasn't to his liking.

In 1845, they'd been sent by the War Department to survey the central Rockies. But they headed straight for California. Fremont, Malcolm said, held the idea that if they could seize California from the Mexicans, they'd all be famous. And he rallied settlers into a patriotic frenzy to take

217

up his cause. Malcolm was just a kid and thought it all exciting. And the struggles he'd had along the way had bonded him to the others. His father had passed when he was a young boy, and his mother had died shortly before he signed on as a soldier. Fremont's men were his family, and Fremont was a father, an older brother, and an uncle to them all.

But Malcolm couldn't help but question some of Fremont's methods. First, he'd never cared much about fame or power so didn't understand Fremont's drive. Plus, he didn't think it valiant to take the land from the Mexicans. People were people wherever he went, and he was happy to have a patch of ground that was free from sharp rocks on which to lay out his bedroll. He expected Mexicans and Indians wanted the same, and it soured his stomach some to take that from them.

Though he'd defended himself and his friends from Indian attacks, he didn't care for Fremont's provocation of the tribes along the way. It was hardly a secret that Fremont wanted to clear the land of Indians.

Still, Malcolm did what he was told. He didn't have anywhere to go and didn't have anything or anybody back home. His friends were with Fremont's group.

On March 30, 1846, they arrived at the Lassen Ranch in the upper Sacramento Valley. Some settlers claimed the local Indians planned on attacking them. "So Fremont moved us up the river to search. It was the fifth of April when we came upon the Wintu."

Malcolm's jaw clenched as he looked off into the forest.

"The bucks lined up with the women and children behind them. Every one of us had a rifle, two pistols, and a knife. Pinned against the river, they couldn't even run. We began to fire. All of us. The bucks were flinging off their arrows, but they were too far off to reach us. I thought that'd be it, but we were ordered to charge. To slaughter each and every member. Bucks. Women. Babes. The old people. And all the soldiers but a few did just that. They ran down every Indian they could catch, no matter who, and killed them dead."

"And you?"

"After I killed one . . . I . . . I couldn't even watch, Effie. But I'm no innocent. I didn't do anything to stop them. I should have. You would have done something. Said something."

"It's easier to claim virtue when you

haven't been tried."

He nodded. "I called those men who did the killing my friends. I knew them. I ate breakfast with them every morning. Supper, too. Shared tents. Stood with them through many a struggle. We buried each other. They were good men, I thought. Don't know now. I've taken the day apart and put it back together in order to understand. More than once."

"Where'd you go?"

"I went to work for Sutter, who was just as bad, if not worse. Now I'm here. Did some drinking in between. Tried to wash what happened away but haven't yet found liquor strong enough. So I've learned to live with it."

I couldn't speak. I fingered my dress, the hem still missing a swatch that I had cut off for the Indian girl I'd met on our way here. Had she kept it? What cruelties had she endured at the hands of soldiers and settlers? What cruelties lay ahead? Did we all possess the cruelest natures under our skins? Had God created monsters in disguise?

FIFTEEN

The work wore on me. I could feel it in the never-ending ache between my shoulder blades. As the nights grew colder, the pain sharpened. But I couldn't let it interfere with the labor needing to be done, both at the claim and in the cabin, as Phoebe had to be nudged or nagged to help with the simplest tasks. Even fetching a cup of corn meal or flour seemed to tucker her out. Mostly, she slept. So much so, we often forgot she was even there. When she wasn't sleeping, she'd be out searching the forest and digging through undergrowth until her hands bled. To ease my mind, I'd send Lazarus with her. Still, I'd worry until she returned. But I couldn't stop her. None of us could.

She'd even refused to brush her hair or bathe. She resembled a woodland creature, her hair wild and matted, her face smeared with dirt, food staining her pinafore.

We all wondered what had become of Duffy. With the work at hand and the hard winter looming, we did our best to brook up our heartache. The absence of his good cheer dulled the very air.

Despite the loss of Duffy, we had to carry on. But it seemed my sister had earmarked her life, as if a book, the day Duffy left. Unless he returned, I wondered if she'd ever turn another page.

I understood they'd grown fond of each other. And I, too, missed Duffy. We all did. But her grief was a widow's grief. It shouldn't have been. They weren't married. They hadn't even known each other for very long.

At our evening meal tonight, Phoebe again sat quietly, picking at her food, almost as if she'd forgotten it was there.

"You're in purgatory," Cecil said to her, shoveling a slice of Beatrice's pie in his mouth as if someone might steal it from him. "It'd be better to know one way or the other about his fate. Hard to cross the river when you can't find it."

In my opinion, his words did little to help. But Phoebe nodded. She lived in her own distance, so perhaps he was right. She was neither here nor somewhere else.

I desperately worried about her, sallow

and thin, her eyes forlorn tunnels.

On most nights, she slept well. I, on the other hand, did not. My thoughts would declare themselves after everyone was sleeping, and they'd patter and chat and argue, playing archery with my peace. Which is why I didn't hear her leave the cabin in the morning. When I'd finally fallen asleep, far after midnight, the slumber had been deep.

Beatrice and Big Al were also up. She in the kitchen, Al outside. Bee hadn't noticed Phoebe leaving, either. She'd thought Phoebe was bundled up next to me under the quilts.

I eased outside to the melody of songbirds and the harmony of the river and found Big Al sitting on a log, shifting a twig back and forth in his mouth while cleaning a trout he'd caught.

I asked if he'd seen Phoebe.

"Set out toward the creek. Figured she was after some water."

Even before Duffy disappeared, Phoebe slept later than any of us. Moreover, she hadn't fetched water in weeks. I reasoned how early she'd fallen asleep yesterday. It had still been light outside. Maybe when the sun rose this morning, industry had tugged at her for the first time in weeks. I only wished she'd brought Lazarus.

To reach the creek, I set off on the path we'd worn down. The dog followed. The shade-thick dew clung to moss and ferns. Mushrooms billowed in bunches. When we'd first arrived, Malcolm had warned us of their fatal poison. I called out to my sister several times with no answer back.

When I reached the creek, she wasn't there. The water was still and dark, the sunlight tucked behind the firs and pine.

"Phoebe!"

Lazarus barked.

Phoebe didn't answer.

Usually, when she was out searching, I could hear her crying out Duffy's name over and over, as if his name were part of her breath.

A red-winged blackbird startled me, launching itself from a tree, its wings a bluster.

I decided to walk around the creek into the forest beyond. We'd looked for Duffy over there, but we'd all concluded it was more likely he'd be found on the path to the neighboring camp, which is where he'd been headed. Maybe Phoebe had wanted to search this area again. Perhaps she'd had a dream. As of late, she'd taken to looking in places she'd dreamed about.

This part of the forest was too dense for

sunlight and probably stayed shady all day. I had to find Phoebe. She wasn't thinking right. She had a habit of landing herself into easily-avoided dangers. Once, when we were young girls, she'd wandered away from me on our way home from school. I'd been walking ahead, chattering with friends. I'd thought she was behind me. But she'd slipped away. When I had arrived home without her, my father's ire had surged. He had to go out looking and didn't find her until after dark. She'd been inside a stranger's barn playing with a litter of puppies.

My sister had a tender, curious heart. Now that heart was shattered. I kept walking and calling out her name. Lazarus sniffed at the ground. Then he bounded after one twitchy squirrel scuttling up an evergreen trunk.

The ground was mostly pine needles, so voluminous in patches, I had to wade through them. Brisk this morning, I pulled my cape around my shoulders. What if Phoebe had run into Indians? What if she'd been taken away? I shuddered at the thought.

Mocking a whisper, the wind ruffled the trees. I snuffed out the sound with my ceaseless calls to Phoebe. I'd said her name so many times, the word almost lost meaning, and unease gripped me.

I felt I'd neared hell's margin. With all the days filled with worry, working the claim, and an unending abyss of tasks, I hadn't dwelled much on our circumstances. I hadn't even been thinking about Boston. But it struck me now how we shouldn't be here. We should be home. I shouldn't be wearing trousers and a man's hat. I should be wearing a frock with crisp ribbons and a crinoline.

I stopped calling out to her and listened, instead. Birdsong. The wind in the trees. The river's raw labor. And then I heard my sister.

I was certain.

Lazarus stood still and stopped sounding off, but his ears twitched. He'd heard Phoebe, too. And she was weeping.

He dashed off in the direction of the sound, and I chased after him.

He darted between trees as if he were a wild animal, not a domesticated dog. As fast as I could, I followed, weaving between the tree trunks.

When we reached her, she was sitting on the ground and leaning back against an outcropping of boulders. She held an object against her chest. Her face was swollen, red, streaked with dirt and tears. Upon seeing us, she looked up and cried without making a sound.

"Phoebe!" I rushed over and threw my arms around her. Lazarus hunkered down and pushed his head into her lap.

She retrieved her breath. "I found his hat and coat. Here, stuffed between these boulders."

I wanted to deny she was holding Duffy's coat but couldn't. Though stiff with muck, it was the same color and make. I saw that his hat, bent, soiled, and folded, lay at her side.

"He's dead, isn't he?" she said. "Someone killed my Duffy. Then hid his hat and coat here."

"I don't know. I don't know."

"He's dead. I promise."

I considered, briefly, arguing that he might still be alive. That he might have misplaced his hat and coat and not to worry. He'd be back soon.

I considered this. But the words wouldn't come.

I saw a beetle dive into a crevice on the boulder and envied the insect.

My sister swiped at her nose. Lazarus began to lick the salt from her face.

"I don't know what befell Duffy," I said. "But he's surely with your savior."

"Isn't my savior."

I didn't challenge her. Phoebe was stubborn so would probably keep her word. I'd have to continue praying for both our souls. But in those prayers, I wouldn't be able to help but question the Almighty about his mismanaged world.

"We will have to get back to the cabin and tell the others." I started to stand.

"You don't understand, Effie. You don't understand how bad it is."

"None of us do," I said. "But anything could have happened to Duffy out here."

"That's not what I'm talking about." She was starting to sob again. "I'm with child, Effie. And we weren't married. We were going to marry up quickly when Cecil got back and could do it proper. But now Duffy's gone."

The shock was the same as if I'd been thrown off a saddle. "Well," I found myself saying, "you'd best get up then. You need to dry your face and shake the dirt from your dress. We need to get back to the others."

Sixteen

After finding his hat and coat, Phoebe refused to eat, climbed up into our bed, and only got up to make water.

She sobbed next to me for two nights straight. Beatrice tried to comfort her by patting her back, praying, and offering silly diatribes about how Duffy was in heaven with the king of all kings strolling down streets of gold, and that she'd see him again someday.

This just made her cry harder.

By the third day, I'd had enough. Phoebe would have to eat. She would have to get out of bed. She would have to care for herself. She'd also have to help with the chores. At first, I tried using tender words. Coaxing her with the promise of a hot bath, boiling up enough water for a good soak in the tub Malcolm had built outside.

She wouldn't budge.

So I did what I had to do. Yanked the

quilts off and pulled her from the bed. "You need to clean yourself up and stop wasting the days."

She screeched and yelled, twisting her arm out of mine. "I loved him! You don't understand. You've never loved anyone!" She threw herself back down and covered her head up with the quilts.

"Your grief isn't more important than living. I can't leave for the diggings because I have to stay behind and help keep this cabin in order, thanks to your laggard ways. And to make sure you don't throw yourself in the creek."

"I don't care what you do. I don't care about anything."

No one except me knew about Phoebe's condition, so I lowered my voice, held her up by the shoulders, and looked her straight in the eyes. "You must care for the baby growing inside you. If for no other reason, you must carry on for the baby's sake. It's all you have left of Duffy."

She screamed and pulled away from me, scooting off into the corner and hugging her knees against her chest.

"We cannot deny what's to come," I said. "And you will need to gather any strength you have left to do right by this child."

Gritting her teeth, she glared. "If Beatrice

hadn't gotten sick, we would have been husband and wife."

"Leave Beatrice out of this," I said.

Phoebe's eyes gleamed with tears. "If we'd married, no one . . . no one would know."

"Know what? That the baby was conceived prior to wedlock?"

She nodded.

"Everyone here can count. I see them do it every day when we bring back the nuggets and dust."

"They couldn't know for sure."

"No one gives a fig about any of that out here."

She began to cry again, and I cursed myself for the lack of comfort I brought to others. My words should have been sugar. As per usual, they were sawdust.

"I did love him, Effie. I promise you. I still do. Always will. We would have been happy."

I went to fetch her some warm chicory. I poured it into a tin cup and tried to be kinder. "Sometimes life blooms in the spring all pretty and yellow. Sometimes it doesn't. And you wait for months for a daffodil that decided to stay put in the ground."

"Sometimes the daffodils get stepped on and smashed," she said.

I handed her the cup. "After you drink

that, go out and have a soak in the water I spent over an hour warming for you. Then comb your witchy hair and clean yourself up. As for me, I've decided I will head out to the bar because today you *are* going to help out. So help me, you are going to do your share! The burden of the household chores shouldn't all be on Beatrice. I swear on everything, Phoebe, if I return and you're still in bed, I'll drag you to the creek and throw you in it!"

I pulled on my boots and heard my sister sipping the hot liquid. I knew that somewhere inside of her was a flicker of who she used to be, the sister who couldn't be stopped, who never listened to sense, who giggled when she should have frowned, who asked questions when she should have kept mum. My sister, whose laugh could cure most ills, was in there somewhere buried in a muddy surge of mourning.

Later, after our dinner of salmon and wild onion soup, Malcolm and I sat on the porch. We didn't have chairs, but the stoop was good enough, and the evening was dusky with a few chunky stars already shining through. The sound of the river folding in on itself served as music.

Phoebe had done as I asked. She'd bathed,

eaten a meal, and helped some, according to Beatrice. It was a start. She was sleeping now. I was glad for this because I needed to tell Malcolm about Phoebe's condition. I also wanted to talk to him about leaving here. More and more, I was thinking we should travel back to the city ahead of the snowfall. I didn't want to leave, but Phoebe could have troubles requiring a doctor. If she did, we'd be stuck and unable to seek help.

"Doe over there is staring at us," Malcolm said. "I'd get my rifle but for the sweetness in its eyes."

The doe's oval eyes and long lashes didn't charm me. Even if we three women went back to the city, the men still needed as much meat as possible with the coming winter. I could already feel the winter wind's first crisp tendrils, and I pulled my cloak shut against the chilly air. Before I could say anything about the deer, Lazarus launched himself off the porch to chase it away.

"My sister is in a state over Duffy Fields," I said. "They were more than friendly."

"I knew your eyes worked." He winked at me.

Lazarus trotted over to us, satisfied with himself for flushing out the doe.

Malcolm patted the dog on the head. "All of us here knew about Duffy and Phoebe's love affair. Our neighbors knew, too. Wasn't a secret on this mountain. Duffy was good at a lot of things, but keeping secrets wasn't one of them."

"You knew they wanted to get married?"

"I figured that's what they were whispering about during meals and after they thought we were all asleep. I'm pleased the man found some love before he came to an end. Duffy was a good fella with a pure heart and a strong back. He was my friend. And I won't forget him. Not for the rest of my days. I can still see him coming up over the hill just as plain as if he were alive."

"He was a very decent man." I paused only for a second. "I only wish my sister wasn't with child now."

Malcolm didn't twitch or shift or offer any gesture showing he was surprised by this.

"What should we do?" I asked. "If we go back to Sacramento City, we can tell people her husband's passed on to his maker. No one will have to know she never did marry, and the babe has no father."

"The babe has a father. Just isn't on this earth. Far as we know."

I nodded. "But what if something goes wrong? Might be better to be near a doctor.

I'll take my portion of the dust and sell our share of the claim to you. We can live off that for a good while. That will cut into the funds we need to get back to Boston, but Phoebe and the baby might be safer."

"Where are you planning on staying?"

"Surely there are places to board."

"Haven't heard of three women, one of them with child, living alone in the city. You best stay here. When the babe's ready to come, I'll fetch some of the Maidu women to help with the birthing. It'll be rough and cold in the winter, but it'll be worse for you in the city."

Big Al had started to pluck a song on his banjo from inside the cabin.

"I think we should leave the mountain," I said after a few moments. "I don't want people finding out Phoebe's unmarried."

"That's what you're worried over?"

"Phoebe worries on it more than I do."

He leaned forward, his hands on his knees. "I might be able to solve that problem."

I clutched the stoop. Was Malcolm suggesting he would marry my sister? Of course he was. Malcolm was a good man. He would do right by Phoebe.

I swatted at the pale moths flitting toward the lamplight emitting from the cabin. To the milky insects, I supposed all light was moonlight.

"I'll have to convince Cecil to perform the ceremony," he said. "And Cecil's a stubborn goat, as you've seen for yourself."

I dug my nails into the board I was sitting on. "You think Cecil will do it? He said he'd never preach again."

"That's why I'll have to use some persuasion. Your sister deserves to be a bride, and Duffy, well he might be in heaven and all, but he'd be grinning ear to ear to see your sister happy."

As he went back inside, Malcolm ducked to avoid hitting his head. Though now shivering, I remained on the stoop with Lazarus's head on my lap.

SEVENTEEN

After tying my bootlace, I'd climbed up a bank of the river with Malcolm to loosen some packed earth. Though backbreaking work, we'd been finding more gold than ever with this method. Stronger now, I was thankful not to have access to a mirror. I must've looked more like a man every day. I felt like one, too. Lately, I'd forgone many of the manners and ladylike ways my mother had taught me. I laughed a little louder, talked louder, and occasionally let a peppery curse word tumble from my lips. Civilization was only a memory, and the girl who'd once lived there seemed a dream.

"When I first asked him," Malcolm was saying while digging his shovel deep into the earth, "Cecil told me he'd do it when pigs flew."

I dug, too, plunging as deeply as I could. If I were only taller, I could do a better job. At my diminutive height, it was hard to get as much leverage with the shovel.

"So I told Cecil I'd once seen a pig fly," Malcolm said.

"Don't be ridiculous." I tossed the contents of my half-full spade into the cradle.

"That's a version of what he said to me. Accused me of making up a yarn. But I told him it was true."

"You've never seen a pig fly."

"I saw one fall off the back of a runaway wagon." He stopped shoveling and looked me square in the eyes. "And I swear on the girl I love that the hog flew a few feet before landing on its hooves. Could've had wings. Don't know for sure."

"We've enough earth," I said. "We won't be able to lift the cradle if we load it anymore."

We picked up the cradle, one of us on each end, and it tilted toward me. We began to rock it back and forth, sifting the heaviest bits from the lighter dirt. We had a rhythm we'd been practicing.

"You're becoming mighty skilled, Euphemia Frost."

I was close to dropping the device because we'd overloaded it just as I feared, but I tightened my grip, trying to live up to his praise. "How'd you finally convince him?"

Malcolm's face glinted in the sunlight, and

a dragonfly with an iridescent blue body landed on his shoulder. "I told him the truth. Cecil likes the truth more than he likes his hat. And you know he doesn't take off that hat for nothing. Not manners. Not a lady. Not sleep. I've only seen him take it off to wash what's left of his hair."

"What truth did you tell him?"

"There's only one truth last I checked. The rest is lies."

We'd almost shaken all the heaviest debris into the bottom of the cradle. I saw a few flashes and twinkles, but I'd been fooled by a gleam before. We all had.

"Only condition Cecil had is that he refused to read from the Good Book, which he swears isn't good at all. He calls it the 'Bad Book.'"

I wouldn't know, as I'd only read parts. A scripture here and there. A verse. A passage. Some parables. I did like Proverbs and Psalms, but I'd skipped around. All that begetting and begatting seemed a never-ending bore. Besides, there were so many other books to read.

"Cecil thinks it'll be the most curious wedding he's ever officiated," Malcolm told me. "Might be why he's willing."

"Why does he think that? My sister is as pretty as the sunshine, and before Duffy disappeared, she delighted in the world. And you're a good man. You'll make a fine match. Nothing curious about it."

Malcolm practically dropped the cradle.

"Well, you're good enough for her." I suddenly felt shy about giving him such high praise. "Offering to marry my sister in her precarious state makes me think more of you. I hope you know you'll be moving to Boston now."

He scowled and shook his head.

Looking for coloration, I crouched down and peered into the cradle. "I believe we have some nuggets in this lot."

"You think that's what I asked Cecil? To marry me and your sister?"

I nodded, refusing to look into his eyes.

"You've got it all wrong."

I stood and brushed off my trousers. "Then who do you intend my sister marry? Big Al?" I said testily. "If it's not you, then I would prefer she not marry at all."

"Why would I marry your sister when I only have eyes for you?"

My skin grew hot, though the day was cooler than most before it.

He kneeled down and drew my chin up, so I could look him in the eyes. "You're so busy looking off into the distance, you can't see a foot away."

I wasn't angry. I didn't know what I was. I didn't know why I stood, kicked at the dirt, and ran off toward the cabin. About half way there, I stopped and looked up at the sky, stretching forever blue. I closed my eyes. For just one glorious moment, I hugged myself and allowed for a sliver of joy. Then I shook it all off, stared down at my feet, and marched straight ahead.

It had been raining hard for almost a week, but we were nevertheless going forward with the ceremony. The roof had only sprung two leaks so far, and we were better off for them, as we were able to catch the water and save it for drinking.

Phoebe's spirits weren't nearly the same as they'd been before Duffy's disappearance, but today I noticed traces of the pluck and joy she once had. The men seemed in higher spirits, too. Maybe the pitter-patter on the roof sounded like folks dancing. If I closed my eyes and listened, I could imagine my father drumming his fingers while listening to Phoebe weave her made-up stories. She always could tell the best stories, ones filled with fairies and magical creatures and happy endings.

I did not consider this a happy ending. I did not consider this an ending at all. My sister was about to marry a ghost.

Once I'd figured out what Malcolm truly intended, I'd protested the notion. Duffy Fields was dead. My sister would not and could not marry a dead man.

"Duffy would have wanted it this way," Malcolm had told me. "They'd planned to marry up. This way he can still have his bride. And the baby can have its father's name."

"But he's not here to make the vow."

"A vow on this mountain can be carried down from heaven by a cloud."

"That's absurd. What if he's not dead? What if he's out there somewhere and finds out he's married to my sister without even being present for the ceremony? What if he went home to Ohio to marry someone else?"

"Duffy didn't go home. And he's not coming back. You know as well as I do that he wouldn't have left your sister for all the gold in California if he'd a choice in the matter. He wanted to marry your sister, and now he'll get his wish from the great beyond. And Phoebe will get her wish, too."

"I never approved of the union. And I don't approve of it now. I particularly don't approve of it now." Marrying my sister to a dead man seemed outlandish. But Malcolm was right in that it would legitimize their babe and make my sister a widow rather than a fallen woman. Once we were back in Boston, no one would know of this farce or that Duffy Fields disappeared before the wedding. Young widows were common enough, so no one would ever think to gossip about Phoebe. Well, not for being a widow at least. Knowing my sister's habits, Phoebe would likely find a way to encourage gossip one way or the other.

But I had a secret I'd even tried to keep from myself: I preferred this pretend wedding over her marrying Malcolm, and this is why I'd ultimately approved. If she was marrying Malcolm today, I'd have to feign happiness. He'd said he only had eyes for me, hadn't he? Maybe I'd misheard him. Maybe I'd only wanted to hear him say that, and it had never happened. Sometimes I believed I was seeing something in the corner of my eye. But when I turned to look, nothing was there.

Still, this ceremony was out of the ordinary and went against all I'd been brought up to understand as normal.

Naturally, Phoebe had not balked at Malcolm's scheme. She'd embraced it. Invigorated, she talked of nothing else, and, with Beatrice, she got busy preparing for the ceremony.

I watched as she chattered and socialized as if this were a real wedding and the most important day of her life. Beatrice had concocted a story to make it all real by saying Duffy was outside, and he wasn't allowed to look at the bride. The thought of Duffy standing in the rain made me want to weep, but Phoebe seemed to like it, and I started to wonder if she'd begin having conversations with her illusory husband. If she'd spend the rest of her days in a make-believe matrimonial state.

We'd managed to get a few eggs from the neighbors, and Beatrice had baked a scrumptious-smelling gooseberry jam cake. We'd also tried to decorate the cabin. This was all Beatrice's idea, and Phoebe had latched onto it. The rest of us went along for the sake of my sister. We made garlands by snapping thin branches off the youngest firs. And we made a wreath, as well. Beatrice crafted a bouquet from small white flowers we'd found in a meadow and another flower I'd never seen before. It looked like a red buttercup.

We didn't have a gown, nor did we have any fabric to sew a dress. All we could do was pin our mother's cameo on my sister's yellow frock, the one I'd scolded her for bringing. Beatrice took great care weaving and rolling Phoebe's hair into a swirled design with finger ringlets dangling over her ears.

When it came time for the ceremony, only I could give her away. My cousin's chatter and giggles stole any practicality or cynicism I might otherwise bring to bear. Phoebe clutched Duffy's hat against her bosom, as I linked my arm onto Phoebe's and walked her under the garland we'd strewn across the ceiling.

I let her go. Now Phoebe faced Cecil, who'd bathed for the occasion and was dressed in what he called his finest suit, though we all knew he only had the one.

Except for the rain on the roof, the cabin was silent. Lazarus dared not make a sound, even when Beatrice went to the front door, opened it, and then shut it again.

This ushering in of my sister's dead groom seemed morose and unnecessary. Everything about this did. But I chose not to dwell on the farcical nature of this moment. I concentrated on Phoebe, who seemed gayer than she'd been in so long. She was staring at nobody, far as I could tell. But her gaze suggested Duffy really was standing next to her.

"Dearly beloved," Cecil said, clearing his

throat. "We are gathered here in this cabin no bigger than a teacup to join these two in matrimony, be it holy or unholy."

I glared at the preacher.

"Holy. It's entirely holy what we have come to do today, which is to say, join Phoebe Frost and Duffy Fields in wedded bliss. Now, Miss Phoebe, please repeat after me: I reckon my love is a bright, red rose."

"I reckon my love is a bright, red rose," Phoebe said.

"That's sprung to bush in June. Or is it July?"

"That's sprung to bush in June. Or is it July?"

"My love." Cecil closed his eyes. "My love is a harmony."

". . . Love," she said carefully, "is a harmony."

These didn't sound like any wedding vows I'd ever heard. But it did sound familiar. I was almost certain he was reciting, albeit badly, a poem. I began to wonder if Cecil had been tippling from his jug of whiskey.

" 'Till the seas hang dry, dear or dear," he said.

" 'Till the seas hang dry, dear or dear."

His voice grew singsong. "And the rocks will melt in the sun."

"And the rocks will melt in the sun."

"And fare thee well. The sands of life do run."

"And fare thee well," Phoebe recited. "The sands of life do run."

"And I will come again, my love." He clasped his hands together. "You don't need to repeat that part, Phoebe Frost. That's what the groom would say to you."

"Okay," my sister said shyly.

"Do you take this man to be your wedded husband, even in death?"

I think we all stopped breathing with this question.

"I do." My sister beamed. "Of course I do."

"Then, with all the preaching I have left in my soul, I pronounce you husband and wife."

Big Al started the hooting and hollering, and then Beatrice joined in. Malcolm, too. Finally, I shouted a big hooray, as did Cecil. Only Oxley stayed quiet. It seemed we were in another place, another time.

Al picked up his banjo and started to pluck a quick and upbeat melody. Phoebe wept, but it seemed from joy. I realized I was weeping, too. We all were. We seemed lost in this fairy world we'd created for the day, where the living can wed the dead, where the two widows could spin about in a light-stepped jig, where a brooding preacher could tap his foot and chug whiskey, where I could freely dance with Malcolm. When had he rested his hand on my lower back? We created our own wind as he swung me around and twirled me under his arm.

Then he quickly leaned in and pecked me on the cheek.

I withdrew instantly, hoping nobody had seen. I joined my sister's and cousin's hands, and we danced a rosy, laughing as we had as young girls, whirling in a circle, Lazarus leaping around between us.

When we came tumbling down ashes to ashes, Lazarus licked my face, and I noticed Oxley stepping outside. He let in a cold bluster and splash of rain before Malcolm could shut the door behind him.

EIGHTEEN

The rain persisted for almost a month straight, washing away all the diggings we'd overturned. When it stopped, a cold straddled the mountain, causing even Beatrice to curse at the wind every time she stepped outside. Perhaps she thought no one could hear her, but her high child-like voice carried.

Malcolm had traded two mules for another horse. I was thankful given Phoebe's belly. Near Christmas, we had to let her dresses out at the waist. Phoebe waddled about and groaned every time she rose from a chair.

At least she was talkative again. After dinner, while I tried to read another volume of Dumas, she chattered about our grand Boston Christmases. "Last year, we ate roasted goose with the crispiest skin and applesauce with sugar and cinnamon. Beatrice, what else did we eat? Do you remember?"

"Winter squash, plum pudding, mince pie, and an ever-so-delicate blancmange. Our cook made the creamiest blancmange!"

Beatrice had plumped up, too, due to her preoccupation with cooking. We were all happy for it, as we enjoyed the meals, and she seemed rosier and more robust than she'd ever been. She'd also taken to sampling from Cecil's supply of whiskey. If we were still in Boston, I would have admonished her for daring to even taste an alcoholic beverage. But the entire surface of the earth and everyone around us had altered. Beatrice might be enjoying a tipple now and then, and I was wearing trousers, both unthinkable back home. When we eventually left here and returned, we would forget all of this nonsense and resume our learned etiquette and civilized conduct. For now, Beatrice could drink whiskey. I could wear men's clothing. And my sister could have a babe fathered by a ghost.

Phoebe asked Beatrice what we'd be eating for our Christmas meal.

"Roasted venison, thanks to Malcolm and his hunting skills. Squirrel soup, too. Thank you, Big Al." Big Al grinned at his success in hunting the rodents. "Boiled potatoes with wild onions and something you'll all enjoy."

"What?" Phoebe asked.

Beatrice smiled in a self-satisfied way. "Apple pie."

"Apple pie? Where'd you get the apples?"

"Mr. Oxley. He purchased them from the neighboring camp. A fellow had brought some over from Rich's Bar."

The rumor was that Rich's Bar was starting to look like a small town with merchants and, as was standard, a gambling hall. It also had a doctor. Two days ride from our cabin, this fact did little to assuage my fear about Phoebe giving birth up here. Still, it was of some comfort to know a doctor lived on the mountain.

Oxley, who'd been, to my surprise, mending one of his shirts, stepped out to use the privy. Phoebe used the opportunity to tease Beatrice. "I think Mr. Oxley is courting you, dear cousin. Bringing you apples. Chopping your wood."

Beatrice glanced up, flour on her nose. "He can court me all winter if he chooses to waste his time."

Phoebe rubbed her ever-burgeoning belly. "Mourning for your late husband need not be for a full year. Nothing's the same out here."

251

"I will always love Aaron." She mixed the dough of her biscuits. "But that's not the reason Mr. Oxley's courting is for naught."

I listened carefully because I didn't trust Oxley and didn't like all the favors he'd been doing for my cousin.

She stopped mixing the flour and looked at us. "I know what love is. I know how it feels. If I do ever marry again, I will have to feel that same thing, which I doubt I ever will. Russell Oxley doesn't provoke even a shadow of that emotion." She tossed a pinch of salt into her concoction.

"Then you should stop flirting with him," I said.

She wagged a spoon at me. "I never flirt with that man."

I rose to stoke the fire. In the cold of the Sierra Nevada, allowing the fire to go out was the worst thing one could do. "You chat unnecessarily with him. You have him run errands for you. He even helps more with the chores. A month ago, he would have demanded one of *us* mend his shirt."

"I showed him how to use a needle and thread, and he happily took up the task."

"You hang up his hat and coat," I said.

"I treat all the men the same."

Maybe she was right. "Have you seen the way Oxley looks at you?"

Beatrice seemed to be considering what I said, which I deemed a miracle. Then she turned back to her dough. "I think you're wrong, Effie. Oxley just has a strange look on his face. He always has had an odd look. Ever since we met him. He allows his gaze to linger a moment longer than he ought to."

"He should pay heed and stop letting his eyes linger on you."

"Oh, Effie, he's been a perfect gentleman lately. Still, he shouldn't expect to court me. I'm not interested. I plan on becoming the best pie maker in California. And once winter's over, I'll sell them in the cities. Every miner near and far will talk about my pies."

"After winter's over, we will be headed back to Boston."

"Is that your intention?"

"Phoebe's baby needs to be raised properly with an education and libraries and civilization. And you can bake pies back home for a proper husband. We cannot possibly stay here. Once they've found all the gold, California will resume its natural state as a desolate and wild wilderness."

Malcolm had built Phoebe a rocking chair, and she was rocking back and forth, listening.

Beatrice began to angrily dollop the dough into a cast-iron pan. "You always know what's best, don't you? You always think you know everything."

I didn't want to bicker so stayed quiet.

"You ever consider," Beatrice continued, "that you might be wrong? You can't decide the futures for me and Phoebe."

"I haven't been working myself to the bone with that pan and cradle for nothing. It's to get us home. It's all we've wanted since we arrived."

"I will do as I please." Beatrice shoved the pan of biscuits onto the fire grate. Sparks flew.

I looked over to Phoebe and saw she'd shut her eyes. I was thankful. Bickering with my cousin was enough noise. I didn't want an earful from both.

"I am only looking out for you," I said to Beatrice. "You told me you hated it here."

"A girl can change her mind."

"Yes, you've always been fickle." I immediately regretted what I'd said.

Beatrice hastily snapped her cloak and scarf from the back of a chair and wrapped them tightly around her before slamming out the front door, a cold wind swooping in. I heard her call out to Mr. Oxley. My cousin had always known how to wield her feminine wiles. She'd wielded them like a sword with my uncle. Then with Aaron. Her wiles also seemed to be working on Oxley. I believed more in Phoebe's tall tales than I did anything that came out of Oxley's mouth, so I wished Beatrice would listen to me. She wouldn't, of course. And Phoebe, sleeping now with her mouth slightly ajar, would never listen either.

They were ingrates, the both of them. Beatrice's biscuit bottoms were burning, and so it was up to me to flip them over. I was certainly growing weary of everything, from biscuits to our very lives, being up to me.

"If it weren't for your hunting skills and Big Al's fishing, we'd starve." It was early January, and I'd just inventoried our larder.

"How much do we have left?" Malcolm asked.

I read from my list. "Two bags of flour, half a sack of sugar, a little over half a sack of beans, one can of coffee, a half can of chicory, some rotten onions, and two bags of potatoes with more eyes than a spider."

"I'll ride over to Brown's Bar and see if they've got extra. Some eggs would be good, too."

"Oh," Phoebe said, her belly jutting out

so much, her dress lifted above her ankles. "I would love to have a chicken. Imagine fresh eggs every morning."

"I'll see what I can do," Malcolm said.

"Not a rooster, though," she said, grinning. "We have enough cock-a-doodlers strutting around here already."

Over the past few months, some of Phoebe's silliness returned along with some of my irritation. But it was better than her lazing on the bedstead for most the day.

Cecil was reading Dickens by the fire. Big Al was shuffling cards. I worried that a gambling bug would grip him should he ever live too near a gambling den, which he likely would someday.

Being forced to dwell in such close quarters was setting my nerves on fire. Malcolm had warned we'd get irritated and hate him for it. But I didn't hate him. I didn't hate any of them. Not even Oxley. I wasn't fond of Oxley, and I would never trust him. But we'd all spent too much time together to not feel joined in a familial way. I might grow to like Oxley more if he'd stop moaning and carping about every little thing. The food, delicious or bland. The weather, hot or cold. The dust. My dog. He'd even complained about the birds singing in the trees. What kind of person complains about

God's gift of birdsong? What's more, he grew puffy and cross whenever his views or ideas were challenged. Even if he was in the wrong. Which he was most of the time.

Although the sound of Oxley or Cecil chewing their food, or my sister's sudden voice out of the silence, or Beatrice's constant humming raised the hair on my arms, I found ways to cope. I'd step outside and take a walk with Lazarus. The winter forest could be quiet except for the river rushing, the crunch of snow under my boots, or a twig or branch creaking under Lazarus's paws. I liked these moments. Sometimes I'd think of my father. If I listened closely to my own thoughts, I could remember how his voice sounded. I could imagine my brothers, too. My mother's face. My uncle's scowl when he was teasing us followed by a quick grin and loud laugh. As time went on, I discovered these memories became harder to recall. I tried to recall them as often as possible, so I could keep them in the front of my mind rather than the back.

This afternoon, after Big Al had broken his bootlace and yelled out a curse word, I needed a walk and was thankful the wind had calmed. The winters here didn't seem as bad as the winters back East. To be sure, when it did storm, the sky raged, and we'd already had snow so deep, it crept four feet up the door. But on many days the sky was a crisp and clean blue, and the sun hung high and bright. The days were cold, but we could still work in the brisk air. The water was icy, the earth stiff and resistant to a shovel, so we couldn't find much gold, but we found enough dust to make it worth our efforts.

I glanced up. A gray and white sky hung above me. I figured it would snow tonight or tomorrow. Now was the time to have a peaceful moment to myself, for I could be locked in the cabin with everyone for an entire week if a storm took hold.

Phoebe had kept her promise and stopped praying, but whether out of habit or not, I still said grace and silently asked the Lord to keep my sister safe during the worst of the storms. The baby would come in March, Phoebe had said. To me, she looked as full of child as a woman in her last days before giving birth. I wished I had someone to talk to about this, other than Beatrice, who didn't seem to fret at all about her cousin's health. Even after everything we'd been through, Beatrice refused to consider potential catastrophes. This was her way. Nothing could dent her natural cheerfulness for long, not the death of her husband, not the death of her father, not the complete dashing of her sunny and unreasonable expectations of California. She'd suffered, yes, but it seemed easier for her than most to emerge from a gloom, almost as if the gloomy mood itself was worse than the actual hardship.

A chunk of snow had dislodged itself from a branch and soared down, nearly hitting me squarely in the head. I would have been vexed if the snow had bent my hat so was glad I'd moved from its descent.

The cold, at first bracing, now grew bitter, so I began to head back through the slushy ground. Bulging purplish clouds swiftly pushed in overhead. Malcolm was calling out to me from the cabin porch. He sometimes worried over me when he shouldn't. I'd scolded him for it, but he'd kept on. I headed toward his voice, which was splitting open the silence. I would never let him know I liked it when he looked out for me.

When I drew closer, I heard Beatrice, too. I couldn't make out what she was saying. Then I heard Oxley. The tone of Beatrice's voice suggested a small disagreement, the words gentle but firm. I eased closer to the noise and listened from behind several thick manzanita bushes.

"You must keep your hands to yourself,"

Beatrice was saying.

"Who told you that?"

"It's polite," Beatrice said. "And you, being a gentleman, will certainly respect my wishes on this."

I heard Oxley laughing.

"Why are you finding amusement, sir? I am serious in my request. As my friend, I know you will honor it."

"Friend?"

I didn't hear what Beatrice said next. I only heard a small burst of noise that sounded as if it had been cut off by a pair of sharp sewing scissors. Racing forward, I saw that Oxley had slammed his hand over my cousin's mouth, and he was pulling her behind the cabin toward a wooded area. She was kicking and flailing her arms, but she seemed unable to twist out of his grip.

Only when I shouted at him to stop was she able to free herself and rush back toward the cabin, passing me along the way. Alone with Oxley, I was stunned into silence.

"You think you're a lady?" he said to me.

I looked down at my clothes, the trousers held up by red suspenders and the oversized shirt, which I now preferred to wear.

Before I could respond, Malcolm, Big Al, and Cecil, all of whom must have heard the commotion, came forth. It had begun to snow, and Oxley, flakes salting his black hair, challenged them with a sour and crooked grin.

"You best take your belongings and share of the proceeds and go," Malcolm said. His fists were clenched. I could tell he wanted to knock the man on his back.

"I aim to marry Beatrice, so I'll be staying."

"You'll be leaving," Malcolm said.

"What you intended for my cousin had nothing to do with marriage," I snapped.

He snarled and puffed out his chest, as if this would intimidate us. The snow had transformed from a light dusting to an errant flurry. "Can't leave now." He held up the palms of his large hands. "The snow will kill me. Besides, you'll change your mind about my leaving when you consider I'll be taking the rest of the provisions with me. You'd hate to starve up here, I'm guessing."

"You can't take our provisions," I said.

"I paid for them. I can take what I want. And I want it all. What I can't carry, I'll sell or burn."

Silence was greatest when it snowed, the ground padded, the birds, even the crows, hidden somewhere in the trees.

Malcolm turned to me. "I should've never brought this son of a bitch into our camp. I apologize, Effie."

"Others might wish you'd never brought us, so don't be apologizing for Oxley. You did what would make us strongest."

"So," Oxley said, "I'll be staying. The judgment is in." He sauntered back to the cabin, and I hurried to keep up, as I didn't want him alone with my cousin. Or my sister, for that matter. I didn't think Russell Oxley cared if a woman was with child or not. He'd have his way and couldn't be left alone with any of us. I vowed from this day on that I'd keep Aaron's pistol with me at all times.

It snowed for nearly a full week. We three girls would stand on the porch and watch the white tassels falling, the fir branches bowing, as if saying grace. The cabin wasn't insulated from the cold, but it was warm enough to be comfortable with the fire and so many of us crammed inside. Phoebe had learned monte, much to my chagrin, and would deal to Big Al, who bragged that he was practicing so he could clean out all the gambling halls in Sacramento City. I didn't think it right to egg Big Al on toward the ultimate demise of a gambler. We'd heard stories about what happened to those men.

But Phoebe was entertained, and it took her mind off the babe flipping around like a flapjack inside of her. That's how she'd described it.

Despite the incident with Oxley, we went on for the most part as if it had never happened. Beatrice, forgiving him almost immediately, resumed her conversations and friendship with the man. And I kept reading the books he'd brought along. I was glad he hadn't decided to take vengeance on me by hiding them or throwing them into the woods.

I enjoyed reading to Malcolm, who'd sit next to me on his bunk and grip the sides when the chapters became perilous. He'd laugh, too, with all the amusing passages, especially in the Dumas stories, which he liked best.

Cecil would spend his time drinking spirits. Then, well into his cups, he'd tell us stories. Some were true. Some made up. Others sounded more like sermons. Today, he was telling one about a woman from his so-called flock. The woman had hair as soft as a rabbit's ears, he said. It was silky, black, and marbled with white.

While running his finger down his scar, Cecil talked about how he and the woman found a bird that had fallen from its nest behind her house. How she'd called him over to offer a prayer for its recovery. The bird died, Cecil said. And they'd buried it, funeral and all. Her children had died, too, he added after another swig from his jug. All four of them.

"I presided over their funerals, too. One by one. Fever. Accident. Whatever scourge was blowing in the wind. Then her husband, finally, too. Then it was just her. The baby bird was all she could stand."

Phoebe asked what had happened to her, the woman with the silky hair.

"You know how the rain washed all our work away, as if we'd never dug or blistered our hands?"

"Yes," she said, holding both hands on her babe inside.

"That there was the woman's life. It got washed away. And so one night, after singing an evensong at service, she went home and drowned herself in the washtub. Hard to drown yourself in a washtub, don't you think?"

We were usually disturbed by Cecil's drunken tales, but this left us all with the melancholy. I wished Big Al would stop playing cards and play something breezy on his banjo. I thought about how nice it would have been to dance with Malcolm again. Dancing with Malcolm would help me forget about the tragedies that seemed to always be nipping sharp toothed at our heels. Maybe dancing would keep them at a distance. We'd spin so fast, troubles couldn't catch us. I'd liked it when he'd kissed my cheek. I'd liked it very much.

I could still feel where his lips had been.

But these were syrupy thoughts. And too sugary to condone.

"I have decided to accept Russell Oxley's proposal," Beatrice announced to me and Phoebe on the first sunny day we'd had in weeks. The men were outside. We were all preparing to head over to the claim and work what we could with the dry day and sunny skies. Even if we found a tiny nugget, it'd be worth the energy.

Phoebe, who was so large she could barely move about the cabin, seemed more startled than I was. "When did he ask for your hand?"

"I forbid it." In this statement, I'd conjured up my father, mother, aunt, and uncle's authority as best I could.

"He asked me on Christmas. And I told him *no,* of course, as I do not love him and never will."

Phoebe rocked back and forth in her chair, faster than usual.

"I have since changed my mind," Beatrice said. "Oxley will provide for me. I have no one or nothing else. I'm becoming plump and will likely become plumper, as I enjoy nothing more than baking these pies and eating them. My best chance at having a comfortable life is to marry Oxley. I have been lucky enough to have loved once, and it will never happen again, so I shall go forward with what the Lord Jesus has set before me in the here and now."

"Oxley tried to force himself on you," I reminded her. "I fear that he will mistreat you for all your days."

"Men," she said, "sometimes cannot control their urges."

My sister stopped rocking. "You're agreeing to his proposal because we're here in this cabin with only these fellows around. You're prettier than any of us. You're even prettier now that you're not too skinny. I don't know why you'd ever marry that lazy scoundrel."

"How dare you question my choice of husbands," Beatrice said. "You married someone who isn't even with the living!"

Tears leapt into Phoebe's eyes, and I ran to comfort her. Beatrice set down her utensils and came over, too.

Phoebe swiped at her nose and took a deep breath before the tears had their way. "We were smitten with each other. We would have stayed that way for all our days. We'll never have time to show the rest of you how true we were."

I lifted her braid off her face and moved it behind her ear. "We all saw it, Phoebe. Even a blind man could have seen it."

Beatrice nodded. But she didn't apologize for her tart words.

"I'm feeling poorly today," Phoebe said, looking up at us.

I touched her forehead to feel if she were warm. She brushed it away.

"It's not a fever I'm having," she said. "It's the baby."

"Your baby must wait." I tried to believe my own words. "Spring is a fine time to give birth. All of God's creatures are born in spring."

Phoebe's eyes sparked. "I was born in December. And you were born in November. Are we not God's creatures?"

"I was born in April," Beatrice boasted.

"I don't know what it's supposed to feel like." Phoebe clutched her knees and bent over. "But . . . Effie . . . I'm scared."

"Are you feeling pains?" I tried to keep

my voice calm and steady though I wanted to scream.

"Strong ones," she said. "I didn't sleep much, but last night they were coming and going, so I thought the baby was only shifting around inside, and that's why it hurt. Sometimes it pokes at my innards."

Beatrice grabbed her Dutch oven and went outside to fill it with water. Before she left, she finally apologized to my sister for what she'd earlier said.

I didn't think Phoebe heard. One eye closed, she was stiffening, gripping the arms of the chair and wincing.

I believed Phoebe was going to die. It'd been over a day since the pain grabbed hold of her and cinched her up in a jagged sack. After so many hours, she was fainting from the force of it. Every time she lost consciousness, I thought she'd died. Then her eyes would spring open, and her screams would fill the cabin. Big Al was crying and cringing in the corner from the sound. I'd yell at him to shush up and go outside. He'd obey, leaving for brief interludes. But it was too cold to stay out there for long. Oxley refused. Instead, he'd torn up some muslin and shoved it in his ears. Beatrice had scowled at him for it, but he'd just shrugged.

Malcolm and Cecil had raced off on the horses to ask the Maidu for help. Malcolm was sure the two women who'd nursed him back to health might be able to coax the baby out, since they had herbs for such matters.

I prayed jerkily, between Phoebe's screams, for Malcolm and Cecil to hurry and return, and mostly for my sister and her babe not to die. *Please don't die. Please Lord, don't let her die. Oh Father, have mercy and let my sister live.*

And then she'd screech, her face contorted, and faint once more.

I wondered now what was worse, dying or being born. Living wasn't exactly the opposite of dying, for living took longer and changed up along the way. Living was good at times. Bad at others. But it vacillated on its course, whether short or long. The true opposites were death and birth. God didn't make either easy, not the coming, nor the going.

Guilt scraped at me. I blamed myself for being here in this cabin, far away from a real doctor. When we first arrived in San Francisco, I should have looked into the future and been more careful before agreeing to winter up here. And when I discovered Phoebe was with child, I should have swept her off this mountain as soon as possible and headed out to live in the city.

Now she could die. She would probably die. What good would the gold, the schemes to get back to Boston, or any of it be if that happened? My own life would be worthless.

I had been selfish. I knew exactly why I hadn't wanted to leave the cabin.

Malcolm. I hadn't wanted to leave Malcolm.

Admitting this truth made me furious at myself.

Phoebe curled up in a ball and began sobbing. Then she fainted again. She was being tortured.

It was another few hours before the men finally returned with two Indian women, who quickly removed their pelts, hides, and furs and neared the bedstead.

One brushed me aside and circled around to Phoebe's head. She quickly opened Phoebe's mouth and shoved something under her tongue. I could only pray whatever Phoebe had been given by the Maidu wouldn't kill her.

The other spread open Phoebe's legs and held out her hand. Beatrice shoved the cloth, which had been soaked in boiling water, toward the Maidu. It seemed exactly what the woman wanted, and she used it on my sister, to clean and pat and sooth. Now the other woman urged me through gestures and motions to assist her. She placed her body behind Phoebe's back, and gestured for me to do the same. With both us partly propping my sister up from behind, the Maidu woman who'd pulled apart my sister's legs grunted deeply and forcefully and motioned to my sister to do the same.

My sister, now alert and wild eyed, seemed to know what to do. Willing up any shreds of strength she might have left, she began to force with her own weak body the child out of her womb.

Then the Maidu woman breathed gently, instructing in her own language for my sister to imitate her. Phoebe understood and breathed. The woman then took a deep breath. Phoebe did the same. Then came a deep grunt. Phoebe followed suit.

This process repeated over and over.

Despite the cold, the men had all gone outside, where they built a fire. This was no place for them. We kept at it, and Phoebe shuddered and grunted and breathed. And finally, after a very long while, a baby boy slipped out, as if it had been conjured up by a magician. He was tiny and motionless. I couldn't help but weep when the woman handed him to me.

My sister screamed. Something was wrong. The worst was over. The baby, the most exquisite little baby boy I'd ever seen, was in my arms. Why was Phoebe still panting and grunting and gnashing her teeth?

The Maidu women also looked alarmed.

When another baby, a girl this time, arrived from my sister's womb, Beatrice and I locked eyes. "Twins!" my cousin said, laughing through her own tears.

The woman who'd pulled the second babe out held her at arm's length. By the grace of God, the baby in my arms had started to breathe and wail simultaneously. And the little girl was squirming and staring straight at the Maidu woman. She was even smaller than her brother but seemed fierce and brave, just like Phoebe.

My sister had fallen back down on the bunk and reached out her arms. I quickly handed her oldest child to her, and she gathered him up to her breast.

I turned and reached for her daughter.

The woman who'd been at Phoebe's head eased up to the other. They huddled around the baby with their backs to me. They were speaking their own language. Malcolm spoke some of their native language, and I needed to know what they were saying. "Beatrice, please get Malcolm."

Beatrice went quickly. Meanwhile, their eyes darted from Phoebe to her youngest babe, and they frowned. Was something wrong with the youngest twin? I needed to know. The women were chattering and kept looking toward Phoebe.

Malcolm rushed in and grabbed the now-screaming baby from the women. He held her protectively in both arms, supporting her neck. He gently spoke in the women's language. I could tell he was explaining something, but I didn't know what. They argued with him. They seemed outraged.

What had we done to make them so upset?

One tried to snatch the baby back, but Malcolm wouldn't let her. Meanwhile, Phoebe was begging for her other child. Still, Malcolm kept hold of the babe, shielding her tightly against his chest. More words were exchanged. While holding the baby girl with one hand, he slipped his other in his pocket, withdrawing some gold dust. He handed the poke to the women, and the Maidu quickly bundled themselves up in their furs and pelts. I watched from the door as Cecil helped them both up on one horse. He mounted the other, grabbed the reins of their horse, and led them off into the twins' first sunrise.

Once they were gone, Malcolm handed the crying baby to my sister. She bundled a baby in each arm, as if it had always been.

"Why were they so upset? Is something wrong with her?" I asked him.

He shook his head. "The Maidu consider twins a terrible misfortune. An event that will curse the entire family for generations to come. If twins are born, one is always killed. Sometimes both."

Phoebe had been staring into the infants' faces and cooing. Now she stopped. "They were going to kill my babies?" Her voice cracked with the question.

"Just the girl," he said.

My heart quickened.

"They meant only good by it," he said.

No matter their intentions, I couldn't bear to think on the possibility. So I wouldn't. Maybe someday the twins would have a story to tell about their close call.

"They sure are a good looking pair," Malcolm said. "Don't know why I'm so darn happy."

Despite what had just occurred, I felt exultant. New life brought joy. I could tell my sister felt the same.

"I tend to think twins are lucky," Malcolm said. "I know Duffy would have been awful proud of siring not only one, but two! I can almost hear him whooping and hollering."

Phoebe laughed and wept at the same time. "I can hear him, too."

"What do you reckon their names are?" Malcolm asked.

"The boy's Duffy Junior," she said. "Can't be any name but that."

"And my niece?" I asked.

Phoebe was staring around the room, as if looking for ideas. Her gaze locked on *The Three Musketeers.* "I'll name her after Constance. From the book. But we can call her Connie."

I agreed it was a fine name, and Malcolm took his leave so we could clean up. He joined the others outside by the fire. Suddenly, exhaustion gripped me. Beatrice had napped off and on throughout the laboring, but I had been awake for nearly two days and a night, and now my head ached and arms felt weak.

I forced myself to stay alert. I washed up Phoebe and the babies. Beatrice, with vigor, gathered up soiled blankets and scrubbed the floor. It wasn't long before we let everyone back inside before they froze to death.

Phoebe fell asleep with a twin tucked in each arm's nook. I climbed up next to them and draped an arm over the three. I closed my eyes and offered up a prayer of gratitude for their lives and vowed I'd see the three safely home and would never, not for any reason, let harm come to them.

NINETEEN

Come April, lilac candied the air and sweet-ened each breath we took. Storms still blocked out the blue skies from time to time, but spring dusted the mountain with wildflowers. Run off from the Sierra snow had chilled the creek to a bone-aching temperature. But we didn't care. So anxious to wash away the winter's cramped quarters, we set aside the morning to bathe in the icy waters. We'd take turns so that two would be left on the banks to hold the twins.

Phoebe leapt in first with her wild whoop-ing and a big splash. I used the moment to broach the topic of Oxley with Beatrice. I asked her plainly if she still planned to marry him. "Or have you recovered from your passing fancy?"

"My plans are the same as before."

"We've money now," I said. "Enough to see us safely home to Boston."

"What life would I have there?"

"You have friends. Friends you've known from childhood. And the familiar streets you grew up on. Civilized roads wide enough for four wagons to ride side by side."

"It's not my home anymore," she said. "I have no family."

"You have us. We'll be together. And we're a larger family than we once were." Looking down at little Duff's face, I noticed he had Phoebe's cat-like eyes. And her curly hair.

"Effie," Beatrice said. "You're a goose to want to take care of me, Phoebe, and these babes. You've always tried to mother us, whether we liked it or not. Maybe you should try looking after yourself."

"You can't marry Oxley. And you can't stay here."

"Russell and I will have a big house and plenty of land. I'll live the life of a lady."

"No one lives the life of a lady in California," I grumbled.

From the creek, Phoebe screeched from the cold, then laughed.

"What about your pies?" I asked. "You love baking your pies. You could make and sell your pies in Boston."

She scowled. "Never."

Phoebe, shivering, rose from the creek and ran toward us. She grabbed a blanket from a warm boulder and wrapped herself inside it.

"Why not?" I asked Beatrice.

"I would be a disgrace to my family name. And to Aaron's."

I wanted to argue but couldn't. She was right. The gossipy socialites in Boston would like nothing more than to whisper about my cousin, once the prettiest girl in their circle. Still, I would have to convince her that she could never marry someone like Oxley.

Phoebe had pulled her dress over her head. She was already fastening up her boots. Beatrice handed Connie to her, and then she hastily disrobed and rushed into the water, submerging herself without a sound.

Duff had fallen asleep in my arms, his chubby arm dangling. He could sleep anywhere. His twin sister was the opposite. Glancing over, I watched Connie clutching Phoebe's wet curls while looking up at her mother's face.

"Connie's happy here," Phoebe said. "Don't you think?"

"She's happy with you," I said. "Wherever you may be."

Beatrice's plump cheeks were dusted with flour while she made a cake. Big Al had visited the neighbors yesterday and brought back a dozen eggs with yolks as bright as poppies. "Russell says we'll only be here a few more weeks," she said.

I stopped sweeping the cabin floor. "He doesn't know what he's talking about."

"Cecil won't marry us, so we're going to find a preacher in Sacramento City to perform the ceremony."

"Everhart Bar still has gold," I said. "It's the miner's code we work it until it has nothing left to give. So we won't be going anywhere for at least a month or more."

Lazarus, snoring, was splayed out in a patch of sun near the open door. Phoebe had just finished nursing the twins and was rocking them in an attempt to lull them both into a nap at the same time, a rare treat.

Beatrice carefully measured out some sugar. "I thought you wanted to leave and return to your precious Boston."

"I certainly do."

"You should get an early start," she said. "The others can keep working the bar after you're gone."

Even if I had a way to travel home tomorrow, I refused to take advice from Beatrice. Her poor judgment led us here in the first place. Now her poor judgment would lead

280

to a sour and pitiful marriage to that dandy, Russell Oxley. She kept talking about it as if it were a foregone conclusion. Even so, I doubted she'd follow through with the farce. Thank goodness Cecil refused to accommodate the pair. Whether it was due to him swearing off preaching or a shared prediction of disaster, I was grateful. His denial gave me more time to keep it from happening.

Why was she so set on it? She didn't need Oxley's money anymore. With all the gold we'd found, we had plenty to travel home and live well into the future. She needn't worry about burdening me because we had enough money for all of us, even if split three ways. With the last few weeks so dry and sunshiny, we'd been able to pull out at least another thousand dollars' worth. I was proud to have dug out the biggest nugget, one larger than an acorn.

Phoebe had managed to get both the little squirrels — as Malcolm called them — to sleep, which is why she whispered, "What if he comes back after we've left?"

"Who?"

Her eyes fluttered, then grew glossy. "Duffy. What if he returns? What if he didn't die?"

I was certain the sun would set tonight

and rise tomorrow. I was just as certain Duffy would never return. Not to here or anywhere.

Setting down the broom, I eased over and kissed the top of her head, just as I'd remembered Duffy doing on the day he left us forever. "If it were possible for him to come back to you, he would be here now."

She nodded and kept rocking.

"He's gone from this world, Phoebe. God rest his soul."

Closing her eyes, tears pearled, then trickled down her cheeks. "Either way, I don't want to leave just yet. I want to wait a little longer."

Beatrice stirred her batter and stayed quiet.

"I'm aiming for the end of May," I said. "We can't let summer get away from us. We'll need the good weather to travel home. Surely, some wagon train will be headed back East by then. Enough of the miners will have grown as tired of this wilderness as we have."

"Okay, Effie." Phoebe tilted her head and pretended to sleep. I hoped she could. Lazarus, being the good soul he was, trotted over from his sunny spot and lay at her feet.

Bluer skies I'd never seen. With the glittering peaks of snow in the distance and rushing notes of the Feather River, it seemed a divine afternoon. And I was pleased to have stopped work early. Surrounded by a green vigil of pine, I enjoyed the stroll back from the bar with Lazarus. So peaceful was the day, Beatrice's scream from the cabin startled not just me but the day itself.

I considered running back to fetch the others. But they were finishing up a dam, and Beatrice had probably spotted a spider or bug. With Phoebe there to stomp on it or swat it with a rag, all would be well. No need to disturb everybody else. My cousin still fussed over the most harmless creatures. I would have thought living out here would have cured her squeamish aversion to insects.

She hadn't screamed again. So my worry waned. Still, I walked faster, ducking under low branches and weaving between thick tree trunks.

The fairy tales our mother had read to us as girls often involved a wood like this. One soaked in green. A flower blooming in a patch of sunlight on a forest floor. A crow cawing somewhere.

My nerves tingled. Probably for no reason. Beatrice was fine. Phoebe and the twins were fine, too.

Still, I decided to run. Lazarus seemed glad to join me.

When I reached the cabin and threw open the door, I saw Oxley, his trousers a concertina at his ankles, lying over Beatrice on the floor.

Startled, Oxley snapped his neck around toward me.

My face flushed, I almost turned around and left.

I looked closer.

Beatrice, her skirt shoved up to her chest, her pantaloons torn and in a haphazard heap to the side, lay motionless. Her hand splayed on the ground. Her palm open and inert.

The metal of the Colt felt cool to the touch. As long as I didn't fire it, it would stay this way.

But fire it I would if he'd killed my cousin or harmed Phoebe or the twins. I knew this as fact. Only I'd be able to level the type of justice he deserved. No vigilante committee would do. Even if Beatrice were alive, I might kill him anyway for what he'd done to her. Maybe I'd do worse.

My nose itched, but I didn't move to scratch it, and my eyes watered with the urge.

Lazarus let out a throaty and mean bark.

Training the pistol at his head, I cocked it and aimed to fire. With only a few bullets left, I was thankful Malcolm had taught me how to shoot. I didn't think I'd miss.

He sneered, shifted off my cousin, and then shoved her aside. "You putting a bullet in me for rolling in the hay with my fiancée?"

The side of Beatrice's face was purplish red at the temple. "What'd you do to her?"

"I had to urge her compliance." He shrugged. "She's alive."

"Move away from my cousin, or I will shoot you dead."

With no sense of urgency, he stood. Then he glanced down at his trousers, as if deciding whether or not to pull them up. I was thankful when he did.

"Where's Phoebe?"

He shrugged again. "I'm glad she left, though. It gave me some time alone with my betrothed."

Lazarus scrambled over and licked Beatrice's face. She remained motionless. Stooping in front of the man would give him an advantage, so I stayed near the door, the gun aimed, my hands steady. "You are to lie down on your belly."

"That some sort of punishment?" He

grinned. I'd never noticed how stained his lower teeth were.

"Lie down," I demanded.

"Or what?" he snarled.

"I'll shoot you," I said.

"Don't need to be shooting me, Effie Frost. I'm just a man. A man with needs."

"On your belly, like the snake you are."

"All right, but it don't have to be like this." He got down on his knees, as if about to pray.

"Do as I say. Lie down!"

Sighing, as if my intentions were benign, he finally stretched out on his belly.

Maintaining my aim, I edged toward Beatrice and squatted. First lowering her skirts, I touched the side of her face with the back of my hand. It was warm, and she was breathing. "Tell me what you did to her."

"I told you already," he said, his voice muffled against the floor. "Just a little roughing up to coax her into her duties."

My hands had started to shake. I stood, keeping the pistol leveled.

Oxley craned his neck and stared up at me. For a moment, he looked like someone else, his sickly smile limp.

"You deserve to die," I said.

Fear jumped into his eyes. Then, just as

fast, it was replaced by arrogance. "You kill me, you'll never know."

"Never know what?"

He turned his head and spat toward the fireplace.

"Tell me," I demanded.

"Gotta promise not to shoot me. You promise that, I'll solve a great mystery."

"The only promise I'll make is to bury you once you die."

He rolled over on his side. Then he rose up on one elbow and rested his chin in his palm. Squinting at me with one eye, he grinned. "I'd bet my share you won't pull the trigger."

"Might not shoot you in the head." I aimed the gun between his legs. "Might just shoot you —"

Interrupting me with an angry scream, Oxley leapt up and charged. Before he could knock me down, Lazarus lunged. Oxley fell, and Lazarus clamped his jaw on the man's left calf.

He screamed again and tried to shake off the dog.

Stepping closer, I told Lazarus he was good boy, which caused the dog to bite down harder.

Oxley hollered and cursed at the dog. At the same time, he tried to shake and pull

Lazarus from his leg. Then Oxley flipped over on his hands and knees and strained to crawl away, dragging Lazarus, still tugging and biting.

"You want any relief," I said, "tell me about this great mystery."

"I ain't telling you shit!"

Over the din, I heard Beatrice from behind me utter a throaty sound. I couldn't risk checking on her. "Effie," I heard her say. "Please. Stop."

I wouldn't stop. I wouldn't order Lazarus to stop, either. This man, screaming and writhing on the floor, had violated and nearly killed my cousin. He deserved the wrath of Lazarus. He deserved my wrath, too. "You want the dog to leave you be, tell me." I knelt, the gun close to his face.

"He shouldn't have said it . . . shouldn't . . . no one calls me a . . . a bastard. Then lives to say . . . it again."

Lazarus shifted from Oxley's leg to his hand and latched on. Oxley, hitting the dog repeatedly on the head, yelled and cursed with the pain.

"You want me to call him off?"

Oxley wrestled with the dog, now wildly locking onto different limbs, tearing into Oxley's skin, snarling and biting. Shredding and tugging. "I followed him . . . Duffy,"

Oxley stuttered. "When . . . he went to get help."

I froze. Then, perhaps because I could no longer bear the noise, I ordered Lazarus to stop.

But Lazarus seemed not to hear and now sunk his sharp teeth into Oxley's upper arm.

"Down!" I shouted.

The dog released him but looked ready to lunge on command. Oxley's breath was fast and heavy.

"Tell me, or I'll let Lazarus loose on your neck."

Oxley moaned. "He didn't even see me for a few miles. When he did, he looked glad for it. Glad I'd decided to come along. Until I had a hold of his throat. Both hands. I didn't even know I had such a strong grip."

For a moment, I didn't believe what he'd said.

Oxley's shoulder twitched, his bloody fingers flexing. Would he kill me, too?

I choked on rage. On my own stupidity, too, for not realizing sooner what he was capable of. Furious, tears flooded down my face. Lazarus hovered near the murderer, and both were a blur. Then Oxley reached out and grabbed my dog, lifting him up by his front legs and tossing him at the fireplace. A yelp cut through the cabin. Then silence. I glanced over. The dog lay unmoving.

Oxley's pant legs were torn and bloody. Blood streamed down his wrist from his tattered hand. Nevertheless, he stood. "I was going to scatter the coat and hat, thinking someone might find them and think a bear drug him off. Changed my mind and stuffed them between the rocks. Far as the body goes, you'll never find it. You could search this mountain for years, you won't even find a finger bone."

Every muscle in my body clenched.

Oxley sprang toward me.

The trigger worked fine on Aaron's Colt, the bullet burrowing into Oxley's gut. I kept my eyes wide open and watched him fall.

Having heard the gun's blast, Malcolm practically knocked down the cabin's door.

Oxley was still alive, but I didn't think he'd live long.

However, Lazarus would. He'd shaken off the impact with the fireplace stones and hovered and growled over the screaming Oxley, who thrashed about, clutching his gut.

I ignored him and rushed to Beatrice. Her eyes fixed on the ceiling, her hands over her ears, it seemed she was wishing to be lifted up by God's talons and spirited away.

TWENTY

Beatrice wouldn't talk to me. Not about what happened to her and not about anything else. But for a few words, she'd almost stopped speaking altogether. A vigilante committee had ridden over this morning to inquire about the details of the killing. Beatrice, her eye still swollen and purple, told them she hit her head on a branch while out for a stroll.

"We were about to eat lunch when Effie arrived. Oxley was mad she interrupted our meal and raised his voice to her," she said. "He was very angry. So angry, I left. I hate to be around folks when they grow cross. I didn't hear or see what happened next."

The men seemed to accept this version. Malcolm urged me to tell the men the truth. Every detail. Including what happened to my cousin. But if Beatrice didn't want others to know, I couldn't spill her secret. I wouldn't want her spilling mine. Besides, I had plenty of reasons to kill Russell Oxley. He'd confessed to Duffy's murder. None could blame me for avenging my sister's husband. So I told the men I'd come back to the cabin early. I told them Oxley was irritated and in a state. That Lazarus attacked him after he'd tried to assault me. That he confessed to strangling Duffy and then hiding Duffy's coat and hat. Oxley tried to attack me again, after flinging my dog against the fireplace. That's when I shot him.

The men were happy to eat a slice of Beatrice's pie while asking more questions.

One of them swiped crumbs from his beard. "Complicates matters that you were alone when the killing occurred."

"I don't see how," I said. "My word can be trusted."

"Got no reason to take your word," another said.

I couldn't argue. And my word, other than Beatrice's, was the only word they had to go on. Malcolm, Cecil, and Big Al had tried to convince them I was innocent, and Oxley deserved what he got, but the committee were dogged a trial be held in two days' time. "Lady Justice must hear out the facts," one said. Far as they were concerned, I could have been a murderer before I'd arrived on the mountain.

Malcolm and I lingered on the porch after they'd left. "Beatrice will come around," he said. "Give it a few days, and she'll lay out the events."

"She won't," I said.

"Good deeds are often punished harshly in these parts. But I won't allow them to lay a hand on you."

I didn't think Malcolm would have a say in what they did to me. Out here, the mere idea of justice — whether justice was a lady or not — helped us pretend we lived in a civilized society. That we were living normal lives. That everything made sense. But we weren't. And our rough and ready courts wouldn't make it so.

I headed back inside and stirred some squirrel stew Beatrice had made. When I walked past her, she wouldn't look me in the eye. Even though her silence might get me hanged from a bough.

She turned her back on me, and I stared at her apron strings while she scooped some flour into a bowl. We had very little flour left and due to the diminishing provisions would have to leave the cabin soon.

It occurred to me I might never leave at all.

"Beatrice?"

She began to hum.

"I could die." I wanted to be as plain as possible.

"Did you stir the stew?"

"Did you hear me?"

"If you don't stir it," she said, "it'll stick to the bottom and taste poorly."

The wind was blowing hard, shrieking through the cracks under the door.

"I stirred it."

"You should keep stirring it."

I walked toward her, grabbed her by the arm, and spun her around. "Did you hear me? I could die! You want me to die?"

Expressionless, she looked down at the bowl of flour.

"You must tell those men what happened."

"I left. When I came back, you'd shot Russell."

A heat snaked up my neck and flushed my face. As hard as I could, I hurled the spoon I'd been holding across the cabin. Then I marched toward the door. When I opened it, a wind caught it and blew it with a bang against the wall. I stormed off into the forest, Lazarus on my heels. Malcolm, too.

My walking became a trot, became a run. I would run off this mountain. I would run and run. Beatrice and Phoebe would be better off without me. I was a murderer, and they didn't need to be burdened by my reputation as a killer. The twins would be better off, too. Weeping was so unfamiliar, I didn't realize I was doing it until Malcolm caught and spun me around, wrapping his arms around me.

"No jury of miners would convict you of such a thing," he said. "They're just wanting to do things proper."

"Can't we go? Can't we leave this mountain now?"

"Then they'd think for sure you had something to hide. Don't you figure?"

I rested my face on his shoulder and wept until I was shuddering. And he held me close like that until he raised my face and kissed me on the mouth.

I'd never been kissed before, not like this, and I was sure I would only ever allow Malcolm to kiss me again.

"You think I'd let anything happen to you?"

I believed he would do everything he could to prevent the committee from wrapping a rope around my throat. "If my demise comes," I said, "promise you'll care for Beatrice, Phoebe, and the twins."

"Time like this, you're still thinking on your cousin's well-being? With her refusing to help you out of this fix?"

"It's Oxley who caused this, not Beatrice. I killed him for it. And I'd do it again. If I am to meet my end because of it, then so be it."

I'd stopped weeping. He kissed me again.

"I'm going to set up my tent outside the cabin tonight," he said.

"It'll blow away with this wind." My hair tickled my face, and I cinched my hat tightly under my chin to keep it from flying off my head.

"I'll make sure it doesn't. Tie it between some trees."

"It's your free will on where you sleep."

"I'd sure like some company," he said.

Maybe because I had nothing left to lose, I chose to join him. I would, at least for one night, do whatever my heart desired.

TWENTY-ONE

"It'll be like the trials back home," Cecil explained while we walked. "Except not one of the boys knows much about the law. Some miners will serve as a jury. There'll be a judge, too."

To carry the twins on the hike to the neighboring camp for my trial, my sister had devised a sling from our red-checked tablecloth. At dawn, we'd set out on foot. All but Beatrice. With Lazarus for company, she'd stayed at the cabin. I had to rope the dog to a tree to keep him from following. We'd trudged quite a ways before he gave up on his barks and howls.

Cecil was doing his best to prepare me, but it wasn't helping. "You'll even get a lawyer to stand up for you. If you're wanting one."

"Can't you be my lawyer?"

Cecil fingered his scar. "I got into enough trouble being a preacher. Don't want to give folks more fodder by adding lawyer to my shingle."

Around ten, we reached a meadow of tall green grass and golden poppies. Malcolm bent to pick one and thrust it behind my ear. "Looks nice with your dress."

I pulled it out and stored it in my apron pocket. "I'd rather be wearing my trousers."

"You should've then," he said.

"A woman in trousers would be suspect. Some might think I was odd enough to be a real killer. I need to look proper today."

"You look more than proper. You look like a lady."

I scowled at him.

"Of course," he said, "you look like a lady in your trousers and suspenders, too." He leaned into me. "You look best of all in the buff."

I blushed from the inside out and fingered the velvety flower petals in my pocket.

On the long walk, we took turns toting the little twins, who cooed some, cried more, and grinned when Malcolm or Big Al made funny faces. Duffy Junior's yellow mop was starting to curl up at his ears. And Connie, we'd discovered, had a dimple on her plump left cheek.

Despite the trial I was about to face, the babies kept us cheerful. Malcolm kept promising I'd be exonerated. It was self-defense, he'd said. Never been a clearer case of self-defense. Oxley, after all, was a confessed murderer, so he deserved the bullet.

Over and over, Malcolm reassured me by explaining how much our neighbors had taken to Duffy Fields. How everyone who'd ever been lucky enough to know Duffy was fond of him. I glanced down at Connie's round face. She looked like her father. I was glad her daddy's killer was dead and buried.

Even if I died for it.

"God's probably good," I said to Malcolm. "Come what may, I'm going to keep that in mind."

"Might be good. Might not be. Sometimes it seems God's got more mischief than the devil."

"I'll be relieved to have it over with. I never want to think on Oxley again."

"You'll be owed gratitude and an apology," he said. "After all's said and done."

"Or I'll be hanged."

"Not a chance."

"Some lives are short. Others are long," I said. "Maybe I have the former."

We walked some before he spoke again. "I can't see myself without you by my side."

"My father always said I'd live a long time.

As a child, I believed him. But I believed a lot of fanciful things back then."

"He was right on that. You'll have to live without me someday. But I'll have the privilege of having you to look at until I shut my eyes for good."

I gripped his hand without agreeing or disagreeing with his version of the future.

We camped overnight at the neighboring claim. The next morning brought a sky laced with sugary clouds. My trial would be held outside. Two rows of benches, constructed from bare wood planks, were separated by an aisle. The judge and I were to sit on a raised platform.

Despite the accusation, the men were polite, one offering a hand to assist me up to my seat.

"Now and then we put on plays or sing songs or have recitations up here," a man in a bright-blue shirt said.

"I love music," I said to him. "My father played the piano." This sort of focus on the humdrum helped distract some from my nerves. It also helped me imagine no one was watching or looking at me. That this wasn't happening at all, and I was somewhere else. Somewhere far away. Back in Boston. Or maybe in my childhood room with the yarn-haired rag doll my mother had sewn for me.

"I'll make sure to bring out Neal if they take you to the tree," the man said. "Neal plays the fiddle better than most. You like the fiddle?"

I nodded, the gravity of the moment striking at me like a sidewinder. How would they take me to the tree? Would they carry me? Would I walk on my own toward my death? Would they bind my arms and legs?

Malcolm, Phoebe, and the sleeping twins took their seats in the first row. Cecil and Big Al sat behind them. With everyone's chatter and murmurs, I could only read my sister's lips while she asked how I was doing. I nodded to her, hoping to convey all was well.

I was glad she couldn't hear my heart thudding.

That she couldn't feel my damp palms.

That she couldn't know I was about to cry.

After everyone was seated, a bulky man settled in a large chair to my right behind a table so freshly built, I could smell the pine. Though his upper lip was shaved, he possessed a full beard shaped like a dark curve. Though older than most men here, he didn't seem old enough to have a judge's wisdom.

The crowd hushed.

"We like to make these hearings quick, Miss," the man announced. "See those fellas to your left?" I glanced over to five men sitting on planks that had been laid diagonally across a few boulders. "Those gentlemen are your jury. If you could introduce yourself, we can get started."

I cleared my throat. "My name is Euphemia Frost," I said quietly. "I'm from Boston."

"You'll need to speak up so the wind doesn't eat your voice," the judge admonished.

I spoke louder. "I am Euphemia Frost. Everyone calls me Effie. I'm from Boston."

"What brought you all the way out here, Miss Frost?" he asked.

"My cousin's husband, Mr. Aaron Criswick, journeyed out here ahead of us to make his fortune, as most of you gentlemen probably did. My cousin traveled across the isthmus to be with him, and my sister and I accompanied her. We intend on going home next month." I didn't look at Malcolm when I said this, as I knew he had other designs on my destiny.

"And where is Mr. Criswick?"

"He passed before we arrived. Typhoid fever."

"I see."

My throat constricted. "Before he died, Aaron bought a share in Mr. Everhart's claim. So I've been working it. In order to earn enough funds to see us home to Boston."

"You've been working the claim?"

"Yes, sir."

"That's gotta be hard on a little lady like yourself." The judge leaned toward me. I noticed how he had baggy eyes. "You were probably musing it might be easier to just have a rich fella's belongings."

I shook my head. "No, sir. I enjoy the work. It's hard, but I like it."

Some of the men laughed. I wished I could growl and bare my teeth like Lazarus.

"Way I see it," the judge continued, "by killing Oxley, you'd get a percentage of his share. Not only that, you could take whatever funds he brought along with him since your cousin was fixing to marry him. Hear tell he had more money than most."

"That's not the way I saw it," I said. "And since you weren't there, I don't know how you could have seen anything at all."

"I've seen desperation drive men to such acts a few times too many."

"I am not a man. I shot Oxley because he'd confessed to killing my sister's husband, Duffy Fields. And I had good reason to believe he intended to kill me next."

"Duffy Fields up and left," the judge said. "Probably didn't want no part in raising wee ones."

Phoebe couldn't help but speak out. "You're wrong!" she shouted.

"Phoebe," I said, "please quiet down." I knew her protests would only make matters worse. I turned to the jury and spoke directly to them. "Duffy Fields was a good man. Better than most. If you knew him, and many here did, you'd argue with the judge's words. Duffy would *never* have left my sister. Or her babies. He loved her."

The judge leaned back in his chair. "So Duffy Fields was a good man, you say? Then why didn't you approve of him marrying your sister?"

This took me by surprise. "Whether I approved of the marriage or not, Russell Oxley murdered Duffy Fields. He confessed to strangling him."

"Confessed to whom?" the judge asked.

"To me!"

"How'd he manage to strangle Duffy Fields? Takes a lot of strength to come at a man like that."

"Oxley said Duffy was pleased to see him." I wiped my palms on my dress. "Aren't I supposed to have a lawyer?"

"Anyone want to be this little lady's lawyer?" the judge asked all in attendance. One small man with round glasses and a dome for a head stood.

"Well, come on up, Basil. You'll do." The judge turned to me. "This here's Basil Grier. He worked as a farrier before the gold fever."

I doubted very much that Mr. Grier's expertise with horse hooves would assist in his lawyering abilities and said as much to the so-called judge.

"Thought you wanted representation?" the judge said.

Everyone was silent while I contemplated my choice. No lawyer at all or the farrier, Basil. I finally said, "Mr. Grier will have to do. May I consult with him?"

The judge peered at me, as if I didn't deserve his or the jury's time.

"How," I asked, "could he know how to defend me if he doesn't know the facts of my case?"

"We all know what happened," the judge said. "Ain't that right, Basil?"

"It's mighty unfortunate," my lawyer said in a hard-to-hear, rattled voice.

"With all due respect," I said to the judge, jury, and crowd, "you do not know what occurred. If you did, I would not be sitting here."

Basil cleared his throat and tried to speak louder. He raised his hand and pointed to a man in the back. "Euphemia Frost murdered this man's son."

The chair I'd been sitting on seemed to bend in the center, as if folding up around me.

Everyone craned their necks to stare at the tall older man the farrier had pointed out. His beige suit snug, his matching wide-brimmed hat stained, the man had a hooked nose and long neck that made his head jut out, as if his skull were too heavy.

With his hands behind his back, the man glared up at me, scowl marks forked between his watery eyes. He then made his way down the aisle and stood at the foot of the platform.

He looked up at me and said, "Why'd you have to kill my son, Miss? He was all I had left."

In the silence, his grief was invasive. How could I tell this man that his son was a no-account brute? The man before me was true in his mourning. I dreaded breaking his heart even more.

His voice now boomed. "Russell didn't deserve to die like that. Dog bit and shot in the gut. My Russell never did harm to a living soul. Would help anyone who needed it whether they asked or not. Nursed his poor mother on her death bed, slept on the floor and went without sleep for weeks due to it. You didn't have to kill my boy, ma'am."

I reeled and looked down at the platform, studying the grooves in the rough board, watching as a small spider with spindly legs hurried along.

"He was a fine young man, Russell was. Just wanted an adventure. I wanted him to have an adventure. He deserved one after his mother passed. I sent him on that steamer with all the pride in the world." The man wiped the edge of his nose. I thought I heard one of the jurors sniffling. But I wouldn't look at him.

I wouldn't look at anybody.

I would hang.

How strange to be living out my last moments on earth. I gulped the air. I looked up to the sky. The clouds had gone from wispy to plump and billowy. Mountain skies were bluer than most, I'd come to realize. The rich blue made the green of the leaves and ferns that much greener.

"You didn't know your son," Phoebe suddenly said. She stood, a twin on each hip. "He was a no-account. He wouldn't help anyone even when asked. Once, when I was well along with my babes, I was walking and carrying two buckets of water, one in each hand. I was struggling and asked for help, lest I spill it. He told me *no.* That he was busy. Well, mister, let me tell you that he was busy doing nothing is what he was busy at. Russell Oxley was the laziest man I'd ever met in all my days."

She handed one twin to Malcolm, the other to Cecil, who didn't quite know what to do with the babe. "Sir, I am sorry for your grief, but your rose-colored glasses are thicker than logs. My sister killed that man because he murdered my husband. Everyone who knew Duffy Fields would say he was the best of them. The very best. There wasn't a better or jauntier man on God's green earth. I dare anyone here to say otherwise. They know in their hearts he'd never leave me here on this mountain. My babes have no father because your son was a killer. Your son was filled with an evil devil. Filled to the brim. And if my sister hadn't shot him, he would have killed her, too. And then my babes would be without a father and an aunt. And I would be without my sister!"

A commotion rose from the audience and jury. Some telling my sister to "sit down." Others chastising her for speaking in such cruel tones to a mourning father. The judge pounded a homemade gavel, which looked more like a broken miner's tool.

Only a few of the faces seemed to be considering her words.

Through the noise, my eyes shifted to the elder Oxley. I saw the man's sorrow was eating at him and how the words from my sister about chewed him up.

"Your son," she kept on, "who wouldn't do a lick of work, was the opposite of my husband. Your son was the worst of them!" Phoebe shouted. "And I must tell you who your son was since the man you describe is a stranger to me. And to all of us at Everhart Bar!"

The judge pounded his gavel again. "You will sit down immediately," he said. "You will not say another word. This man's anguish shall not be made worse by your spiteful tongue."

"I will not sit down! Everyone needs to hear what I have to say. Is this man's grief worth more than my sister's life? More than my husband's life?"

"You will sit or be tried right along with your sister!"

"I dare you sumbitches to try me," she yelled, tears spilling from her eyes. "I will sit by my sister, and I will stand by my truth!"

Malcolm, with his free hand, pulled her back down. Fuming, she resisted at first but sat stiffly while glaring at the jury. When I'd told her what had become of Duffy, she'd wept for an entire day and night. Then she'd risen the next morning, nursed her twins, and carried on with the day, as if it were ordinary. It's what mothers did, I supposed. What they'd always done in the face of unspeakable sorrow.

Oxley's father was openly crying. I had to look away.

But what I now saw puzzled me. Lazarus was bounding down the aisle. He leapt onto the platform and sat by my side. Then I saw Beatrice, holding the bridle of the bay, which was walking behind her. Headed towards me, she was struggling to catch her breath. Her hair had sprung from her braids and spilled out in wedges over her shoulders. Dirt patched her chin and forehead. Somehow, she'd also torn the sleeve of her dress.

Basil Grier stepped toward her, and they spoke. Now he turned to the judge and jury. "Judge," he said, "Mrs. Aaron Criswick has just arrived on horseback. She would like to give her account, as an eye witness, she claims, of the killing."

"I rode all night, Effie." Beatrice's eyes were wild, as she looked around at the men's faces. "I have decided not to care what these ruffians think of me. They need to understand what kind of man Russell Oxley was."

Oxley's father spat at the ground. "My son was a gentleman. He would have worked harder than any of you. Why, you wouldn't have been able to keep up with my boy!"

I had been imagining what it would feel like to be hanged, to be forever separated from Phoebe, Beatrice, the twins, and Malcolm.

I had been certain, despite Phoebe's pleas and my cousin's sudden reckoning, I would die here. But now an idea occurred to me. "May I speak?" I asked the judge. "Or will Mr. Grier have to speak for me?"

"Long as you don't have unkind words for the deceased," the judge replied.

Beatrice looked around. "I need to tell everyone what happened. And the truth, I am sorry to say, is unkind. It's unbearable."

Again the crowd began talking, admonishing all of us, looking around, some trying to comfort Oxley's father.

I stood. "Thank you, Beatrice, for riding all this way, but you need to hush." Thinking of her in the forest alone, except for Lazarus and the horse, I was thankful she'd made it through without being attacked by any number of things. That she was willing to reveal the reality of what Oxley did to her in front of this crowd of foolhardy men broke my heart. And I wouldn't allow it.

"When was the last time you saw your son?" I asked the elder Mr. Oxley.

The man's face was stony.

"I am sorry for your loss, sir, but I must know when it was you saw him last."

The man looked up at the judge.

"Please answer," the judge said.

"The day he left on the steamer to travel around the Cape. Happy with the high step of the traveler. It was a blue-sky day, the sea smelling like good fortune."

"When was the last time you heard from him?" I asked.

The man paused and wiped his nose with the side of his hand. "Russ sent me a letter from the ship. Said he was enjoying his time. Even said the food was good. And he'd made a friend, who was making his time aboard more enjoyable. But I haven't heard from him since. That's why I made the journey myself. I've been looking for my boy. A fellow in Sacramento told me he was up in these parts, mining with Everhart. Didn't know he was kilt till I got here."

I forced myself to look the man in the eye. "Sir, if you could describe what your son looked like, I would very much appreciate it."

"I don't quite understand why you feel the right to interrogate me."

A thick wrinkle materialized on the judge's forehead. "It's unusual," he said. "To be sure. But all of this is. Given that this is life or death, I think it fair to air matters out."

The breeze picked up and blew a few hats off. The clouds moved as if being chased. If I were to be hanged, I hoped for rain. Dying in the rain seemed preferable to a blue sky.

Yet maybe I wouldn't die. Maybe if what I was thinking was true, I wouldn't die at all. Not today, at least.

"He wasn't squat or lanky — just a right-sized man," the father said, a fondness spiking his voice. "He had corn-colored hair, round brown eyes like his mama, and didn't have to shave much. One of his ears had a point, same as my ear." He took off his hat and pulled back his thinning silver hair to show everyone his ear. "He was a sharp dresser, my son. He liked to look clean and

313

nice. He was right fond of a white hat his mama had given him. He had a good complexion, too. Always sunny looking, my boy was."

"The man I killed," I said, "and I did kill him, sir, I admit to that, had black hair."

"No, ma'am, Russ's hair was on the lighter side."

"The man I shot had light-blue eyes. Duffy used to say he had eyes like ice."

"You must not have looked closely enough."

"We all saw his eyes. Even some of the folks here saw them the day he came for the gathering." The men started talking loudly enough that I had to speak over them. "His eyes and his hair! We at the Everhart Bar were unfortunate enough to see both every day."

"That's right, Effie," Big Al shouted. "Oxley had hair the color of a burnt log and eyes like a Siamese kitty cat. We all remarked on it."

Oxley's father tilted his head and squinted at us.

"Russell Oxley, at least the Oxley we knew, did dress in fine clothes, and he seemed near the same height as your son, but he did not resemble in the slightest the man you are describing," I said. "Not in personality and not in his features. I never examined his ear, but with all my soul he otherwise must have been a different man."

"How can I believe you?" the senior Oxley asked. "Any of you?"

The judge banged his gavel. Everyone simmered down. "We'll have to dig him up, I expect."

Lazarus wagged his tail at the prospect. He'd been trying for days to dig into Oxley's grave, probably in search of a good bone.

Twenty-Two

The judge had tasked us with the gruesome duty of digging up the body. We used the same shovels we used every day to work the claim. The same shovels we'd used to bury the man. At least it had rained some, the black loam soft and easy to turn.

Oxley's father, whom we'd learned was called Hutch, folded his arms over his chest and stood back with the judge and jury to watch us dig. If the body was his son, his heart would break all over again. But we hadn't buried his son. I was sure of it.

Hutch Oxley's son must have met up with the man I killed. Perhaps this was the friend he'd written home about. At some point, probably on the voyage itself, his son had died, likely at the hands of the stranger we were digging up. Maybe Hutch Oxley's son had died of natural causes. Maybe the man in the grave had used the opportunity to assume Russell Oxley's name, his belongings, and cash. But I didn't think so.

I knew the man I killed. He was vicious. Cruel for the sake of cruelty. The way he'd described killing Duffy was the same way one would describe hunting a deer for food or catching a trout in the river.

The more dirt I turned over, the more I believed that Hutch Oxley's son had been murdered by the imposter in this grave.

The man I shot had suffered for a full night and day, leaking from the earth before finally shutting his eyes for good. Though his wailing and carrying on had upset the babies, Phoebe had wanted him to suffer even more. But the man's anguish hadn't brought me pleasure. When he'd finally passed, I'd been grateful.

Crueler sorts might have tossed the body into the woods and let the wolves and bears have their way. But we'd laid him on a pallet and covered him with a dark-green wool blanket. We'd now excavated enough of the soil to expose an edge of this blanket, soil bunched in its folds. We increased our efforts and soon revealed a toe. A foot. A knee.

Though we'd tied our kerchiefs around our noses and mouths, we couldn't contain the putrid odor.

"We're going to uncover the head, Mr.

Oxley, and you tell us what you know." Malcolm's voice was muffled by the kerchief. "Then we'll need to cover him back up fast as we can."

Cecil flipped his shovel upside down and reached it into the grave. Death seemed a secret we were about to reveal. Cecil edged the nose of the spade gently under the blanket, then raised it from the dead man, exposing a bloated face with blue and red splotches. Whether he was recognizable to Hutch, I didn't know. One thing was certain. The man had raven-black hair. In life. And in this grave.

The eyes were shut, but the shape of his nose and mouth were intact. I had a morbid moment of relief when I considered it fortuitous I'd shot him in the gut rather than the head. If I'd aimed for his temple, his father might never know the truth, and I'd hang from a tree.

I looked to Hutch Oxley for his verdict. A verdict that would either end with my death or reprieve.

The man's mouth hardened into a crisp line. His neck stiffened. Then he spat down into the hole. "That's not my son."

He turned and walked away, his hands clasped behind his back.

With twilight already upon us, we wasted

no time in covering the body back up, packing in extra dirt, and setting as many stones as possible on top of the mound. We didn't know who the man was, only that he'd murdered Duffy and likely Hutch Oxley's son. I didn't say a prayer for the body in the grave. But I did pray. I prayed for Hutch. For Phoebe. For the twins. For Duffy and the genuine Russell Oxley, God rest their souls.

Dark now, we headed back to the cabin, all of us, Malcolm, Cecil, Big Al, and me. Judge, jury, and Hutch, too. Phoebe and Beatrice, each holding a baby, met us on the porch with expectant eyes.

"I won't hang," I said. "Not today at least."

"Not ever," Phoebe said, leaning against a post, as if needing it to hold her up.

I didn't counter this with a last word or thought. This land was lawless. It had committees who lacked ration and reason and made decisions based on hunches and rumors. Anyone could die here, either from disease, a vigilante committee's overzealous efforts, or from a scoundrel not caring about anyone's life but his own.

Being apart from Malcolm would at first sting, but we had to leave this place. Come morning, I'd make plans to get us off this

mountain and out of this godforsaken
country forever.

Twenty-Three

Hutch Oxley was as decent a man as his son's killer was depraved. We all agreed he was due the killer's share, as his son's stolen money had financed our provisions. But Hutch refused to accept the nuggets and dust without pitching in. So for the past few weeks, he'd stood side by side with us at the diggings. Good with his hands, he'd even built a sturdy rocker that had proven useful, as it had helped us find a few of the largest nuggets yet. Our company now had plenty to secure our futures, be it in California or where we hailed from.

With his share, Big Al planned on heading home to Missouri to buy a farm. I was happy to hear this, as I knew the gambling bug would bite him hard should he stay. Cecil, on the other hand, would remain in California. His scheme was to buy up some lots in San Francisco. I'd told him he was daft. That city seemed reckless and unsound. Once the Argonauts' fever broke, I predicted the sloppy, fog-choked place would empty out, and its unfinished buildings would slide into the bay.

As for me, Phoebe, Beatrice, and the twins, we'd at last be going home. Thanks to Hutch Oxley, who'd offered to fund our passage in a first cabin, we'd be traveling by sea around Cape Horn. Though I would have preferred to keep my feet planted on the earth, Hutch promised the journey would be shorter and safer than overland travel, especially with the twins. He'd described his own passage here. How he'd seen thousands of dolphins and three rainbows in one day. And what a thrill it had been to sail from one side of the equator to the other. He now insisted on paying for our voyage as a reward for the justice I'd wielded for his only son.

"What if he's still alive?"

"My son's with his mother. If he were alive, he'd find a way to get word to me. I owe you a debt for avenging him."

I'd killed Oxley for my own reasons. "You owe me nothing."

He'd disagreed, and I'd finally accepted his generosity. I hadn't told anyone yet. Not even Malcolm. While out this evening on our after-supper stroll with Lazarus, I decided to let him know our plans.

"Hutch offered to pay our passage home. We'll be traveling around Cape Horn."

We did not stop walking, but Malcolm let go of my hand to swipe at a fly.

"Seems the best route," I said. "Especially with the babies. Fastest, too."

He stayed quiet. The pine needles crunched under our boots. Our shadows were short, and an owl was already waking and launching from the treetops. We'd reached the boulders where we first found Lazarus. Malcolm stopped. He turned and pulled me toward his chest. "I'd like you to stay on, Effie."

"You have known my wishes from the day we met. I belong in Boston. So do my sister and Beatrice."

He released me from the embrace and cleared his throat. "I want to marry you."

Leaning down, I scratched Lazarus behind the ears.

"You want to marry me, too," he said.

I didn't answer. I didn't know how.

"Will you marry me, Euphemia Frost? Stay with me in California? We can make a good life here together. I promise."

His eyes still looked like they belonged to a bird of prey. Hooded by dark brows. Deliberate. I would never forget them. I would never forget him. "I don't want to marry you or anyone else," I finally said. "And I won't be staying in California. I never wanted to come here in the first place."

"Fella told me that Sacramento City and San Francisco have doubled in size since we were last there."

"I didn't like those cities when they were smaller. I will certainly dislike them now. Double the scoundrels and sin, the way I see it."

"All right then. I'll come with you to Boston instead."

"You'll take care of Lazarus for me after I go?" I asked. "I wouldn't trust anyone else."

"I'm either going with you, or you're staying here."

"I will be going," I said firmly. "Without you."

"I can't believe that. You couldn't leave me because I'd find it impossible to leave you."

"If I had any ambition to be someone's wife, I'd marry you tonight. But I don't possess that particular ambition. I never have and never will."

"If you'd marry me tonight, then you must love me."

"A girl should never marry without love.

324

But neither should she marry for love alone. I read that in one of the Bronte books. It said that being single won't provide many joys, but sorrows will be meager, too. In marriage, however, a girl could have more sorrows than she could possibly bear. And I've already had enough sorrows in my life. So I won't marry at all." I turned to look at the sun setting over a vista of treetops.

"So what's the point of living?" Malcolm asked. "If you're going to avoid joy to avoid sorrow?"

"I wonder what this mountain will look like in a hundred years."

"Might not change much," he said. "Sort of like what you've got planned for yourself."

"This mountain with all its trees, flowers, and creatures would probably prefer not to change."

Malcolm shook his head and then turned his back on the violet-tinted sunset and me. Lazarus followed him when he walked away. Even the dog seemed fed up.

TWENTY-FOUR

When I opened the cabin's door to fetch my shovel, pick, and pan, I was met with singing. A quartet of men, two of whom had served on my jury, was serenading me with an off-key "We Won't Go Home Till Morning." A dozen or so others stood in a line behind them with their heads bowed and hats held to their chests.

Then one from the line stepped forward. The judge, himself.

He straightened as if about to make a speech. All I wanted to do was go back inside and shut the door.

"Miss Euphemia Frost, we've come here today to thank you for your bravery and to apologize for our frail attempt at justice."

"Apology not accepted." I stepped off the porch, grabbed the water bucket from a tree branch, and brushed past the men.

Malcolm headed out after me and caught my arm. "Effie, we've got plenty of water."

"We can always use more." I shook him off.

"Our neighbors came to make amends," he said. "And to celebrate our engagement."

"We're not engaged."

"I didn't dream you'd turn me down. Arrogance, I suppose," he said. "Either way, they wanted to apologize, and I bragged before I should have that we had plans to marry. So a shindig to surprise you seemed a fine idea."

"Tell them to leave." I kept walking, Lazarus beside me, as the creek was his favorite place. "I've no need to be in the company of soaplocks and rowdies."

Malcolm followed. "Don't see why we still can't celebrate your innocence. And our fortune at the diggings. Found more gold in the past week than we did in the whole month of April." He caught and spun me around. "Let's head back. They're all staying over. They're going to roll out blankets and set up tents, and we're going to have a jamboree to write home about."

"I refuse to pretend that I accepted your proposal."

"Wouldn't ask you to pretend and wouldn't expect you to, either. These men will find it reasonable that you'd give me the mitten. It'll lead to some teasing, but

I'm up for it."

We walked back, and the neighbors were already busy unpacking from their saddlebags eggs, apples, bacon, onions, potatoes, jugs of spirits, even fresh cream. Beatrice went about cheerfully collecting the food in her apron.

It seemed we would have this jamboree tonight whether I approved or not. But I had to insist we not celebrate my so-called innocence. The only innocents here, far as I could tell, were Duffy Junior and Connie. And even they tenderized most nights with their crying, which pierced the air and seemed a devilish gesture for ones so young.

I didn't mind as much celebrating our efforts and success at the diggings. All our pokes were full, our futures, like heaven, paved. So I gave in and helped decorate the clearing in front of the cabin with wreaths and pine boughs. We hung lanterns from the branches and dragged logs over to serve as seating. Beatrice, with Phoebe's help, spent most of the day preparing a meal that rivaled Christmas dinner. The tasty and juicy way she'd roasted the venison had everyone craving more. After the meal, the music began. Soon Big Al was plucking out a feisty version of "Old Dan Tucker." The fiddler, Neal, played along. An Irish took out his tin whistle and joined in. We danced, and many sang along. Cecil seemed to be singing a different tune while jigging with his spade. No one much minded. Hutch also seemed to be enjoying the evening. He'd taken several slugs from a jug of brandy. Even I had sampled Cecil's whiskey. So had Beatrice and my sister.

I would have never tried whiskey in Boston. And I would have scolded my sister good if she'd dared let alcohol touch her lips. I wouldn't have danced with Malcolm, either. Not in the way we were doing now. Spinning around, arms locked, laughing. For just a second, I forgot all the others were here. I could only feel his hand on my waist and his lips on my neck.

The moment vanished, and I untangled myself and broke free, dizzy from Malcolm and the whiskey. The others might gossip. Might think we really were engaged. When we weren't and never would be.

I weaved through the men toward Phoebe and the twins. She held both while chattering with a few of the younger miners, who simply stared at her with awe while fiddling with their shirt buttons. When I approached, they edged away.

"You chased them off," Phoebe said. "And I was enjoying our little parley."

"Did they have names?"

"I should think so."

"You recall what they might be?"

She looked down at her son. "I just know one's too slender for the shirt he's wearing, and the other has grass under his nails."

"You shouldn't be chatting away with random strangers. They'll get the wrong idea."

"I don't care what ideas they get."

"You should care."

"It's you, not me, who has always lived your life in a jail made from the rules of others."

"I do no such thing. I wear trousers now. I work the claim alongside the strongest men." I glanced over at Malcolm, his face aglow while adding a few logs to the campfire. "I've had other experiences, too. Ones I keep to myself."

"Even a long life's short," Phoebe remarked. "And there's no sense living just to please another's idea on what living is supposed to be."

Tonight I'd worn my hair down. The color of tree bark, it fell to my waist. To patch up my best dress's rips and tears, I'd crouched behind the cabin where no one would see me with a needle and thread. I'd even stained my lips red with the juice from a berry. And when Malcolm and I had danced, I felt pretty and mirthful. But I also felt guilty. And ashamed. As if it were wrong to enjoy myself when others — people I loved — no longer could.

Phoebe didn't add to her lecture. The babies asleep, she arched her face toward the sky, a dark bathtub of stars. Malcolm soon joined us, bringing over some crackling they'd cooked over the campfire.

I thanked him, and he sat next to me on the log. Phoebe and the twins on one side, Malcolm on the other, I felt content in this moment to be with them. If Beatrice sat with us, it would be a perfect night. But she was standing near the fire surrounded by a semicircle of men, all holding their hats and gazing at her, as if she were Aphrodite.

"I have something to tell you, Effie," Phoebe said.

There was no guessing at what Phoebe might say, as her imagined world was built from dips and turns. Perhaps she'd lecture me further about how I should or shouldn't live my life.

"You're not going to like it," she added.

I took a breath.

"I've decided to stay in California."

I'd told Beatrice and Phoebe last night about Hutch's offer and that we'd be leaving soon.

"So," she kept on, "the twins and I won't be going back to Boston. Beatrice won't be going, either."

I should have stopped her from imbibing Cecil's whiskey.

"We like it here," she said. "And Beatrice's pies can help earn us some income once we buy some land."

"We'll be leaving with Hutch Oxley," I said. "So please make Beatrice aware."

"You're not listening. I can and will stay in California. It's my life and my choice. You may be my sister, but you can't make me go back to Boston unless you've got some strong rope and the handiwork to tie some mighty fine knots."

"You will return with me. You, the babies, and Beatrice. The arrangements have already been made with Hutch." I reached out to touch Connie's soft arm. "You cannot possibly raise your children here."

"Why would I walk backward when I can keep seeing new things and having new adventures? I can't slip back into Boston society and pretend I'm some tea-sipping debutant without a care in the world except what hat's in fashion."

"We will not discuss this again," I said. "You will return with me. All of you. We've planned it out."

"*You've* planned it out. You didn't ask us once what we wanted, so I'm telling you now. We love you. We always will. And we are forever grateful because we certainly would have died without you. That's the truth. But we can care for ourselves now. We won't be going."

I stood and smoothed my skirt, shaking out the crumbs from the crackling. "You and Beatrice are both fools. And I will be happy to be traveling without fools as companions. It should make for a pleasant journey." My throat ached from the held-back tears, but I couldn't let her see this. I couldn't go back into the cabin, either, as it was full of people. So I walked away from them and headed into the dark woods.

Phoebe didn't follow, but Malcolm did.

"All your life," he said, "trouble has come knocking on your door, then invited itself in."

I nodded. How could Phoebe be so cruel? My cousin, too?

"But now it seems you're the one making trouble."

"I'm not —"

"You've got this notion of going back to a home that no longer exists. And you plan on dragging everyone else with you despite their urges against it. You can't see past your own face. You don't want to go back to Boston any more than Phoebe or Beatrice. Fact is, you love this mountain. You love it more than any of us. I can see it in your eyes when you wake up to catch the dawn glazing that peak over there. I can see it in your eyes when you look at me."

"I do want to go home. And it's a real place, unlike this gilded fantasy."

"Maybe you're already home. You ever thought on that?"

It was too dark to see his face or for him to see mine. "Phoebe and Beatrice can do as they please," I told him. "I'm leaving with Hutch Oxley. I am going home, and I won't return."

I could barely make out his silhouette. But I did hear him clear his throat and felt the breeze when he left.

TWENTY-FIVE

Cecil was drunk. "Everyone knows that God protects drunkards and lovers," he said, quoting from Dumas, while I finished packing my belongings, neatly folding my freshly laundered trousers and flannel shirt. I was pleased that Big Al had allowed me to keep them.

"You should avoid the whiskey during the day," I told him. "You're becoming a sot. And sots are useless."

"Just hard to see you go, Miss Effie. I've come to enjoy your company. Your words always set me straight. If you were a man, you'd make a fine preacher. Better than I did the job."

"Quit your sniffling. You'll set everyone off with your emotions, and that wouldn't do at all."

"Regret's a funny thing," he said.

"Regret's not funny at all."

"Well, it's an odd thing, though, isn't it?

An odd thing to feel."

"If it weren't for regret and shame, people would shrug off all decency and restraint."

"Don't know why you have to wrap up regret with shame. Shame's different. A good dose of shame isn't all that bad to keep folks from running roughshod over their fellow man. But regret's the odd one." He sat on the edge of our bedstead, a blade of grass in the side of his mouth. "It's odd because you don't see it coming."

"There've been plenty of times I knew I'd regret something. I regretted coming to California. I regretted it then, and I regret it now."

"You do? Seems you made the most of it. And, rough as we are, I like to think you've grown fond of us."

I was hoping Cecil would make his goodbye quick, yet he'd drunk far too much whiskey to make my wish come true. But we needed to leave soon, and I had many goodbyes to say. Hutch had already saddled his horse and packed the provisions. I needed to do the same. Only I'd be riding a mule. I preferred mules to horses and always would for the rest of my days.

"No," he continued, "You don't know true regret yet. Haven't made mistakes like I have. But you're about to."

"I need to ready my mule," I said.

"You're about to make the biggest mistake of your life. Later on, you'll think on this moment before you go to sleep and again when you first wake up. You'll want to come back here and try it again, but you won't be able to. Not ever. And so you might take to whiskey like me."

"I would never take to whiskey," I said.

"Then you'll take to something else. Something just as bad. Could be meanness. Some take to meanness. You've met those folks. Surely you have."

I left him there and stepped outside. Malcolm was already readying my mule, taking care to make sure I had everything I'd need.

I reached up and felt the brim of my hat. I could lose many things, but I would never lose this hat.

He was squinting in the sunlight. I thought perhaps it was making him cry.

Beatrice was holding the sleeping Duffy Junior on her shoulder and patting his back. His fist was clinched against her full bosom. I would remember them like that. I wanted to hold him one more time but wouldn't wake him for a goodbye. It wouldn't do. Connie was awake, and now Phoebe was handing the baby over.

"Kiss her goodbye. I bathed her this morning, so she'd smell good for you."

I held Connie and rocked her gently, allowing her to grab hold of my finger.

"You'll miss me," Phoebe said. "And you'll miss her. You'll miss us all."

I handed Connie back, kissing her cheek. My tears had left it wet.

"Why are you crying?" Phoebe seemed angry.

"Didn't know I was," I said.

"Well, you are. I'll be, you've got tears just like the rest of us."

"I want to go home, Phoebe. You can join me there once you've given up on the notion of California. Because that's all it is. A notion. I'll have everything ready for you, the twins, and Beatrice. I'll send for you."

Phoebe threw one arm around me and squeezed with the baby between us.

"We won't be apart long," I said.

"We'll be apart for the rest of our lives," she said.

I refused to believe this. I wouldn't go if this were true. And Phoebe was always one to tell tall tales, exaggerating every detail to make the story as dangerous and thrilling as it could be.

Beatrice didn't move when I went to kiss her on the cheek. "You stay sweet, cousin,"

I said. "As sweet as your pies."

I went to Lazarus and kneeled down to embrace him. Then Big Al led him off and tied him to a tree to keep him from following.

Malcolm, holding the rein of my mule, was whispering something in its ear.

"He doesn't speak English," I said.

"Maybe I speak mule."

"Maybe you do."

Malcolm looked more handsome than he'd ever looked before. He'd put on a waistcoat and had trimmed his moustache and beard. "I shall never forget you, Malcolm Everhart. I hope for all your dreams to come true."

"Only ever had the one dream, and you were in it."

I kissed his cheek, but he pulled me close to him and kissed me hard on the mouth for all the world to see.

My face red and my heart bickering with my head, I climbed on top of the mule and followed Hutch out of camp. As I rode away from everyone I loved, I heard Big Al, his voice as high-pitched as a woman's, shouting goodbye. I would always wonder why they called him that.

TWENTY-SIX

The wind whirled and whipped about while we set up camp on that first night. It was nearly impossible to get a fire going, but Hutch had managed. All we had to eat was cold. But I was too tired and too worn from the emotion of that morning to care that our food was cold.

I recalled the San Francisco harbor, how crowded it had been when our steamer had navigated toward the dock. How amazed I'd been not to have collided with one of the many abandoned ships. I felt that same fear now. The fog thick. Not knowing what was out there. All the people I loved back at the cabin.

But I had to shake free from this melancholy. I was going home. Where I belonged. Where I could finally make sense of the world.

Hutch didn't help my mood, though, as his sorrows were stronger than mine. And in the light of the fire lantern, I saw the fresh tears on his face. Perhaps the flurry from the jamboree and hard work at the claim had distracted him from his grief. But now, on our long ride off the mountain, there was nothing to hold it back, and his grief had charged forward like a bull in a small pen.

"You know what ticks at me about all this," he said, while I split some cold beans between us. "That my boy's name was dragged through the mud. I've told you how outstanding he was. What a good man. You would have liked him, Effie. My guess is you wouldn't have turned down a proposal from my son like you did Malcolm's. My boy was noble. Like you. It was my idea he have an adventure. Thought he could have some fun. We all need the ability to enjoy ourselves. And he was just so damn serious and cautious all the time."

"I might have liked him very much." I wanted to comfort the man. And was trying my best. The truth was that I could only ever love Malcolm.

"Oh," he said, "you would have. You two had the same way of thinking on matters. You don't submit to delusions. Nor did he."

"He sounds very practical."

"Indeed," he said. "These beans are tasty.

Even cold. Your cousin sure can prepare a delicious meal."

"You want the rest of mine?"

He was grateful. I was glad the food didn't go to waste. Nothing should be wasted out here, as everything seemed so hard to come by. He finished eating while the fire crackled and spat bits of bright flickers into the night sky. The small clearing where we'd built camp seemed the only place on earth. An illuminated patch of earth with only two inhabitants. The surrounding forest was dark and seemed a fable, almost as if the earth ended where the light did.

Loneliness was the result.

After I'd made the decision to leave alone, I understood it would come with the deep ache of absence. So I wasn't surprised by the pain I felt. I hadn't yet discovered a way to cope with the ache. I would in time. Of course I would.

"You know, Effie, I've been saying to myself ever since I arrived that Russell at least had a grand time on that ship. His letters remarked on it. He was indeed enjoying the adventure of the journey. Still, I can't help but regret ever putting him on that boat. I try not to let that regret fill me up, though, because I've got to keep living with myself. I can't walk out of my body and live somewhere else, now can I?" He set about wiping our bowls with his kerchief.

"I suppose not."

"Regret's like a toothache. It nags and makes about everything around you loathsome."

"You shouldn't regret wanting some joy for your son. How could you know the future?"

I rolled out my blanket and used my bundled up cloak as a pillow. Without the noise and shifting about from the twins and Phoebe, I figured I'd have a better night's sleep than usual even if it was on the hard, cold ground.

"Goodnight, Hutch. I thank you again for helping me get home. It's all I ever wanted."

"Happy to have you along if you're still happy to go."

I lay down and stared at the fire. I would stare at it until it turned into embers. And then my dreams would flare.

Dawn was hoisting above the horizon when I woke to Lazarus's wet tongue on my hand. I had barely slept so I tried to push him away.

I shut my eyes again, and he climbed on top of me and started licking my face and frantically wagging his tail.

Sitting up suddenly, I threw my arms around the dog as he nuzzled his face under my chin.

Hutch had already started the fire, and he was squatting in front of it and brewing some coffee. "Must have shown up last night. Mutt's decided he's coming with us, I'm guessing."

"Lazarus!" I scolded. "You were supposed to stay!"

Since we'd tied him up, I'd felt confident that after he'd stopped howling, he'd forget I ever existed. He loved the twins, after all, and I didn't dream he'd ever leave their sides.

"I can't take him with me. It's impossible."

"Maybe we can leave him at the ranch in Marysville."

Lazarus would like that. Plenty of table scraps. Other dogs to play with. "No," I said. "He needs to look after the twins."

Hutch handed me a tin cup brimming with coffee. The brew was so thick, sediment floated on its surface.

With Lazarus's head now in my lap, I sipped the hot beverage. I was happy to see the forest lit up again, the world opening like a locket. "I'll have to take him back to the cabin."

"Well, it might set us back a day, but if you think that's best."

"I'll take him myself. I wouldn't want to interfere with your arrangements."

"Coffee's a little strong," he said.

"It's good. I like it strong."

"So," he said, "seems you might have changed up your plans."

"I might have."

"On my way up this mountain to find my boy, I saw an eagle of some sort circling in the sky. He then soared down like an arrow and hooked his talons onto a jackrabbit, lifting off while the jack struggled and wriggled to free itself. I didn't know what might happen. But the hawk dropped it. And the jack sprang away. Too cumbersome, I suppose. But the hawk didn't hang around after. Just soared off looking for a leaner meal."

"I apologize that you have to travel alone," I said.

"I'm not alone. My boy and his mother are with me while I walk the earth. So I'll keep on walking long as I can."

EPILOGUE

They were going to burn the house down, for heaven's sake. I didn't want a party, but they hadn't listened to me. So I'd been steered from my sunny room with the picture window overlooking our ranch and escorted downstairs to singing and carrying on. Then I was presented with a vanilla cake, on which were lit one hundred candles. It looked as though it might explode. Which one of them decided I needed a candle for each year? I noticed little Gladys Fields grinning like a devil. Must've been her. Out of all my great nieces, she was the feistiest. And she might have been my favorite.

That child. Well, now less a child and more a young lady. She always was up for trouble. Trouble and joking. Day and night. Just like her Grandma Connie. Connie left us too long ago. The Spanish Flu took our Connie. Duffy Junior couldn't stand the world without his twin and went along to his maker not long after. "Weren't they a delight?" I said to Phoebe. Then to Malcolm, "Remember when you saved Connie from the Maidu?"

Oh, sure, these young folks around me think I'm mumbling and talking to myself like some old addled fool. But I realize Phoebe and Malcolm are gone from the earth. Doesn't mean I have to stop talking to them, now does it?

Did Gladys think I had enough gust to blow out these candles? I didn't. Not nearly. I doubted I could blow out even one.

Some of the youngest ones scrambled over to help. Together, we extinguished every last flicker. The cake could be eaten now, and maybe they'd let me go back to my room, where I could live in my head, the only crick-free part of my body left.

Or maybe my head had as many cricks as my arms, legs, heart, back, and feet. And I was too doddering or forgetful to notice.

After the candles, they guided me over to my favorite chair, plush and the color of a peacock, and Betty jumped up on the ottoman at my feet. She came from a long line of good dogs so deserved the soft spot. I'd kept a pup from each litter descended from Lazarus. Betty, I expected, would probably be the last in a long line of near perfect canines.

So many here today. For a woman who never had a child of her own, I sure had plenty of kin. Some from Beatrice, who had the three boys after she married the newspaper man, Harry Ramberg. She quite enjoyed her life in San Francisco after our time in the cabin. Once she went back to the city, she bought herself some land, built a home, sold her pies, and before long married her best customer. They led a cultured life there, which surprised me, as I'd always believed San Francisco would just burn to the ground and fall into the sea. I was glad it never fell into the sea, though it had burnt to the ground on several occasions. And the great earthquake of 1906 wreaked havoc, but Beatrice and Harry stayed and invested their money into helping rebuild the city they loved. Malcolm and I always did have a high time visiting them. And their boys grew into good men. Her youngest, Frost Aaron Ramberg, was still alive, and I used to enjoy coming off the mountain for a visit. He'd take me out to dinner and occasionally to the theatre. Frost enjoyed my stories about the muddy streets in those early days and how his mother's first husband was buried on Powell and then moved several years later to the Yerba Buena Cemetery and then to another, as the city grew. I didn't understand why they didn't leave the dead be and build over their graves. Phoebe was the only person who'd agreed with me on that. We buried Beatrice in our family cemetery on the ranch when she passed in 1916, a year to the day after Harry left us. Died in her sleep. Peaceful as a dove.

But it was mainly Phoebe's army at the house today. When Phoebe died ten years ago, she'd told me she'd lived long enough. Then she shut her eyes and never opened them again. I blamed the cigars she smoked. But maybe she'd been right. She'd certainly lived enough for ten people. Phoebe never had another child, but the twins had broods. Connie had six. And Duffy Junior had his ten, including two sets of twins. Then those children had children. And so on. With Phoebe's travels, wild ways, gallivanting, and writing her stories, the twins spent a good deal of their childhoods on the ranch with us. We liked it that way. I loved them as if they were my own. I certainly did. I loved them still. And would until I took my last breath. Phoebe never did remarry, but she'd had plenty of love affairs. It was even rumored she'd had a brief and torrid romance with Mark Twain. She'd spent some time in Virginia City, so maybe the tittle-tattle about the pair was true. Maybe it wasn't. It was hard to know with my sister.

I did believe, despite her many dalliances, that she only ever loved Duffy Fields. She'd said so on her deathbed. "See, Effie, we were true."

I missed Phoebe more than most. Sure wish she could've come to this party. But she'd really had enough of living, I suppose, just like she'd contended. I hadn't. I just kept on.

One of Phoebe's grandchildren, Duffy's oldest, brought over a beer that one of the young ones had brewed up in their cellar. That absurd law prohibiting spirits dumbfounded me. So much of the politics these days had my head spinning that I just couldn't keep pace. I still read the paper on days I could find my spectacles, but the hate in some hearts made me think people all had their own myths and lacked sense or a strong mind. With what was happening abroad, I feared another war was afoot.

I thanked the boy, as the beer was cold. Probably shouldn't think of him as a boy, as he was over sixty years old. The beer tasted good. Malcolm and I sure enjoyed a beer or some whiskey now and then. When children never came for us, we'd just got on with our lives on the ranch and had a time of it. We'd dance in our living room and talk sometimes until dawn. Since Beatrice's and Phoebe's young ones stayed so often, we never lacked the company of children and didn't mind not having our own after we'd accepted the fact of it. We had each other, and that was enough.

The problem with beer is that it made me sleepy. I shut my eyes, recalling when Malcolm and I finally went back to Boston. We were older. Can't remember how old. Maybe I'd been forty-five or so. We'd traveled by train. The food had been divine, and we had quite a lot of romance in our sleeper cabin.

But Boston had stunk of fish. The sidewalks composed of crowds of elbows. I'd recognized nobody and felt underdressed. Malcolm, too, had seemed awkward in his denim, flannel shirts, and cowboy boots.

We'd eaten a scrumptious roasted chicken dinner in a restaurant with blue velvet curtains and crisp, white tablecloths. At the other tables had been women wearing fine imported dresses and men sporting coattails.

They'd been strangers. The city a stranger, too.

Home had been sitting straight across

from me, and I had no regrets even with Malcolm passing when I was just fifty-six. He'd been out fixing some fence, and one of the ranch hands found him face down in the rain. Heart attack, they told me. But we had our time, and I kept him with me. Everything I'd seen since, I'd seen with him. Every new idea I shared with my beloved. Every curious detail. And the mundane ones, too.

I didn't know if I'd see him again. Didn't know if I deserved much else but the life I'd been able to lead. But even a long life is short, Phoebe once said. And it felt that way to me.

ABOUT THE AUTHOR

K. S. Hollenbeck is the author of *The Sand Castle* and *Closet Drama*. Her writing has appeared in multiple journals, including *Willow Springs, The Cream City Review, Arshile,* and *Rattle.* She grew up in gold country and could hear the Feather River tell its stories from her childhood window. She currently lives near Joshua Tree National Park.

Printed in the USA
CPSIA information can be obtained
at www.ICGtesting.com
JSHW080148040424
60478JS00005B/5